A SKYLINE MURDER MYSTERY

FLOOR 24

MARTIN HILL ORTIZ

OLIVERHEBERBOOKS

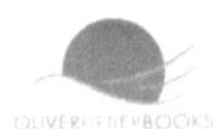

I am Martin Hill Ortiz, residing in Puerto Rico. In Puerto Rico, the mother's maiden name is automatically appended to the paternal surname.

I am Hill after my father, Milford Lee Hill, 1925-1977.
I am Ortiz after my mother, Adelina Alcaria Ortiz, 1929-2014.

This book is dedicated to them both.

CHAPTER 1
SOMEONE DROPPED A PEN

Alan

TEN IN THE morning on a hangover Monday, and I had no proper excuse for staying sober. After all, I'm a diligent drinker and, ever since America went dry, a watering hole had sprung up along every other block in lower Manhattan and every one of those oases had a shot glass etched with my name.

In the year of our Lord, 1926, Decoration Day fell on a Sunday and the Pulitzer boys at the *Evening World* gave us veterans the next day off. Any two free days demanded a binge.

My lodging was a fourth-floor walk-up on West Street in a run-down building overlooking the Hudson and the docks. When the season warmed—and the end of May stank the same as summer—my flat became a steam bath and the waterfront reeked with heaps of day-old fish and the sulfurous haze from steamers' smokestacks.

I'd lost my right hand in the Great War. I knew of a

soldiers' bar on Pine Street where I wouldn't have to tell my story, where I could say, "I punched von Richthofen in his propeller," and we'd all laugh and drink up. Then I'd say, "I slammed my hand down on the Kaiser's pointy helmet." Only civvies wanted the truth, and they hadn't paid the price of admission to the dark tale of my past. That price was Ypres or Marne, although some other battlegrounds sufficed.

Even though it was a holiday, I put on my Monday shirt, starched so thoroughly it improved my posture. No yellowed collar for me today. A light gray dress jacket with extra pockets sewn to the inside right flap, easy access for my one hand.

The clouds promised rain, but Manhattan weather seldom keeps its promises, so I left behind my umbrella. By the time the storm arrived, if it did bother to show, I'd be indoors with an iced drink sweating in my hand and a blissful dead smile on my face.

A construction crew had plowed up a trench next door to my building, the start of a foundation for a sun-blocking monster. A steam shovel rumbled, and men yelled at the tops of their lungs to hear one another. I passed along the trimmed rim of the pit crossing over to Washington, zig-zagging on up to Edgar.

Edgar is the most nothing road in Manhattan: sixty feet long and nary a door to post a street number. Don't have a home? Tell people, "I live on Edgar." No job? Well, you get the picture.

I had stepped off the curb where Edgar met Trinity when the rain hit. Fat drops, great gobs. My riverboat hat sheltered my eyes, but my jacket and pants grew leopard spots. I clutched at my collar.

Heading up Trinity, the overhead tracks of the El provided some cover but only in the roadway. I loped along behind a taxi which was, in turn, slowed by a cart and horse. A geezer in moth-eaten Union blues, probably dragged from the closet for Decoration Day, spanked the horse's haunches to keep it moving. The pair of them looked to be a few hoofbeats from the glue factory.

I turned onto Exchange Alley. Not really an alley, the walkway served as a shortcut between financial centers for the foot traffic of the well-heeled and the hopefuls, traders riding the twenties boom. Out West they have rodeos for buckaroos. At least those bull-riders have the sense to know that everyone, eventually, gets tossed to the dirt.

The passage was a deep crevice and the tall walls blocked out all but a sliver of the sky, thereby protecting me and the herd from the insult of the slanting rainfall. To my left, the Adams Express Building, four hundred feet plus. I'm a bit of an aficionado of building design; I've written several features about their histories. This one belonged to the "Let's Poke Holes in a Box" school of architecture. Above the ornamentation of its bottom three floors, it was a tall dreary slab of terra cotta brick with a thousand or two look-alike windows.

The entrance to the Adams Building faced Broadway. By the time I made the turn to pass in front, the rain had weakened to a drizzle. The storm had been no more than a showy boxer: all bluster and dance and only one punch. I imagined a genuine drencher was on its way, but I hadn't that much farther to go. The brief rain had scared open some elbow room, thinning out the sidewalk sloggers.

Without a downpour to prod me onwards, I slackened my pace. I managed just a few more steps when, without warning, an object plunged in front of the brim of my hat, bursting at my feet. My breath stopped and so did I.

It was a fountain pen, the spear of its nib had crumpled and broken free, separated from its splintered wooden barrel. Ink spattered my shoes and the cuffs of my pants. The pen had struck the ground with such violence that I could only imagine it had fallen from a great height. One more step, and I'd have been skewered.

I looked around. None of those passing seemed to have noticed or else they didn't care about the meteor strike. I extracted a handkerchief from my vest pocket, gave it a shake to unfold it, and then carefully picked up the moist barrel. It was embossed with gold-leaf lettering: *Carolyne Fritch Designs.*

I looked up, backing to the curb. On this side of the Adams Building, each floor presented four clusters of four windows each. The intensity of the fleeting squall had caused nearly all the tenants to batten their hatches. There was one exception, high up, a single open window with a red curtain dangling out. I counted up the floors... 10...20...24.

I'm not so determined a boozer to lose sight of a good story. I had an itch of curiosity. How was it that this pen came close to impaling me? If that open window is where the pen fell from, why was it the only one to not shut out the rain? Maybe I could pitch a story to my assignment editor: "Death from the Sky!"

And this Carolyne Fritch. Was she a steely-willed matron? An uptown socialite with a side business? A lady architect? Part of what prompted me to investigate was this featureless, commanding, and mysterious female.

I'd been invited: I'd use the pen as a calling card.

Chase Bank made up the first floor. I wove between its walnut desks with their money-pinchers and headed to an array of elevators. A directory confirmed my destination: Carolyne Fritch Designs, 2406-A.

Carolyne Fritch, you nearly killed me.

Several of the elevators were on the ground floor and loading, each manned by an eager operator. I entered one empty of passengers, figuring I might get an express trip.

"Floor 24."

The operator, a youngster uncomfortably squeezed into that sort of uniform that looks better on an organ grinder's monkey, pulled shut the outer gate and safety grill. He cranked the control lever upwards. With the speed of these modern cabs, the journey would take less than a minute. After a firm jolt with the launch, the ride progressed smoothly.

I don't like taking off my hat in public. My straw-colored hair, when damp, looks like a spit-out wad of hay. I tipped the front brim up to halo height.

"Carolyne Fritch," I said. "Do you know her?"

"Nah," he said, "too many names and faces blow by to nab any."

"Alan," I told him, to add another moniker to his list of forgottens.

"Victor." His gaze fell to the floor and his lips puckered to the side. "You've got some oil spots on your shoes."

He then focused frowningly at the dripping handkerchief in my left hand—and not at the stump of my right wrist.

"Is it your job to scrub the elevator?"

"Uh-huh."

I dug in my pocket, then handed over two bits.

"Thanks, mister," he said, fluttering his lids with surprise. His amazement passed. Tugging down on the control lever, he drew the elevator to a smooth stop. "Twen-tee-four."

The elevator let out into a central hallway that connected the building front to back. I oriented myself, reviewing the twists and turns that had brought me to this point, and then headed left. The hall ended in a T, with corridors to either side that ran the length of the offices which faced Broadway. So many identical rooms, so monotonous. The owners advertised these sort of buildings as "towers" so the residents would think they were in an urban castle and not notice that they'd actually been slotted into a tall warehouse.

One door to my right hung half-open. Its plaque read: 2406-A, Carolyne Fritch Designs. I gave the door a nudge and took a peek.

No one home. I stepped inside. The narrow space, more like a hallway, had been cut in half from a wider office with a slapdash wall set between. The room stretched out along a slim path that wove between blocks of furniture. A reception desk stood vacant, unreceptive. The vast paper calendar covering its top was empty of notations and unchanged since January. 1926—at least it got the year right.

A coat tree held a lady's polka dot waistcoat with puffy sleeves. I hung my hat on one of the tree's pegs, resigning myself to wait.

I asked myself, what the hell was the purpose of my quest? What would I say? Tut-tut, you should be more careful. Someone from your office nearly killed me. Yeah, that would make for a friendly icebreaker. I dropped the handkerchief and pen, my calling card, in a waste bin.

Nonetheless, I decided that, since I'd come this far, I might as well take the full tour, threading my way down the length of the office.

A tilted drafting table displayed a large-scale drawing of a screw. I was disappointed. I had imagined Carolyne was designing skyscrapers, rather than street corner hardware. The pencil ledge held an Eversharp and a blob of gum eraser: no pen. The eraser was clean, never smudged.

An executive desk was set at the far end. The only item on top: an ashtray with a pyramid of crimped cigarette butts. Beside the desk stood a tall tripod with an empty U-brace, devoid of a camera. In the back, the maw of an open window, its curtain rustling. There had been no breeze at street level. Even the wind favors those who look down on the rest of us.

All in all, the room presented a flash-powder photo of a working space where no one ever worked. I heard the tick-tock of the wall clock and honking from the street far below.

I felt drawn to the window: it seemed to hold a mystery; it seemed desperate to tell me something, its curtain a wagging, albeit mute, tongue. This is where the pen fell. Raindrops on the sill. Why didn't Carolyne close you with the rain? Being open, why were your curtains not tucked in, not tied back?

Behind the desk, in front of the window, lay a single high heel shoe, ruby red, fancy, its style built to reveal skin or a naughty glimpse of a sheer silk stocking. A single slipper. I thought, *a Cinderella offering.*

I leaned against the sill, then poked my head out into the dizzying height. Across Broadway stood the Columbia Trust Building, its roof matching this floor. A dozen of its windows hung open with noggins jutting out, all facing down. The same was true for this building, heads seemingly without bodies stuck out from the windows around and below. Altogether this seemed queer, off-kilter, like a vertical cabbage patch.

Like the other spectators, I turned my stare down to the street, where, directly below, lay the contorted body of a woman. From this height, I could just make out her polka dot dress, the black and white in sharp contrast to the scarlet puddle she wore as a crown. Nearby, I spied a sliver of red, a shoe that matched the color of the one I just found. A small crowd clustered around her, an oval frame for a macabre painting. A blue-coated police officer looked up.

I had heard nothing. The fall and the initial reactions must have occurred during my elevator ride. I imagined the screams that drew people to their windows which stirred a commotion that drew in more and more.

A woman's voice from a nearby window, nasal and snarled: "That dress. It's Carolyne." The polka dots matched the waist coat hanging on the coat tree. "She would never have jumped."

I looked at the speaker, just one office to my side. Slowly, she pivoted her head my way, to where she must have known Carolyne worked.

"Murderer!" she cried, then let loose a full-throttled shriek.

That scream saved my life.

Startled, I drew my head into the office, just as footfalls thumped near and a pair of hands met my backside, shoving, thrusting me down. My chin banged the windowsill, my shoulders and chest skid forward. My balance teetered over the edge. Without turning, I flung my hand out, grabbing hold of the curtain to keep from flying.

The same woman screamed at me again. I yanked on the curtain, pulling myself back and bringing myself to my feet. Immediately I spun, intent on giving my attacker a chop to the throat with my forearm—but he had turned, running for the door.

For a moment, I stood frozen, other than my heaving chest. My blood boiling, my fury stoked, I gave chase.

CHAPTER 2
THE SPIRALING DESCENT

Alan

BY THE TIME I'd rushed into the hall, it was empty. Down at the end of the corridor, the stairway door swung closed. I sprang forward, but as quickly as I'd begun, I was forced to a halt. The same lady from the window appeared in front of me, her mouth blasting like a steam whistle. She spread her arms as wide as the wings of the *E pluribus* eagle, with fingernails like talons, ready to snare me. I had no time for this nonsense. I shoved her against the wall, bowling past.

I crashed against the door at the end of the hall, pausing my mad dash. I drew a breath. Seizing its knob with an already sweaty palm, I tore it open.

The stairwell dove down in dizzying, diminishing squares, a sharp-elbowed helix: twenty-four floors and whatever basements. I leapt from the brink of the top stair, throwing myself into a Cubist's abyss: Fool Descending a Staircase.

My prey tattooed each step, his footfalls creating a frenzied, thundering drumroll. I followed in pursuit, galloping and bounding down steps and across landings in a plunging steeplechase. The inside handrail was set on my left side, by my left hand, my only hand. I yanked on its bar to whip around each corner, all the while gaining on him.

Below me, stretched out in infinite regressions, the handrails became pistons, and the stairs became the teeth of gears. Seemingly spinning as I circled ever downwards, those gears ground and gnashed, ready to crush me. In the far depths of the well, pale dots pointed upwards, faces framed by blue caps and collars: the police.

"Stop, right there!" The order came from above, another officer.

And I did stop, my sides heaving as I asked myself, Why am I chasing this killer? What would I do if I caught him?

I wouldn't have to catch him, I told myself. I only needed to see his face so I could describe to the police who did it. If all that I had was the story of a phantom, I would be the most-likely suspect.

With the goal of merely getting a glimpse of the killer, I readied to renew my chase. Only then did I realize the only footfalls came from the policemen above and below. There was no sound from the object of my pursuit.

Each floor had a nook with a firehose. The killer must have ducked into a blind spot allowing me in my frenzy to pass him. Or, he'd exited onto a floor. Of course, he did. Why run straight into the arms of the one place he knew the police to be?

The policeman stopped two floors above me. We studied each other's faces, his expression mirroring my fear. He drew his gun—and turned.

Someone leapt against him, throttling him, and heaving him against the handrail. I began trotting up, but before I could get there, the attacker heaved the copper over the banister. The policeman held on, desperately clinging to a baluster.

By the time I'd arrived, the assailant had fled. A door stenciled with the number 16 slid shut. My instincts screamed at me to get the hell out of here as the police pounded up steps toward me, but my better nature took control. I leaned against the railing, extending my left hand and right sleeve, something for him to grab hold of or cling to.

In this moment of terror our gazes met. He looked so young. I read that same plea of "not now" on his face that I'd seen in dozens of doomed soldiers. He swung one hand up, grasping the points of my fingers. His other hand let go and swatted at my right hand—which wasn't there. And then, before I could pull him up, his grip slipped. He fell, searing me with his stare as he plummeted downwards. His body shrunk to fit through the needles' eyes of evermore constricting rectangles of the stairwell.

With the death-fall of their comrade, the police, now only a few floors below, doubled their pace, their steps clattering toward me in quick-time. I slipped into the hallway of the 16th floor.

No sign of the killer. A single person stood in the hallway; a lady positioned in front of an open office door.

This one didn't scream. I ran her way, fully intending to storm past.

"Come with me," she said, her voice a stage whisper. "You need to hide."

But how could she know? I slowed to a walk, my steps choppy, my mind numb. I wanted to ask a question, but nothing came to my lips. She grabbed me by my sleeve. I'd seen two deaths in the last few minutes, and I could have been dragged anywhere, even by a toddler, so when she pressed the back of my shoulder, she had an easy time herding me into her office, shutting and locking the door behind me.

The space was much wider than Carolyne's workplace; it ended in a bank of four windows. An antique armoire, large enough to serve as a family crypt, stood to my left near the entrance. Its partly opened door revealed empty coat hangers and a built-in safe. Halfway down and off to the side was a glass-domed teletype machine with a silent ticker tape printer. Four stern ladderback chairs surrounded an octagonal game table. Other chairs, plush and plump, bordered tea carts. A liquor cabinet shared space with a humidor. Along the papered walls hung Turner watercolors—originals, or else damned good copies. All in all, the place reminded me of a gentleman's club shoe-horned into a storage room. It seemed so out-of-place that I imagined I walked into the plot of a histrionic melodrama, one where I had died, and this was the waiting room of hell.

"You're the man who stuck his head out of the window," my hostess said.

"Yes." I felt dazed; I could think of nothing to say beyond dumb agreement.

"I was looking out this window—my job provides me with plenty of time to daydream—then, suddenly, I was awakened by a shriek from floors above. I stepped to the window, my hands pressed to the pane, when I saw a woman in a polka dot dress whisk by. At first, I thought she had jumped, but after taking a moment to review in my mind that crisp image of her fall, I could see she was already limp, lying flat, her neck arched back, and her eyes closed. I recognized that she was dead before someone tossed her away. Hearing screams from the street, I opened the window and looked out. All the other oglers were looking down to the cement. I looked up to see where she fell from."

"I didn't kill her," I said.

"You don't have to tell me. I'm certain that you're innocent."

"You are?" I sounded doubtful.

She drew a gin bottle from the cabinet, filled and handed me a glass: along with my innocence, my need for a drink was another thing she instinctively knew about me.

"Thanks."

She said, "The roof flares out like a hat brim. Anyone falling from there would be dropping to the street and this woman passed by within reach of my arms. As for what window she fell from, one directly above had part of its curtain hanging out. After about a minute, you appeared, peeking out. Now, why would a killer look out one minute after the fall when the screams had brought so many to their windows?"

A good detail, and one in my favor. The rim of the gin glass trembled against my lips. My pulse thumped in my ears.

"But what made me certain you were not the killer," she said, "is that a moment later, your head and chest sprung out the window. My heart skipped, thinking there would be a second victim."

"I almost was. Someone pushed me." I clutched my empty tumbler. I could have crushed it in my hand.

"That's what I thought."

"You're a good detective."

She smiled. "A short time afterwards, I heard the commotion coming from the stairway and while I stood in the hall, I saw one man run out the stairway door and pass by me, heading to the back side of the building. A few moments later you appeared."

"You saw him?"

"Only a flash. He held his arm in front of his face as he came from the stairs, like this, like Chaney in *The Phantom of the Opera*." She raised her forearm to eye-level. Her demonstration included the phantom's wide-mouthed chomp.

"He threw a patrolman down the well of the stairs."

"Down the well? Oh my."

A tumult in the hallway. The clamoring of feet and shouts: the police. One ordered, "Check the doors!"

"Shh!" She raised an index finger in front of her lips. It was tall and slender with a perfectly sculpted, mirror-painted nail. Her lips were lush and ruby-red, whimsical even in a pout. Contrary to the bob cuts *en mode*, her auburn hair poured down to her shoulders and swaddled them like a sable stole.

Her blouse was jazzy and revealing. It had a plunging vee and see-through chiffon sleeves. Her skirt looked both elegant and sizzling, as though ready-made to brew a scandal at the Met.

"You shift your eyes when you look at me," she whispered. "Are you a bashful boy?"

"Another war wound," I said. Back when I had two hands, I had confidence with women. Frankly, I was a jerk. She glanced down at my wrist.

I looked into her eyes: coffee-brown and a deeper tumble than the stairwell.

"Lorraine Marquette," she said as softly as a purr.

"Alan Priest."

"Shh!"

The police rattled the doorknob and knocked. We kept silent. I could hear others milling in the halls: tenants emptying out of their business caves. Lorraine squeezed my hand.

That gesture and her beauty dizzied me. Only with effort could I draw my thoughts away and begin to puzzle over the oddness of this set-up. This office, a fancy parlor, empty save for one worker: Lorraine—and she was gussied up for the ballroom at the Ritz. That hairdressing alone must cost a hefty sum to maintain, more than what fit in with an office girl's salary. Was she the boss of this outfit? Was she some well-heeled swell? And yet, she didn't wear any jewelry. That could have been a personal choice, or else, and this I guessed: she wasn't rich. She was dolled up for a reason, but what was it? At eleven a.m. on a Monday. In an otherwise empty office.

And why would such a stylish dame hide me from the police? She could vouch for my innocence by saying she saw my head poking outside the window and describe that moment when I was pushed, instead of risking becoming an accessory to my flight. Why not tell them about Lon Chaney in the hallway? What was her angle?

I chided myself. I should keep quiet and be glad I'd run into her and had this chance to hide, and not tear into her motives. I don't have to suspect everyone.

No, that's not me. I don't know how to trust.

With the thumping of doors moving far down the hallway, she spoke at a normal volume. "Don't worry, soldier. You're safe with me. I'm allergic to police."

I wanted to ask why. I decided to approach the matter indirectly. "This is a real tony get up," I said. "What do you do?"

"I'm part of the decoration," she said.

"Well, then it's a very beautiful place."

She brooked a smile, but her eyes sharpened to knife points. I had said the wrong thing. For some reason, my compliment had riled her.

CHAPTER 3
A FULL-MOON WOMAN

Lorraine

WHEN I TURNED fifteen my mother warned me: you are a full-moon woman, you will bring out the baying wolves. Because of your beauty, men will sprout hairs on their palms and spring claws; their drool will thicken into sap. Lorraine, she said, you will attract the ardor of so many men, you might even find love.

What a load of crap.

Beauty inspires infatuation and infatuation merely makes the lying more sincere. The rakes and the shy boys, the high-hats and even the bellboys, all become addlepated ninnies.

If my knight in shining armor ever did exist, he and his armor got crushed to the size of a needle and tossed into a haystack.

Alan seemed sweet, and I thought he might be different, until he chose to make that same sort of obeisance to my beauty. Fortunately, he followed up with a different track.

"Your accent," Alan Priest said. "I can't quite place it."

"Chicago," I said, making the "o" and my lips as round as a Mercury dime, "by way of finishing school."

Finishing school. My mother's desperate attempt to transform me into a fortune hunter, an adventuress. To magnetize me and toss me into a bucket of rusted bolts and nuts. Mostly nuts.

Having money doesn't make a man tedious, but talking about money does.

So, wearied by the Yankee *riche*, I tried my hand at landing one of the British aristocracy. Men with combed beards who smelled stale like smoking jackets, even when naked.

Mr. Priest smelled like Sandburg's Chicago: stormy, husky, brawling. And he had big shoulders. He tucked his right arm under his coat as though I hadn't noticed his missing hand.

"I told you I'm decoration," I said. "So, who are you?"

"I'm a reporter."

"I don't like reporters. They tell secrets."

"For every confidence I publish, I keep ten more unsaid."

"Then promise me, I'll be a story that you will never tell." As I spoke those words, I felt my heart pang. With my illusions of wealth and nobility circling the whirlpool of a commode, I realized what I wanted most in life: someone to whom I could whisper my secrets and my sins. Someone who would keep them forever enfolded in his depths.

Alan stared at the window with such a fierce silence, I thought his gaze might punch through the glass.

"A short time ago," I said, "when I looked out that window, I took in all of those who peeked out of their windows. Their floating heads seemed as if they were swimmers at the beach; dog-paddlers treading a tall wave. I imagined a giant guillotine blade skimming the face of the building, decapitating them, punishing them for their morbid thrills, their heads raining from the sky. Does that make me ghoulish?"

I suppose beauty is like wealth. Craziness is excused as eccentricity. That's why he said, "Unconventional."

Liar. I'm crazy. I was about to confess something more, but the words stuck in my throat. I didn't tell him: the moment before the woman passed, I was lost in a reverie. I was imagining myself jumping, feeling the flight and the crush at the end.

Instead, I said, "That instant when I saw you, nearly launched out of the window, your face showed shock, exploding in disbelief."

I suppose some lingering distress must have overwhelmed him at this moment. He turned wobbly-legged, dropping back into a smoking chair, a splash of gin lipping the rim of his glass.

"Being a reporter," he said, "and a veteran, I am used to witnessing horror. It takes me a moment to adjust, but my training locks in and I look for answers. Who, What, When, Where, and How. That's what I've got to do here. But, before I step out that door, before I risk encountering the police, I'll need to know where I stand. Lorraine…"

He spoke my name with the intimacy that suggested

he had the right to ask a favor. I felt that he did, but then I'm a sucker, and he shouldn't have presumed to know that.

"Floor 24," he said. "Room 2-4-oh-6. The police will be all over that place by now. They'll be asking questions, taking statements. I can't go there, but you can. Tell them you saw the victim fall. And listen in. Maybe you can find out whether others saw the real killer. Whether it's safe for me to go to the police. They might think the lady had jumped, but they know the policeman didn't."

"I can tell them I saw the man escaping from the stairs and running down the hall ahead of you."

"We'll save that. They'll ask you where I went, and I don't want you to say you hid me or else have them catch you in a lie."

I'm a good liar, I thought in protest, annoyed that he didn't trust me.

I studied Alan. That matted hair. He seemed like the scruffy dog who haunts the steps outside my apartment building, the one no one wants to adopt but whom everyone keeps feeding day-old biscuits. So damned lost and mangy. Charming, but mostly because he wasn't trying to charm.

Besides my life needed a pinch of zing. So, I told him, "I'll be your spy."

CHAPTER 4
THE ADVENTURES OF
MATA HARI

Lorraine

I HADN'T SUPPOSED that getting to the 24th floor would be so difficult. The police posted men in front of the stairway where their fellow officer had fallen. I smiled and nodded their way. They smiled back, their chins dipping so that, without looking, I knew that, as I passed down the hall, their eyes were following my fanny.

A sign announced that they had stopped service on the elevators. So, I strolled down the long central hall to the Trinity side of the building: the same direction in which I had seen the killer run. I stepped into the backside stairway and peeked upwards, cringing at the thought of an eight-floor climb.

I dropped my gaze down the well and contemplated its depths. At the bottom was the pink speck of someone looking up. As a hunch, I held my forearm in front of my face. He responded with the same gesture. *The Phantom of the Opera.* It was him, the killer. Why was he hanging around? Perhaps he was trapped, what with the police manning the exits.

And by my gesture he knew it was me, the witness. Unlike my sliver of a glance when he ran past, he had seen my full face: close-up and startled. I'd been standing in front of the office where I worked.

A sudden panic seized me; my shoes felt nailed to the floor. I suppose that if I were some other, some sillier woman, my spine would have turned to aspic, and I would have melted dead away. But I have too much grit in my bones. The morbid half of me allows me to stuff my fear in a carton. My panic becomes like a scream sealed in a box which I can set aside to open at a later time. Oh, look! Under the tree, a gift-wrapped scream.

It would be useless to call the police at this moment. "You see that spot sixteen floors down? I know it's him." And he would hardly wait there to be caught.

The speck disappeared. I held a breath and listened, trying to determine whether he was climbing my way. No sounds.

I headed up the stairs, a long trek in high heels but happily my shoes made the only clatter in the echoing stairway. I imagined Mr. Priest massaging my shins: I had earned that much of a favor from him. Would he be the kind who'd prefer to stroke my legs inside my silk stockings or would he prefer my naked calves? I've known both.

I've concluded that every woman has three levels: the decoration, the flesh, and the soul. Most men think they want the flesh above all, but, in reality, it's that illusion of glamor, the silkworm threads that excite them the most. It's the garter hook that snatches hold of them, allowing me to reel them in. When they open the flesh, it's only to gobble up the carnal meat of a woman. So few want to unwrap the soul inside. No man had possessed all of me. None have tried.

I thought of Alan's one hand and how he seemed to hold all his shame and anger clenched inside an invisible fist and I wondered whether he'd be too bashful to massage my legs. Sad, but maybe true.

———

The twenty-fourth floor was abuzz like a hive of wasps. Milling about the hallway were officers in bluecoats, businessmen stamping their feet in impatience, and chatterbox office gals yakking it up, overjoyed to have gossip so juicy and so tragic.

One man, a little man, stood in the center of all things and seemed to be in charge. He had jet black hair and that sort of droopy mustache you'd expect to see in the before-picture of a tonic ad. A blue-capped officer stood near him, holding what must have been the little man's bowler. One bluecoat with sergeant stripes whispered in the man's ear. I heard him say, "Detective."

"Keep the press on the first floor," the detective said. "We've shut down the elevators, but we'll need to guard the stairwells front and back."

The detective then turned his attention to an elevator boy, his name Victor, I recalled. "So, did this man ask for Miss Fritch herself or for Miss Fritch's office number?"

The elevator boy said, "He asked *about* Miss Fritch, like he wanted to get to know her, like he had plans."

The little man scribbled on a pad. "And what did you say in response?"

"I didn't tell him anything. Our tenants' lives are sacred. Private. He was about this tall." The boy raised his hand to a Priest-ly height.

"Did he have any unusual marks, tattoos, scars?"

The boy thought for a moment. He would certainly recall the missing hand. He shook his head, "no," then a bright light came to his face. "He had oil stains on his shoes, and he said his name was Alvin."

"I saw the killer," a woman announced. Her hair stood tall like the fuzzy dome of a Beefeater. Half-shell glasses on a silver chain rested in front of her bust. She wore flamingo pink lipstick. "He tried to kill me, too." She sucked in a deep breath as though shocked by her own melodramatic proclamation. "First I heard Carolyne falling out her window, then a wild scream which trailed out becoming tinier and tinier until there was this loud splat."

Several in the crowd gasped, then fell silent.

"That's not true," I said, my voice small but amplified by the sudden hush.

The detective pivoted and directed the full bore of his attention my way. "Why do you say that?"

I pressed my lips closed but everyone waited on my answer, compelling me to speak. Damn. I doubt that Mata Hari had ever uttered anything so foolish. Or maybe she did. Fact is, they caught and executed her. I'd come here with one mission: to listen. Now, in less than a minute, I'd become the focus of attention.

I'm a good liar, I told myself, but I might as well tell

the truth. "She couldn't have screamed. She was dead before she fell."

"That is correct," the detective said. "And how would you know?"

"I saw her fall by my window on the sixteenth floor," I said. "Her body was limp, and she made no sound."

The little detective sucked on his lips. He was a good three inches shorter than me, and he dipped his head and held me with his eyes: a bull pawing his hoof, readying to charge.

He said, "Before being lifted by the elevator carriage to this floor, I had a moment on the street to inspect the corpse. Even in death, she had a beautiful face. Well, half-a-face: one side was jelly. She had rope burns on her throat. I stuck a finger under her collar and checked her nape. The red stripe made a full circle. That type of strangling, they call it garroting, a G-knot. Taught in the army and shared amongst the gangster breed. She was dead before the fall. You said you are from the sixteenth floor?"

He had an odd way of phrasing things and a hypnotizing cadence. His question took me by surprise. I nodded: easier to do than kicking myself for having admitted to being on the floor where the policeman was killed. With this visit, that made two murder scenes.

He pinched his nose and sniffled or else used his hand to hide a smile. "So curious that you happen to come here. The elevators are shut down, not an easy trip. I believe you have an interesting tale to tell."

Mata Hari. Executed by firing squad. I'd so much more prefer a guillotine, my head tumbling into a basket. A quick darkness—as long as I had the discipline to keep my eyes closed and not take a final peek back at my severed neck.

"Lieutenant Santarelli," he said. "Gilberti Santarelli." He raised his eyebrows and pursed his lips, and it took me a moment to realize that he wanted me to respond with my name.

"Lorraine Marquette." I felt the eyes of the gaggle of gossipers pin me, the chill of their whispers brushing my skin.

"Shall we speak in private?" he asked.

He guided me to the office of Carolyne Fritch and shooed out an officer with a Brownie camera who was across the room photographing a red shoe beneath a tripod.

The detective sat down in the leather swivel chair behind the reception desk and lofted a flat palm. I thought it was there to take my hand to kiss it. I'm bad at reading the gestures of my species. I soon realized that he was directing me to take a seat.

I made a dainty adjustment to my skirt and sat. I leaned forward and pouted and clutched the fabric of my blouse above my stomach to tighten it against my bosom. I wanted him to think like a man and not like a detective.

He ignored my well-schooled charms. "Let me tell you a story, Miss Marquette." He leaned back in his chair, the tilt-joint wincing for lack of oil. "This area of town used to be the Second Precinct until they shuttered the headquarters. Since it is mostly all businesses and skyscrapers down here, we have but few pedestrians come nightfall. Some troubles along the docks, sometimes fights spill out of the gin-joints, but as for the rest of this plat, an easygoing time. These big towers have their own security guards who do half our job, the annoying half: rushing bums and giving the wallet pinchers a punt with an iron-toed boot.

"So, Tammany made this into Precinct 2A and moved us up to the Fourth, which is a long walk away. I don't like to walk. But they were right. Nothing happens in the former Precinct Two, and now I've got time for family. Do you like your family?"

Again, his question caught me off-guard: I thought he was never going to pause. What was his question? *Do I like my family?* It's complicated. I hesitated to answer for long enough to suggest that I was searching for a lie. "Yes," I finally said.

"And so do I." He jotted down a note in his book. I peeked. His writing was indecipherable. "One-half hour ago—was it only a half-an-hour?—the light flashed over a call box on the corner of Rector and Broadway, but I could see the disturbance even before lifting the receiver. Officer Baylor trotted past me in the direction of a crowd a block away, a dreadful group of spectators which had gathered, the way vultures circle a carcass. Motor cars and horse traffic also stopped to gawp. So, I rattled the phone's cradle, cutting the connection. No need to talk: I had my assignment. I advanced toward the commotion.

"A jumper, I thought, some woeful Joe. Jumpers make my life easy. They get what they want: a showy exit. I get what I want: an easy case. Suicide: killer and victim united, forever one and the same. No one to cuff and book and I'm home in time for supper. My wife is a superb cook.

"So, I hurried over to the victim and saw it was a

woman. That saddened me. I pride myself in being a gentleman, a descendant of Italian knighthood, and when a member of the fairer sex is troubled, I regret not being there to spread my coat at her feet like Sir Walter Raleigh before the Queen—although I doubt in this case a coat would have broken our victim's fall."

He must have read the credulous look on my face because he said, "To the point. As I told you, the victim had deep marks on her neck. So, I knew I was on the hook for a murder case and a cold meal tonight."

"Mmm," I said, feeling the need to punctuate his speech with sympathy, to let him know I was still awake.

He wrote some notes on his pad, and I glanced about the office. A drafting table. Again, that lonely, abandoned shoe.

The detective continued, "So Baylor rushes inside the building, where he meets with the switchboard exchange and the ladies inform him of a flurry of calls from the victim's floor. On his own initiative, he was first up in the elevator. I, being senior officer, recognized that this building was massive, and in need of more than a few flat-footers to trample the carpets, so I had a lady operator patch me through to HQ. After delivering my request for more men and while waiting on the cavalry, I marshaled the bank guards and building security, a half-a-dozen in all.

"I told the elevator boys to shut down their cabs to seal in the witnesses sand hopefully trap the killer. The guards and I took to the stairs: a long haul, but I figured that was the only escape route.

"I figured correctly! The killer came bounding down

the stairs, straight toward us." His cantering speech came to a halt. His lips puckered and his eyes watered.

"Officer Baylor..." he made the sign of the cross, "a man of initiative and someone who will never know the joys of family, encountered the lady-killer in the stairway and his gumption was rewarded by being hurled down from an Olympian height. He fell by me, near enough to touch. But I could not save him."

Santarelli dipped his head back, balancing the tear that rested on his cheek, at first making no effort to wipe it away.

"And so, I ask you," he said, leaning forward, "how is it you came to this floor with its murder from the 16th floor where another one took place?"

"Just curious, I suppose," I answered. He jotted this down.

"You are a curious woman, indeed." That snap of sarcasm told me that, despite his flights of flowery speech, he hid a bulldog inside his suit. "My lengthy speech was designed to stir your emotions and get you to open up. I failed. You said that the lady victim fell past your office window on the 16th floor. What office?"

"The Anglo-American Fellowship Foundation."

"And what is that?"

"A gentleman's parlor."

"A gentleman's parlor? In an office building?"

"A specialty club."

"And what do you do there?"

"I'm a hostess."

"Ah!" Santarelli perked up, his smile sly and knowing. "Hostess, gentlemen, specialty: I enjoy words which lie so vividly that they tell the truth. You keep the gentlemen clients pleased." He took a break from questioning to write down several lines of notes.

I felt a surge of fury. I despised him for all his assumptions, for how he had reduced me to some giggling lap-sitter. Nevertheless, I had a good deal of practice in showing deference towards those whom I loathe. I smiled coyly. Some women can cry on demand. I blushed.

"How is it that you are hosting a gentleman's club at eleven, let's say, eleven-fifteen in the a.m. on a Monday?" he asked. "In so attractive an attire?"

I hate police. They think authority makes them superior. And they're so nosy. "Monday is our least busy day, and that's why I was there alone. However, there happens to exist a small but avid group of enthusiasts in Great Britain who follow American sports. Today is the running of the Indianapolis 500. I am on duty to forward to them, by teletype, the ongoing account of the race. Otherwise, the reports would not be sent across the Atlantic until the news services bring them, tomorrow. Sometimes local members will come to the parlor for a cigar and the sports updates. I greet them and serve charm and tea."

The detective wrote several lines with seeming glee. "Enthusiasts, sports, parlor. From this I conclude that you work in a bookie joint, albeit a dignified one with an elegant hostess. And talented, I might add. To service a teletype, you would need to write in Baudot code. Miss Marquette, I would so much enjoy visiting your office."

"My boss will demand a warrant."

"But you will not," he said. He mashed his mustache against his face with the heels of his hands. He snuffled and gave a satisfied, conclusive sigh, widening his eyes and saying, "You will invite me in. Here is the reason. I propose that the murderer, when he escaped, did not kill my man and then exit on the 16th floor by chance. How did he disappear? He had a destination, someone he knew. Someone he trusted to hide him. All of this is mere conjecture, but happily it can be proved or disproved with a visit to your workplace."

Mr. Templeton, my boss, told me that if the police ever raided our betting parlor, I should not say anything and wait for him to send me a lawyer. And now, even though I'd intended to tell Santarelli nothing, I had jeopardized our operations by spilling nearly all my job's secrets, or at least enough for Santarelli to toss us in the slammer as bookmakers.

"Don't worry," he said, reading my mind. "I'm not interested in your money schemes or the contraband liquor you must certainly keep on hand. It is only the killer whom I seek."

Santarelli had seen through my evasions with such ease, I was hoping he could see when I told the truth. I was harboring Alan, not the killer. "The murderer is not there," I said.

"That may well be the case. But I have a suspicion that the police on the 16th floor never searched your office. When they came by—knock, knock, knock—you were there but you were not there. Am I correct?"

My expression must have answered his question because he smiled and said, "I fancy that, after all, I may be home in time for dinner."

CHAPTER 5
A RAPPELLING NOTION

Alan

ALL MY BEST efforts at being a drunk had come in the past two years. Before that I was too annoyed by those who felt sorry about my war wound to flounder in self-pity. But then…yeah, it was a woman who pushed me over the edge. I hate clichés. I kill the ones I write, and it kills me to be one. Misery burns double when it comes from being a chump.

Her name was Toddy. She kissed like an angel.

Given enough practice and devotion, two years is plenty of time to achieve a certain level of expertise in my chosen field of inebriation, and now that Lorraine had left me alone with a generous and defenseless liquor cabinet, I planned on plying my skills. On the one hand, she had already poured me a glass, so didn't that say she wanted me to help myself to a snootful? On the other hand: I don't have another hand.

The ticker tape machine spat out a tongue of paper. I

expected Morse or else something as indecipherable as Braille. Instead, it showed a string of letters and numbers. IND 500. COOPER POLE. LOCKHART IN. I spent too long trying to decipher this, my mind on its way to being mushed on mash.

The window beckoned me. This is where Lorraine saw Carolyne Fritch fall. I imagined that moment, a streaking flash of a plunging woman. She passed, her body lumpen, her dress and hair swept upwards, passing through the air as though a wind howled from below, that wind having fingers but no grasp.

I parted the window and looked out. This artificial cliff, a vertical slab of rock, with my head projecting like a clinging toadstool. Vertigo spun my eyes and gravity pulled my gaze downward.

Sixteen floors below, Carolyne still lay on the sidewalk. Now covered, the top end of the sheet was blotted with blood. Red Cross Sisters in stark white gowns floated around the body. They looked like a corps of fellow ghosts preparing her for transport to the next world—or else at least to Bellevue Morgue, New York's way station to the afterlife. A meat wagon waited, its tailpipe belching smoke. Two attendants unfolded a canvas stretcher.

Is this what God sees when He looks down on our dramas? I'd make a lousy deity: I felt a cold, thudding nothing. I stirred the image with my missing hand.

Behind me, the ticker tape began to clack away again, its paper snake coiling on the floor.

Someone knocked, beating the door, giving it a fair bashing. "Hul-lo? Hul-lo?" A man with an English accent. Again: thump-thump-thump.

I kept silent. The only sound was the clacking of the type keys.

"Lorraine, my precious one, is that you?" he said. "I heard your footsteps."

I thought, what if he won't go away? What if he brings the attention of the police? Or perhaps he'll recruit the house detective with the skeleton key.

Lorraine is in there. I heard her, officer. You say there's a killer afoot?

The only escape was out a window. This was not as suicidal as it sounded. As part of army training, I had been taught to improvise rappelling down an embankment, one hand on the rope, one holding a gun. If I had to, I could use the curtain cord to lower myself down to the window, one floor below.

"Hul-lo? It's near racing time."

I hadn't made up my mind to slip out the window, but, I thought, I might as well be prepared. I stepped on the bottom end of the curtain cord loop and bit down on the stretch passing by my face to make it taut for cutting. My teeth often serve in place of a second hand. I took out my pocketknife and sliced. I freed the cord by drawing it through a pulley. Twelve feet. I tied one end to the radiator and looped one end around my right elbow.

The door rattled again. I looked out the open window. Insanity. I cinched the cord around my forearm, tight enough to burn skin.

Then, to my shock, the door opened. Lorraine entered, along with a hefty man in tweed and a small Italian-looking man in a business suit. The last-mentioned raised a detective's badge. More officers stood outside the door.

I hadn't counted on that: Lorraine had turned me in. I threaded a leg out the window and sat on the sill.

"I'm sorry," Lorraine said. Her eyes had a look of fright.

The small man calmly looked me over. I must have appeared crazy or suicidal or both, balanced on the window's edge and tied to the radiator.

"Oh, don't do that," he said, seemingly more annoyed at me than concerned for my safety. "I can't think of anything more futile. If you don't die, we'll merely capture you on the floor below."

"That's crazy, Alan," Lorraine added.

They were right. I unwrapped the curtain cord.

CHAPTER 6
A PLEASANT CONVERSATION

Alan

UPON THE RECOMMENDATION of Detective Gilberti Santarelli, I agreed to fork up the cab fare to take the three of us to the Fourth Precinct Station. It was either a taxi or else a trip in the paddy wagon accompanied by hostile police.

"Mr. Priest," the detective explained, "my fellow officers believe you killed Officer Baylor and Carolyne Fritch. I'd prefer to speak with you in private before they break your neck. A pleasant conversation, and certainly not the sort that includes the pummeling they are wont to provide."

Mighty obliging of him. A cop-killing was the kind of crime where officers go deaf when one pleads for a lawyer. Fortunately, I had on hand a stash of bills to pay for booze and there's always a Yellow Cab across from the Adams Express outside the Securities Exchange, although I suppose most of the hacks don't expect their fares to wear handcuffs.

Santarelli sat in the middle, on my left, chained passengers on both of his sides.

"I'm a reporter with the *World*," I told him.

"I'm a *Herald* man, myself," the detective said. "Not so lurid."

"You call them, and they'll tell you, I'm working on a story."

A bluff, but I figured if my people at the *World* learned I was headed for a grilling, the police might fear the exposure and hold back on the knuckle dusting. Swope, the chief editor, might even come to my rescue.

"A newspaper story?" the detective said. "I find that improbable."

He didn't say why. In fact, nothing more was said until the cab pulled up to the corner of Varick and Ericsson. I skimped on the tip.

Santarelli unhitched his wrist from Lorraine's. She wouldn't have to enter the station in cuffs. He wanted to be on her good side when he told her she had a choice: witness or accomplice, then offer her a deal. *We know you were flim-flammed into hiding him. Just tell us he confessed, and you can walk away.* Could she be pressured to lie? Even though she led the police straight to me, my gut said no. Still, she wore a poker face, inscrutable.

Santarelli waited to uncuff me until we got out of the cab. With one hand missing, he could hardly lock my wrists to each other, so he waited for a gorilla to arrive and clamp a paw on my shoulder.

The Fourth Precinct sports a stylish shell for a station house. With a limestone facade and three stories in height, it looks like a bank for snooty patrons. The fact that it serves as a police station is made obvious by the number of bluecoats milling about out front and the paddy wagons sharing stable-space with the horse patrol. In contrast to its grand façade, the inside was austere: a main tunnel passing between bleak cells. One side accommodated officers who worked out of cubbyholes; on the other side, lock-ups and hotboxes for offenders undergoing inquisitions.

My reputation preceded me. I received the welcoming snarls and lethal glares fitting a cop killer. The desk sergeant shot me with his finger and then blew on the "smoking barrel." A detective strangled the knot of his tie and lolled his tongue. We have the electric chair in this state, I wanted to tell him, but maybe they were saying they'll shoot me, hang me, and then fry me.

In my early days as a reporter, I had covered the police beat. I figured I was first headed to booking: some print-ing, along with a snap photo of my unbruised mug to place in the Rogue's Gallery at HQ and to hand out to the press. Then came the line-up where a bit of ink on the fingers always helped witnesses pick the correct choice. I wondered whether they had rounded up that shrieking-eagle lady I'd met in the hall. She'd have yet another opportunity to point at me and scream.

My figuring proved wrong. Santarelli and Marquette continued on down the hall while the simian hustled me into a grilling room and slammed the door at my back, throwing the bolt.

A single bulb in a socket over the door illuminated the space, its light so anemic I could make out its tungsten twists. No windows, no ventilation. A small peep slot in the door. The smells of sweat and mold choked the air. They mixed with the stench of piss and fossilized vomit going back to the Roosevelt days. All this mixed together in a late-May cauldron with me tossed in to simmer. *Double, double, toil and trouble.*

The cell itself was empty save for three chairs, two for the zookeepers and a flimsy one for me. I backed mine to the wall before I took a seat. I don't like it when the knuckle boys sneak up behind me.

The bolt clacked. The door opened. Detective Santarelli, alone. He set a stenographer's pad on one chair and took out the nub of a pencil from his breast pocket. He pinched his mustache, sniffled, and then settled in the remaining seat.

The ape-man shut the door and threw the bolt, sealing us in. I could see the back of his neck through the peep slot. He stood guard.

I decided to let Santarelli speak first. He obliged.

"Mr. Priest," he said, "I have three questions. If you answer them to the best of your ability, my interrogation will be complete."

That sounded too good to be true. "Shoot."

His soulful eyes locked on me. "Do you believe that the children of mixed-race parents are the most beautiful?"

"Pardon me?"

"Did you not hear the question?"

"I did, still..."

"Do you believe that the children of mixed-race parents are the most beautiful?"

Whatever I had presupposed, I had not expected that sort of question. After my initial shock wore off, I raised my eyes toward the stain-blotched ceiling and tried to fashion a serious response. "I suppose there are many ways to be beautiful."

He wrote several lines composed of a strange scribble.

"Can you tell me why you asked that?" I said.

"Yes. I find the answer to that question provides me with the measure of a man."

"And how did I size up?"

"Better than most. I've found that those of the criminal element, and Dr. James of Harvard agrees with me here, behave out of a deep sense of rejection. In turn, they reject others who are different, a pecking order, they call it. Some who answer jump right in, tearing apart half-breeds, mulattos, or whatever names come to their tongues.

"Others will sneer at the question. You did not. Some will shape their answers toward what they think I want to hear. That is valuable to know and flavors all future exchanges. I believe you answered sincerely and with consideration."

He leaned toward me, his fingers woven. "Second question. When you were ten years of age, did you continue to sodden your bed with urine in your sleep?"

I thought I had readied myself for his game, but this question was a bunch of hooey. Reflexively, I let out a dismissive scoff. As to any real answer, frankly, I froze.

What should I say? Should I insult this Santarelli and his Dr. James? I looked around the windowless room, then at the door with the glimpse of the brute's hairy neck. I thought of its bolt. There was no way out but through this man. And, by hesitating for so long without a reply, I had commented on his question.

"Excellent," he said. "You disrespected the question. This is a question I reserve for the more intelligent of those who I interrogate. By scoffing, you have shown your-self to be a hard-edged cynic and you wondered whether I was some simpering socialist with dubious notions regarding insanity or someone in the complete thrall of the Viennese alienists. If someone of your sensibilities *had* shown respect for the question, I would have pegged him as a liar. Oh, and please do not report on my questions or their reasons. That would sap them of their usefulness." He jotted down some jots. "Now that I have appraised your soul, I can judge the integrity of all subsequent responses."

I had to concede that he had a method. I wasn't ready to concede its merit. "Third question?" I asked.

"Oh, yes," he said as though he'd forgotten. Again, he leaned in. "How did you feel when you strangled Carolyne Fritch?"

Again, he caught me by surprise. "I DIDN'T KILL HER." I gave my words a 60-point headline.

"Hmm." He wrote down several lines of scribbles including what I recognized as exclamation marks.

"Do you believe me?" I asked.

"Even before I entered here, I had decided you were not her killer. Firstly, the timing of the elevator ride and your ascent. Strangling to death would take a good two minutes and you had not the time.

"Secondly, she was strangled as by garrote. An impossible feat to perform by a cripple with one hand."

I thought of arguing: I am not a cripple. I *could* twist a garrote. Instead, more sensibly, I said, "So, I'm free to go?"

"Oh, no. I told you that, in exchange for three honest answers, my interview would be complete. It is. While I believe you are innocent of the murder of Carolyne Fritch, I still believe you may have killed Officer Baylor out of panic, merely out of the fact that he was chasing you. My colleagues will grill you regarding that, and not so pleasantly."

"I didn't do it," I said.

Santarelli stood, nodded, then backed away. He kept his eyes on me as he rapped on the door. I heard the bolt slide back. The door parted and the gorilla man entered.

"Booking?" I asked.

I hoped.

CHAPTER 7
MR. GOMORRAH

Lorraine

I'm a nasal woman. Or else I mean whatever is that Word-A-Day word which says that odors speak to me. I should be able to recall it, my father is a doctor, or was before they took his license. I stared at his medical books years before I could read them, studying pictures of tumors and wounds and naked men and women and operations performed on all their squiggly innards. Now I remember the word: *olfactory*.

I'm an olfactory woman. Seeking out smells, some days I enjoy strolling through Chinatown wearing a dress that provides a scandalous glimpse of my knees, my calves slicked with dark silk stockings, with seams that gallop up the back of my legs. Catching eyeballs with a swivel and, after giving them a good rattle, tossing them back with a bump of my hips.

On those streets I can inhale all the wonders of the Orient: Marco Polo spices sizzling in fry pans; smoldering punks of incense; pungent fish husks dried until they turn translucent and then strung out like garlands of lanterns... I feel steam and industry erupting from pipes and perspiration irrigates the furrows of my brow.

When I met Alan, I sniffed a touch of self-conscious cologne, one which declared that, yes, he performed his morning ablutions—thank you very much—but which never apologized for his sweat. He had the lonely breath of yesterday's liquor and today's tooth powder.

As for me, I add a dash of perfume to my baths, just enough to leave a hint, but I never dab it on my skin. I never want an artificial scent to announce me. I can smell honesty. And dishonesty: I could smell the woman next to me.

We sat at a long table in some sort of witness waiting room. It was situated at the end of the hall where I saw them shove Alan into a dim and dismal hotbox.

Here, the lights were pleasantly bright, and the air charged with the fragrances of stale tobacco and freshly brewed coffee. An officer brought me a cup of the latter and lumps of sugar in a tray along with a gosh-eager smile. I think he was smitten with me. I doubted very much that they were treating Alan with such royal courtesy right now. I avoided eye contact and left out a thank you. He whisked away.

The woman at my side also smiled. She used perfume the way a kidnapper uses chloroform: to knock you senseless.

"I'm Patrice," she said, her eyes crinkling, her nose wrinkling as she peered my way. "Patrice Somerset." She clasped a gold lamé coin purse as though I might steal it.

Perhaps she thought, with some hypocrisy, that, unlike her, the reason I was tangled up in this case was because I was up to no good. Nevertheless, she said, "Lovely to meet you."

"Lorraine," I returned her false sincerity. "The pleasure is mine."

She was the one who had told Santarelli that she'd heard Carolyne Fritch scream while falling. The one who said the murderer had tried to kill her in the hallway. She with the tall hair and half-shell glasses.

"I saw the killer," she said. "He had one hand. Like a pirate."

So, she had seen Alan. "He had an eyepatch," I added. The more confused her description the better chance Alan had of being set free.

She thought for a moment, then said, "Yes. I saw that first and then I noticed his hand. His hand that wasn't there."

She gobbled up the story so readily that I felt guilty. I shouldn't toy with her. This could be an opportunity for some valuable inquiries.

"Did you know Carolyne Fritch?" I asked.

"Very much so. We were practically best friends."

"Was she married?"

She blinked blankly. "I don't know."

"How long did she work there?"

Her eyes darted about. "Definitely a while. More than a while. I'm not sure."

She glanced at my coffee. I guarded it with both hands.

"What do you know for sure?" I asked.

Her eyes flitted around a bit more and landed on a thought. "She has a brother. Or, rather, she claimed he was her brother, but from the way they goggled each other, all moon-eyes, that look alone would have changed the city of brotherly love into the city of brotherly Gomorrah, if you know what I mean. His name was Ivan."

"Ivan Fritch?"

"I don't know." She massaged her coin purse. "All right. I didn't know Carolyne that well. Not well enough to speak to. Still, what happened to her is wrong and that's why I came here to help."

She came here to feel important, to feel as powerful as her perfume. From that sad purse, I could imagine her entire story. Its contents were probably no more than the few dimes that she meted out for her subway fare from home to office and from office to home. A *petit four* from the corner bakery, but only occasionally; she guarded her waistline like it was the River Marne. Friday nights she splurged on a picture show which she saw alone.

An officer was passing by. "Could you please bring some coffee for my friend?" I asked.

"Does this look like a diner?" he said and continued on.

My coffee had been just another fawning offering to the altar of my beauty. I passed Patrice the cup.

"Thank you," she said. "I get the genuine jitters if I don't down a noontime helping." She whisked a fly from the pyramid of sugar, pinched a pair of cubes, and then crushed them in her fist, the grains sprinkling into the brew. In the absence of a stirring spoon, she plunged a finger into the muddy depths and swirled.

She sipped at the rim. "Ugh." Her face turned bitter. Then she gulped down a full swallow.

"Carolyne did have a best friend," she said, "Daisy Yinger. She worked down the hall where she wrote jingles, the kind for ads. She didn't come into work today, but how much work does it take to write two, maybe three lines? Poor thing. I'm positive she'll die of shock. I suppose I could go break her the dreadful news." She perked up at the prospect. "So dreadful."

"Have a seat here," an officer said, directing a scrawny man to the far end of the table. The newcomer was in his mid- to late thirties. He wore a checkered coat that flared at the shoulders. He doffed his sporting cap and took off and folded white kid gloves. His brown hair was combed straight back and slicked with pomade. A wispy mustache hung over his thin smile.

Patrice nudged me, whispering, "Mr. Gomorrah."

Ivan? He didn't seem particularly broken up over his sister's death.

He tipped his chin up and used the sharp ridge of his nose as a gun sight to aim a double-barreled stare. His intense interest appeared directed at me.

"Do I know you?" I asked.

"In your dreams," he said, and cracked a count-my-teeth grin.

A common masher, street-corner quality. From this distance he was odorless or else Patrice's perfume had knocked my sniffer senseless.

"You're Ivan?" I said. He seemed startled that I should know his name.

"Why, yes, yes, I am. But you're not one of them dolls

from the 24th floor. I do believe I'd remember a lassie with your luscious chassis."

In man-think, he was complimenting me. "I'm Helen Nash," I said. Patrice appeared ready to correct me. I gave her ankle a kick.

"Helen," he echoed. "Like Helen of Troy."

Help. "I'm sorry for the loss of your sister."

Ivan seemed to remember where he was. "Oh, yes. That. Terrible. Terrible. I was just coming to see her, and I didn't even need to go into the building—thank God. I have this thing about elevators: coffins for the living. She was right there, laid out on the cement right there, out in front. I had to identify her. Imagine that. Awful. Terrible."

"Did you have a chance to call your family?"

"Call? Them? No, it's just the two of us. We're a pair of plucky orphans." He smiled the same toothy grin, this time for sympathy.

Thank heaven for bad liars. He couldn't even put his sister in the past tense. She was nothing to him and continued to be.

Could he have been the killer? I considered raising my arm in front of my face. But I had seen the killer's eyes, and these weren't them. Then I recognized with horror that my flash of memory had been replaced with an image from *The Phantom of the Opera*. If I were to describe the killer to a police artist, they would arrest Lon Chaney.

Still, the killer had snatched a good look at me, and Ivan didn't seem startled when he saw me here. And Ivan is a horrid actor. While his lips say one thing, his every true thought registered on his face. Mostly as leers. Sex was his only truth.

"What sort of operation were you and your sister running?" I asked. "That wasn't a design office."

He squinted. Before he could answer, an officer appeared at his shoulder. "Mr. Fritch?"

Ivan looked up at the cop, beaming with the radiance of a pimple. "Yes?"

"We have a few questions."

"Sure. That's why I came here. My poor dead sister." He put on his cap and stuffed his gloves in a pocket of his baggy pants.

The officer guided him, passing Patrice and me. "I'd like to see you at the funeral," he said to me. "We could have dinner and talk some more about poor Carolyne." He passed me his calling card, black with white flowery lettering.

Fritch Financials, Inc.
Ivan Fritch, President
and Pecuniary Agent

Fiscal Speculations &
Fiduciary Miscellany

Sinclair Bldg.   RECtor 3353

"President, that's me," he called back as he was led out the door.

And that was that. Patrice and I sat quietly for a spell. She finished her coffee. My coffee.

"You were asking those questions because you're investigating this case," she said, softly. "I'd like to help."

CHAPTER 8

A SUMMONS FROM A DARK FRIEND

Lorraine

"So, we come to you, Miss Marquette," Detective Santarelli said. He had saved interviewing me until last—and thank God for that. I had time to collect my wits and breathe real air. This grimy, spore-ridden room clutched at my throat. "Why did you tell Mr. Fritch that your name is Helen Nash?"

"Self-defense," I said. "You've never been a woman."

"Not necessarily true. I share the Hindi belief in the rebirth of souls."

I stifled a giggle. "Reincarnation? A bit unusual for a cop."

"In my line of business, I've seen too many lives with abrupt endings: spirits that never had a chance. The human soul is too abundant to exist only for its brief stay here.

"Mine is not so unusual a creed. It's close to the Christian belief, only in the case of reincarnation, the souls return to earth."

"Heaven is nicer," I pointed out.

"Hell is worse."

He was certainly a peculiar sort of detective. He smelled of baby powder and baby cream. Either he had recently been born into this body or else he had an infant at home and shared the diapering duties. Or maybe the baby smells were part of his shaving ritual. "So, you were once a woman?"

"In one of many incarnations, undoubtedly. My wife is from the Far East, and we endeavor to merge our beliefs. But I've strayed from the subject at hand…" He hovered his pencil over his notebook. "I have three questions, and if you answer them to the best of your ability…"

"I saw the policeman's killer," I intervened.

"Pardon me?"

"He ran out from the stairway door shortly before Alan did."

Santarelli's brows knotted. His lips moved silently. Finally, he spoke, "And what did this man look like?"

"He covered his face. Like this." I demonstrated. "I saw only the top of his head."

"His race? His eyes? His height? What color of hair?"

He had already passed three questions. No matter. I closed my eyes and concentrated. "White. He's just a bit taller than me. I'm five-eight. His hair…he had hair. Dark but not black. His eyes…" Lon Chaney, The Phantom in black and white, stared at me, bored a hole in my skull. "I have nothing."

"Did he limp? Did you see a scar?"

"No. No."

"For how long did you see him?"

"A second. Not even that. Time didn't stop. He just swept by." I remembered Carolyne's fall much more clearly.

He leaned in. He seemed meaner than before, a paternal sort of anger. "Why did you wait so long before telling me?"

"I thought I was protecting Alan." But that didn't make sense. In general, the reason I didn't want to talk to the police about anything was to protect Alan. But this? Something which exonerated Alan? Waiting made it sound false, contrived.

I suppose I've had an aversion to the police bred into me since I was a child. And yet, it was more than that. In truth, I felt ashamed. This was my big moment to capture history, as though I was there at the murder of the Broadway Butterfly, or had seen the Wall Street bomber, and I had nothing by way of the memory but that of a villainous opera fan from a year-old photoplay flick.

"It could well be that Alan Priest is innocent of all charges," Detective Santarelli said, "while you, madame, will still go to jail for protecting him, for hiding him, and for interfering with my investigation."

I hadn't thought of that: Alan free, and me behind bars. How ironic. From time to time, I've imagined myself in prison. Usually on death row. Whenever I read of killers frying on the electric chair, I'd pictured myself in their place. I've even sat in a rigid chair and acted it out. But I'm morbid that way. These charges, of course, would lead to no more than a few months in lock-up. Not as long as Mom. Not as long as Daddy.

Some raps on the door. Santarelli left me stewing in my thoughts as he went to answer it. He whispered to an officer. The exchange became heated but still stayed below the threshold of my skills as an eavesdropper. The two were so secretive, so disrespectful. I had a right to listen in! When they finished talking, Santarelli bowed his head, like a father-confessor weighed down by the sins of the world.

Alan Priest appeared in the doorway.

"Miss Marquette, Mr. Priest," the detective said, "I have misjudged the two of you. You have the darkest of friends in the highest of places."

We do?

"There's one person in New York who can free a suspected cop-killer," Alan said. "Arnold Rothstein, the king of New York, has finagled our release and has insisted that we pay him a visit. Let's just hope it's a two-way trip."

CHAPTER 9
THE BIG BANKROLL

Alan

IN MY ESTIMATION, early motor cars looked too much like carriages. Some were tall and boxy, like broughams. Others were coaches, or buggies, or buckets on wheels. They should have come with a whip to give the motor an occasional lashing. Finally, in recent years, automobiles took on a style of their own. Liberated from clopping hooves, they proclaimed the gospel of speed.

The Pierce-Arrow which waited for me and Lorraine outside the Number Four Precinct Station had a jazzy sleek cabin extending behind a six-foot-long hood which caged a rumbling beast. Lean angles and sharp edges were designed to slit the air. Oak paneling shared space on the doors with sweeps and stabs of metal. The running boards were broad enough to play hopscotch. Its leather-covered top sealed out the rain which had finally decided to come down in full force.

"No one summoned by Rothstein is innocent," Detective Santarelli called after us as we boarded the back seat. He looked sad and soaked as we left him standing on the station house steps. Although eccentric, I deemed him a good man and a conscientious detective. He despised Rothstein and despising Rothstein was a sign of honesty.

———

Once we'd settled in, the auto pulled out: a fast yank followed by quick jolts as the driver jumped from first up to the high gears.

Two mugs and a driver sat in front. They wore pinstripes stretched over shoulders that were as solid and as blocky as gravestones. The driver had a wild mop of orange hair. The two mugs stared our way. One of them had the bulk of a dump truck. None of them sported a gun or even bothered to clench a fist. No one runs from Rothstein.

Lorraine swept the moisture from her skirt. "Who's this Rothstein?"

"You've heard rumors of a circle of people who secretly run New York?" I asked. "They exist…and Rothstein owns them."

We were driving at a breakneck pace. In this rain, on these slick streets with trolleys and horses and foot traffic and New York automobilists, we'd be lucky if there would be part of us left over for Rothstein to kill.

I told Lorraine, "Once upon a time there was an honest policeman, went by the name of Inspector Dominic Henry. After Rothstein had personally shot and injured three of his officers, Henry decided to arrest Rothstein and file charges. When the case came to trial, the judge apologized to Rothstein for the inconvenience and set him free. Inspector Henry, however, wouldn't let it end there. He charged Rothstein with rigging the trial. A grand jury was convened. They handed down an indictment. Inspector Henry was tried for perjury and sentenced to five years for telling the truth. Nobody stands up to Rothstein."

One of the ugly mugs in the front seat grinned my way. He seemed to like the story and liked the fact that people told it. It meant fear.

The motor growled as we waited for the cross-traffic at Union Square to clear. The windshield wipers flopped back and forth, slopping the rain to one side and the other. One of the mugs mimed shooting me with his index finger, just like the cop at the precinct. I was popular all over.

"Alan," Lorraine said calmly with the wide eyes of a child, "is Rothstein going to kill us?"

"He'll probably talk to us first."

"But why us?" she asked.

"Save your gum-flapping for the boss," a mug said, "or I'll…"

"Show the glamorpuss some repute," the carrot-topped driver intervened. "She might be some or some other big shot's moll."

"That's right," Lorraine said. "I might be."

The mug sneered my way. No reason to show me repute.

I leaned close to Lorraine and whispered, "Just the fact that Rothstein wants to see us changes the whole story.

Whatever Carolyne Fritch was involved in, it wasn't a nickel and dime operation. Rothstein doesn't waste his time unless there's thousands, or tens of thousands in play."

Lorraine replied, "I like your lips next to my ear," and filled my ear with the breeze of her breath.

Danger possesses an erotic sort of tension. I'd noticed this in my reporting. Some gangsters thrived on it, near death as an aphrodisiac. I sensed this in Lorraine. I felt it in my own blood. If she'd let me, I would have grabbed her and lost myself in kisses. If only Tom, Dickless, and Hairy weren't racing us to our doom. If only...

She squeezed my thigh, just beyond where I lay the stump of my wrist, my ghost hand being the most sensitive part of my body. Maybe I was crazy, but I had never allowed a woman to go there. My right hand had no skin, no muscle, no bone to protect it. I've never allowed anyone so near as to be inside me. I brushed her hand away.

"The screws didn't go so harsh on you," one of the mugs said to me.

After Santarelli had stepped out, my trunk had taken some choice jabbing. I said, "They didn't bash in my face, if that's what you mean."

Wrong thing to say. He took this as a personal gibe: his face was lumpy, rearranged. His eyes deadened. He was a massive chunk of concrete, his head brushing the uphol-stered ceiling. He crunched a fist.

"My apologies," I said. "For your face. I mean, for the comment."

"You're an idiot," Lorraine whispered to me. And then to the ugly mug, "What's your name?"

"Friends call me Icepick." He growled when he spoke to me, but for Lorraine, he showed the eagerness of a nine-year old.

"Fascinating. How did you get that name?"

"'Cuz there's the Italian Icepick and I'm not him and I'm not Italian." And then, even more earnestly, "There was this girl once, she called me Bucky."

I could see what Lorraine was doing: easing the tension. I thought I'd join in the small talk. "So, Bucky. Seen any good motion-picture shows, lately?" Both Bucky and Lorraine gave me baleful glares and I couldn't figure what I'd done to deserve them.

———

We pulled up against the curb alongside Lindy's, a delicatessen just north of Times Square, patronized by celebrities and gangsters and the official unofficial head-quarters where Rothstein conducted his business. The crowd along the sidewalk had thinned to those hooded beneath umbrellas, a smattering of shuffling, strolling mushrooms.

Icepick offered his hand, helping Lorraine from the car. I followed in quickstep to shorten the time I had to spend in the rain. A pair of the two-ton goons tucked down the brims of their hats and chaperoned us through the revolving doors.

Who did I expect to greet us? Legs Diamond sporting a tommy gun?

The noontime customers were involved in their private dramas. Waiters orbited the patrons who sat in chairs ringing their round tables, those tables encompassing their round plates, and, in the center of their solar systems, those plates circumscribing isosceles wedges of cheesecake.

Being noon, Broadway players, having just woken up, crowded the scene. I recognized Harpo seated across from Alexander Woollcott, the former with a grin as wide as a piano, his teeth being the keys. They laughed out loud as though sharing a bawdy joke. Will Rogers, wearing a rumpled suit, slouched in his booth, squinting at news type while jotting down notes.

The hoods escorted us upstairs, to a second floor I knew must exist, but only on the principle that, from the outside, this building had three stories. At the end of a hall there was a door covered with ornate padding, perhaps to deaden the noises within.

Icepick gave the door three hardy thumps. A panel slid open, eye-level.

The door parted and two slouching giants bellied their way up to us. They frisked me and then Lorraine. The goons who delivered us headed back down the hall and the fresh pair took their places at our sides. Behind us were two suede-covered chairs, the burgundy leather stretched tightly over wafer-thin cushions.

"Sit"—one of the giants squirted the word through the side of his mouth. It wasn't a suggestion and so we obeyed.

They stowed their hands beneath the flaps of their jackets, near their side holsters, and all of us waited.

"More than rum, more than gambling, racketeering, and protection, Rothstein deals in information," I told

Lorraine. "He thinks we know something about the murders."

"Or maybe he knew Carolyne," Lorraine said. "Maybe he believes we killed her and wants to get even."

I should have thought of that.

During the brief instant that the door in back opened, I glimpsed a poker table. I recognized Mayor Walker and the starlet on his lap.

Rothstein entered, walking tall, shoulders back. He was the King of New York, the mayor's mayor. Hell, Jimmy Walker was a circus act, a dog trained to do back flips. Here was the genuine ringmaster.

Rothstein gazed at us. He didn't have lips, just a crack between his jaws that allowed him to open them to whatever size he needed to swallow us.

"Mr. Rothstein," I said, standing. A goon pinched my shoulder.

"Arnold!" Lorraine said. She took to her feet.

"Miss Marquette." He gave her cheek a peck.

I was gobsmacked. "You two know each other?"

"We've met," Lorraine said. "I didn't know you were the famous Rothstein."

"Not too famous, I hope," he said. "Walker wants the stage lights. I want everything else." His smile looked more like a wince. "I've run into Lorraine at the Anglo-American club," he said to me. "There's no such thing as an independent betting parlor in New York. At least not for long." His goons chuckled.

"Sit," he said. Again, not a suggestion. The chairs were rather tall, the seats elevated to just the right height for chopping at the back of one's knees. "Good. Are you comfortable?"

"I suppose," I replied.

"Well, you shouldn't be. Those are speaking chairs. You'll only be comfortable when you tell me what I need to hear."

Among a half-dozen sobriquets attached to Rothstein, people called him "The Big Bankroll" and he didn't take long to show us why. He extracted a massive roll of bills from his pants pocket and skinned off five Franklins, which he laid in a neat marching row atop the coffee table, just beyond my reach.

"Let's call this a down-payment on our friendship," he said. "As a friend, you'll tell me what you know about Carolyne Fritch and her death." He saw me eyeing the bills. "Go ahead and take them." He waved a hand over the five hundred.

If I pocketed the money, he would own me for life. If I didn't pocket the money, I would have refused his friendship.

The Big Bankroll. They also called him The Brain, The Fixer, The Man Uptown. Mr. Death.

"What if I don't know a thing?" I asked.

"Such a suggestion would be an insult," he said. "Everyone knows something."

"Carolyne has a brother," Lorraine spoke up, popped like a cork. "Goes by the name of Ivan. I met him at the police station. He said they were orphans."

"You see?" Rothstein said, smacking his hands together in a single soft clap. "Sharp, clear, and to the point. Your turn, Mr. Priest." He directed his gaze my way.

I had to offer something. "Carolyne's office, it was a lie," I said. "The calendar had no appointments. It hadn't been changed since January. Nothing appeared smudged or used. The drawing, the draft of a screw, it was on the top page of the sketching pad. There was no ruler, T-square or stencils." As for the last of these observations, I just now realized that they had been lodged in my brain.

"The reception chair squeaked," Lorraine said. "They never oiled it. I doubt that they ever used it."

Rothstein stepped forward, hovering over us, looking down. "If the office was a lie, then what was the truth?"

"I don't know," I said, and Lorraine agreed by shaking her head.

The door in back opened, just a slit. A man in an expensive suit peeked out and asked, "Do we skip your deal? Or is it time for a break?"

Rothstein raised a halting finger and time itself stopped… He inhaled, exhaled, inflating and deflating himself and delivered a frown to the back room and then toward us. He said, "Before you came here, Mr. Priest, I called up your chief editor, Mr. Swope. Herbert. He and I have gambled with each other for so long that we've run out of space in our ledgers. He's one of the few people whom I allow to win. I asked him if you were his friend and whether he would take offense if an accident should befall you. He said he is not your friend, but that he would vouch for you and expressed concern for your well-being. In my life, in my business, I have made many friends. But there are a mere handful I would vouch for.

"Take the money and shake a leg. Use your newshound nose to sniff out the story and when you've scared up the answers, remember, you're working for me."

The greenbacks on the table frightened me. I spoke in their direction, "What makes you interested in this case, Mr. Rothstein?"

The man tilted his head and smiled as he swatted his eyelids shut: about as innocent as Satan. He gave his chin a silent toss in the direction of the bills.

Lorraine grabbed them.

CHAPTER 10
GUNPLAY AT THE CAPITOL

Alan

THE ORIGINAL TWO mugs waited for us in the hallway. Icepick—the man with the messed-up mug—blocked our way while the other one slid behind us. The latter said, "Let me check with the bossman for word on your riddance."

He left us with Icepick.

Good riddance, bad riddance: didn't they mean the same? I mulled these over.

Meanwhile, sweet old scramble-face glared at me with a twitchy sort of snarl. I had an idea of how to get on his good side: ask his expert opinion. He was a professional killer. I figured he couldn't have been the one who killed Carolyne, not behind his boss's back, so I plunged in.

"I have a case," I said, "and I could use some insight. Why would a killer strangle a person to death and then afterwards throw the body out the window of a tall building?"

Icepick brooded over this.

"The dead one," he said, "is he a fella or a dame?"

"A woman."

"A hot tomato?"

"Never met her."

He churned this new information in the cement barrel of his brain.

Finally, he said, "Oh, she was a hot tomato, all right, a real sizzler. And the killer came in all juiced up on account of how she had been cheating on him and she was asking for it. Asking for it twice." He raised two fingers.

Lorraine sputtered, not bothering to mask her disgust. "Maybe the killer was a gorilla. A no-brain thug. A lady hater."

Icepick's face squinched at that judgment, barely containing his anger. "Or it might-be, have of been, could of was, I wanted to kill her three times but felt all sweet and big-hearted and could only snuff her twice."

I didn't like the way he switched to first person. Or the way Lorraine switched to the second: "Or maybe you tried to make it look like suicide only you were too dumb to know the throat marks would make the murder obvious."

"Oh, no, I had smarts, I had double smarts, so I wanted the body found far away and off from where I throttled her so they wouldn't finger the scene back at me and my place."

Icepick held up a pair of mangling hands to demonstrate. His partner nearly walked into them, stopping to thump the big man in the chest. "Boss says, let 'em hoof it."

"You're not even giving us a ride?" Lorraine said.

I grabbed her wrist and yanked, ducking beneath the strangling hands. I whispered, "The fewer rides they give us, the less chance we end up visiting the bottom of the East River." We hurried down the hall.

Icepick called after us, "Hey, buster, did I win the puzzler?"

I looked back and said, "Sure, Icepick, umm, Bucky."

He chuckled, congratulating himself, and his expression turned positively angelic. Hell, who knows? He might even take a day off from killing people.

———

Diners, the lot of whom had ignored our first passage, gaped our way as Lorraine and I descended the central staircase. She was a one-punch knockout, gorgeous: elegant and royal in a city that celebrated the rage of the moment. Manhattanites worshiped appearance but the moment your star dimmed, they tossed you aside. Or else out a window.

Lorraine knew she was being watched and soaked it all in. I felt like some sort of celebrity. I let go of Lorraine's wrist and she tucked her forearm beneath mine. We wove our fingers together. She even caught Jack Dempsey's eye as he posed for a photo, his bare knuckles playfully kissing the chin of his latest wife. Flash powder exploded.

"Did you notice the tripod in Fritch's office?" I said to Lorraine, speaking softly through smiling lips as dozens looked on. "What do you suppose they photographed? Were they into nudie shoots? Something more graphic? Blackmail?"

She hmmphed. "Men—you look but you don't pay attention."

"How so?"

"A camera's tripod has a mounting plate. That tripod had a U-joint. It was set near the window to hold a telescope."

I pictured it in my mind. "Lady, you're a genius."

"Yes, I am."

So, what was Carolyne Fritch looking at?

———

In the great elsewhere—outside the city—where the down-to-earth folk live, rain nourishes the soil and freshens the air. Leaves tremble out of gratitude.

In Manhattan, the rain is dumped into a giant asphalt stew pot and then simmered, drowning the streets in a pool of humidity. This damp air mixes with the odors of piss from the occasional horse and alleyway bum, but mostly with the fumes coming from the consumptive cough of motor cars and the stifling stench that percolates up through the sewer grates.

The motor-car horns blast continuously. The sky-high towers cast those below in a valley of shadows. It's crazy how much I love this place.

"I suppose we ought to talk to Mr. Gomorrah," Lorraine said.

"Who?"

"Ivan Fritch, Carolyne's brother. He passed me his business card along with a five-minute leer."

She handed me the card. Black with raised white

lettering, an effect I'd never seen. It had a font with snarled loops and flourishes. I sniffed it to see whether it was perfumed. It wasn't. Pecuniary Agent. Fiduciaries. Two-dollar words to dazzle the gullible. I'd never met him, still I doubted he knew what either term meant. The Sinclair Building. That was square in the middle of the financial district, across from the Federal Reserve. No office number was listed: this card was his office.

"He's a confidence man," I concluded. "Was he slick?"

"Slick? Not exactly. Slippery. Boneless. If you added a little mucus, he'd have passed for a slug."

"Let's give him a call and arrange a financial consultation."

"I told him my name is Helen Nash, my standard ploy for mashers."

I scanned the street, searching for a pay phone. The folks at Bell must have deemed this stretch of walkway too busy to crowd it with a booth.

Across Broadway, the Capitol Theatre marquis bally-hooed their latest cinematic thrill: "*A Good Bad Woman.*" Huh.

"Starring Gail Collinswood," I pointed out. "I suppose I'll have to see it."

"Are you some sort of a fanatic of hers?"

"Nah. She's my mother."

"Honestly?" Lorraine asked me, but to avoid answering, I skipped into the street, sliding between the traffic, finishing up on the far side of the boulevard. Having made the transit in one piece, I waved to Lorraine who gave me another one of her "Are you stupid?" glares.

Only after a trolley had glided by and the cross-traffic

signal light turned red, did she deign to follow, not hurrying, expecting that any lagging vehicle would stop for her and knowing that they would.

"When you said you had to see the flicker, I didn't think you meant right at this moment," she said.

"These film palaces, they're always good for finding a phone box." I didn't mention that I also wanted to test whether a skinny guy in a black overcoat was tailing us. He tagged along, passing between hooting motor cars, none of which slowed for his passage.

———

A matinee crowd was drifting in. I plied the usher at the front door with a story about waiting on our friend who was supposed to join us, and couldn't he please let us in to drop a call to my friend's house, and he could watch, and we certainly weren't no door-crashers, no how.

He told us to buy tickets.

I bought a pair, a fifty-cent robbery. Still, I suppose, this joint had a lot of upkeep. This was the brashest, most spectacular cinema house in the world. Chandeliers in the lobby, a grand staircase, and more seats than the Metropolitan Opera, over five thousand of them, all covered in velvet. This was motion picture entertainment in the sort of spacious arena from which the Babe would have trouble in trying to swat one out, where Caruso's voice would float so far that it would be reduced to a mouse squeak. They had a massive organ for belting out the accompanying music. If you were saddled in the back seats, you'd probably need opera glasses to read the film's dialogue cards.

They ran a stage show before evening performances, a top-notch jazz band, and they spoke of launching a classical orchestra with its own wireless program. I supposed that our four bits would serve to underwrite culture for the masses.

Lorraine studied the lobby posters as I found a phone and dropped a nickel.

"RECtor 3353," I told the operator.

A single buzz.

"Good afternoon." A lady's voice.

"I'd like to speak with Mr. Ivan Fritch."

"Mr. Fritch is in a meeting. May I take a message?"

"Tell him I'm calling for Helen Nash, who has several grand to invest, and who would like to meet for some financial consulting."

"Do you wish to make an appointment?"

"We'll be down that way around two. We'll call back when we're in the neighborhood."

I tugged down on the phone's cradle.

Another nickel and I asked for RECtor 3354. A business of any size will have two or more phone lines and usually the second number will be one up from the main one.

"Doubleday, Page & Company. Booksellers."

"Where are you located?"

"At the corner of Nassau and Liberty, in the Sinclair Tower."

"Next to Fritch Finances?"

"Who?"

"Never mind."

As a final measure, I checked the telephone directory for anything Fritch. No businesses and no person with that last name.

———

A lobby poster of coming attractions assured us that John Barrymore *IS* Don Juan.

I told Lorraine, "I've arranged a meet-up with Mr. Gomorrah. I made you sound like an easy mark, too good to pass over. But first we've got to ditch the snoop on our trail."

"Someone's following us?"

I pointed—discreetly. He stood there, outside the door pretending to read the *Morning Herald*.

Now, in my newshound capacity, I've shadowed an alderman or two. I've found them eager to trade up for a better story after I had cornered them in a bordello.

First of all, real people when reading newspapers open the full column, rather than focus on a horizontal slice of the front page, one rolled up tightly enough to swat flies. If they hold it at arm's length, they peer, squeezing their eyes near shut. He stared somewhere beyond the page, where he could keep us in the periphery of his vision.

Still, he seemed to think he was fooling us, so I grabbed Lorraine by the elbow, and we made a slow promenade to the side exit.

Our tail rushed to the entrance and fobbed a coin into the hands of an usher. The usher pushed back directing him to the ticket booth.

We stepped out into a grimy alleyway. The door shut behind us and I realized how stupid my choice was: not only had I announced that we knew we were being followed, I stepped into a shooting gallery, a narrow concrete canyon with no witnesses.

Our tail rounded the corner to the front of the alley, unholstering a gun. He leaned in and began charging. Lorraine and I rushed toward the dead end, looking for an open door.

We had luck. A delinquent guarded the back exit to the Capitol, charging a dime to admit those in the know. I would have gladly tossed him my wallet but settled for dropping a dollar at his feet. Lorraine and I slid by.

I looked back to see the junior delinquent stooping to pick up the coin. Our pursuer bowled him like a ten-pin.

We chose the wrong direction to run, hastening along the backside of the screen as it displayed a Metronome newsreel. I thanked God the feature hadn't started. I don't know if I could have braved a fifty-foot-tall projection of my mother's head at that moment.

The organ player accompanied the snippets of world affairs with somber, sonorous tones and the audience responded to our shadowy crossing with hoots and catcalls.

Enter the villain, stage left. Our pursuer brandished his pistol as he followed us behind the screen: to the audi-ence, a menacing silhouette. The crowd oohed and booed. Someone shrieked.

We ran out beyond the far side of the screen. Several steps scrolled down alongside the stage. The startled organist froze on a single note, a heavy hand pressing a bass chord. The house lights brightened.

Sloping up before us in the immense theater chamber was a tidal wave of felt-covered chairs. It began at our feet and rose in banks, level by level, cresting in the balconies. The matinee patrons, although numbering in the hundreds, seemed sparsely scattered throughout the vast auditorium. Many of them stood, seemingly uncertain as to whether they should stampede or stay still. Teenaged lovers broke from their snuggle-pupping. The box seats emptied. Ushers came tumbling in, padding down the stairs.

Lorraine and I reversed direction, cutting in front of the stage. The shadow with the gun stopped in its tracks. I suppose he realized that he'd become the film star: an unwelcome christening. If he peeked out from behind the screen, he'd have hundreds of witnesses.

He slowly turned his gun to the screen and fired a single shot. Those in the crowd screamed and shouted. Jostling became shoving as they stormed the aisles, clotting and blocking our escape path.

I looked back. The gunman pressed an eye to the hole and rotated it, until it aimed our way. That first shot was to drill a peephole. He backed up and unloaded his gun, spearing the screen and sending bullet after bullet our way.

Whether shot in the back or due to the shoving, someone in front of us fell against the stairs. The swell of panicking patrons trampled him.

Policemen began heading down the steps, pressing

against the tide. Lorraine and I ducked behind a row of seats, quick-crawling our way to the center aisle.

The newsreel came to an end with Calvin Coolidge bashing the bow of an ocean liner with a champagne bottle. When the last frame rolled up, the screen blazed, stark white.

A silhouette of a gunman would have given the police perfect target practice but the projector lamp cut for a moment, and when it came back on, the shadow with the gun had vanished.

Lorraine and I scrambled to our feet. A policeman clipped my shoulder as he rushed past me. I slung my arm around Lorraine's waist as we joined the bustling crowd.

Moments later, in the lobby, we both gasped, giddy with relief. I was trembling more than she was.

CHAPTER 11
THE BUCKET-SHOP BUNCO

Lorraine

"Rothstein wouldn't bother forking over five C-notes and then send someone to kill us," Alan said. "So, who was our stalker?"

Neither of us had a clue. But I liked the question. Alan and I were caught up full tilt in the thrill of a mystery. None of the false smiles of a gentleman's parlor hostess. If I wanted to scream or claw the stalker's face, I could, and I felt like scratching the eyes out of some villain right now just for the liberating hell of it.

Hanging around Alan was a pulse-pounding experience: arc lamps blazed in my mind. My heart banged against my chest as though locked behind a dungeon door, wanting out. Maybe my heart has always been locked in a dungeon.

I leaned against him tingling, a patina of sweat cooling my skin, as we rode in the back seat of another Yellow Cab. This time we plummeted down Broadway heading for the Financial District to meet up with Mr. Gomorrah, the lizard of Wall Street. Alan says he's a con man—but aren't con men supposed to be charming? Or so I thought.

"I suspect Mr. Fritch runs a bucket shop," Alan told me. "He fobs off penny stocks that aren't worth a penny."

"So, how can you be sure he's a con artist?"

Alan ticked off the answers, saying, "I've written a story about these operators. Fritch sounds like it could be a name, but there are none in the directory, not even Carolyne or her design business. Ivan's fancy-pants business card uses four-bit words when nickel ones will do. Fiduciary is setting up a trust, not some sort of fiscal hocus-pocus or whatever he thinks it means. He chose the financial district to make it look like he rubs shoulders with the high rollers but he doesn't list his office on his card. He doesn't have an office. When we get there, we'll find that Fritch uses an answering service to take his messages, or maybe he bribes the building switchboard."

The list was impressive, and it did seem to make sense. "That means, when he flirted with me at the police station, that was because he saw my expensive clothes and wanted to skin me for my money."

"Most likely."

Being ogled for something other than my body felt strangely complimentary.

"He's dazzled by you and now he thinks he can scam you for a bundle. What we've got to do is con the con."

I noticed the taxi driver was glancing back in his rearview mirror, his eyes shifting from the road to us, probably wondering who the hell he had on board. He'd have a nifty half-story to tell his family and friends.

I said, "So the plan is, when I meet up with him, I'll get him to talk?"

"Precisely. First, he'll tell you his office electricity is out or some such thing and why don't we do business at the nearby deli? And then he'll dazzle you with charisma."

"I doubt that. You haven't met him."

"While he's delivering you some fairy tale about fortunes to be made, you'll need to steer the conversation to Carolyne. What business she ran. Now, I've had some experience as a reporter prying out stories. He'll spin some tales, so you'll have to be patient and persistent—but subtle—to tweeze out the truth. Reel him in. Save the accusations until after you've cornered him in a lie…"

And Alan went on. I'm sure he meant well, but he was lecturing me wrongly on a topic I knew all too well. The way to get any man to talk is to hang on every word he says. He'll go on for hours. You can't shut him up. He'll soon delve into some sob story, and after the magic words "Poor baby," and a squeeze of the hand, he'll confess to his every secret sin.

Alan went on to talk about the Sinclair Building. He had a thing about buildings and their histories as though every one of them was the character in a novel he was writing. Maybe he was writing a novel. I've heard it's a fever among newsmen.

The Sinclair Oil Building, originally the Liberty Tower, had been bought by Harry Ford Sinclair, who stole oil from the Teapot Dome in Wyoming. Being rich, he never went to jail for his crimes and went on to sell the oil to Japan, who, if you believed General Billy Mitchell, would be fighting the next war with the U.S. of A. and blah, blah, blah.

Men and their towers. I bet those Viennese head doctors would have something to say about that. I gave Alan a listening ear and he could have gone on hours except for the fact that the cab ride came to an end, and it was time to ring up Ivan Fritch.

Fritch was a confidence trickster, and I was there to con him, and I liked the idea of that. I might even be sitting across from a murderer, and, strangely enough, I liked that even more.

———

I stood across from the Sinclair Building, my purse mashed between my hands, hoping to appear like an innocent rube waiting to be fleeced. I wished that I'd had a bow to put in my hair, one that would make me look like I just stepped off the express train from Hicksville. Of course, if Hicksville was worthy of an express train, it wouldn't exactly be backwoods.

No matter. All that necessary play-acting turned out to be unnecessary. As he crossed the street, I could see by Fritch's hungry eyes that he saw me as a scrumptious bonbon, ready to be gobbled. I had no need to sell: he'd already bought.

CHAPTER 12
A FINE PAIR OF LIARS

Lorraine

HAVING PLAYED hostess to a hundred Baron von Monocles, I've sometimes lapsed into despair, believing that true gentlemen no longer exist. Maybe they succumbed to the scourge of the European war and the shattering of empires. Knights without orders of chivalry, abandoning the tin cans of their armor alongside the motorways, leaving them there to rust.

The classiest man I'd ever seen stood on the stage of the Cotton Club. Duke Ellington in a spotlight: breathtaking. His felt tuxedo shimmered as though it were the sunlit surface of a black pool. His white silk shirt popped like flash powder. His cufflinks and eyes twinkled and dazzled. When his eyebrows rose, they were strong enough to lift a thousand smiles.

And then there was the creature sitting across the table. His checkered coat flared at the shoulders making it appear as though he might actually have shoulders. The matching sports cap slanted to one side and his leer leaned the other way. Together they balanced his tilting head, preventing it from toppling off his neck. He seemed distracted, as though he had happened upon this restaurant booth while searching for a shanked golf ball.

This restaurant. Three blocks from the Federal Reserve in what must have been the anti-financial center of Manhattan. The tablecloth had a red-and-white checkerboard pattern with blotches of food serving as the checkers. The menu began with chicken broth for three cents, broth with chicken for six cents, and two side biscuits for a nickel. If you tried hard enough, you could blow an entire quarter on a meal.

Alan sat in the booth behind me, a second pair of listening ears.

"If you pass along the secret words," Fritch said, "they serve sparkling wine here. Quality stuff, pink, white, red: all different colors. Maybe the pink is when they mix the two. The owner is a Jew. Are you a Jewess?"

His sentences hopped about between thoughts in a way that challenged me to follow. "Catholic," I said.

"Not joined up to one of them Orthodoxies, I hope. I've got nothing against Jews or Catholics or any of their breeds, except for them Orthodoxies. Spooky gowns like Masonites. Shaggy beards. The Klan, God bless them, they ought to focus their zeal on them Orthodoxies."

I took a whiff of the aroma drifting in from the kitchen: sauerkraut broth and ammonia. I wondered which one they used to clean the floor and which one they served. Or maybe a mixed pot served both purposes.

"I told you I have a few thousand to invest," I said. "So, why did you invite me to the worst restaurant in downtown?"

He sneered at the menu and brushed away a few sticky crumbs. "Because you're not Helen Nash and you're not rich. You didn't suppose that I'd jabber with the cops about you? There I am in their stinking hot room on that stinking hot seat, and I'm easing along with my story about my dear dead sister and sneaking in a few questions of my own along the way, questions about that broad, that high-class broad, who they tell me is Lorraine Marquette. That's your name it seems, and you're a witness and a suspicious one, under suspicion and all for helping a cop killer. Still, I had to meet you, to size up your game, to cipher out your angle."

So much for playing the rich socialite who gently drew out answers. Time for another strategy.

"And you aren't Ivan Fritch," I said. It was a guess, but only partly a guess. The man sitting across from me was a con artist, right? And what bunco man would use his real name?

"What makes you say that?"

Time to go all in on my bluff. "I, also, asked about you at the station. An officer recognized you and remembered that you'd been arrested for grifting."

"What a pain. The police remembering me and all. Jinxes my con. Right now, I got a flatfoot on my tail, standing on the corner outside on account of they're still eyeing me over Carolyne's swan dive. He thinks I don't see him. Maybe I'll have to ankle my way out of town." He concentrated on the menu. Not really. He was just avoiding eye contact. "So, here we are, a fine pair of liars. What do we talk about?"

"So, who are you?" I asked.

"Trade secret."

My nose twitched. I changed the subject to something else I wanted to know. "I pay attention to smells. How is it that you don't have any odors?"

This question perked him up. "Bicarb, I swear by it. In my shoes, under my arms. A depth charge to my belly come sun-wake and I'm fully neuterized for the day."

He attempted a smile, but still, there was something deeply bilious about him, surging from his soul: a well-spring of repugnance.

I decided to up the stakes. I said, "I also play the con. I'd guess by the quality of your clothes and choice of restaurants that I'm better at it than you." I popped the clasps on my purse and let him ogle the five C-notes.

This lit a pilot flame of lust inside his eyeballs.

A waitress came for our orders.

"We're still pondering," Ivan said.

"Yeah?" she said. "Well, we ain't got pondering on the menu."

"Here," he slid his palm across hers, leaving a coin. "Take a dime for your time. Now go scare yourself." He flicked her away.

He told me, "You know, I can do the high-end hustle." He pinched his collar as though tightening a tie. "I figure with your style and my know-its, we could partner up, someplace far from here. Miami. Everyone's making a killing in Miami. You've got a sponsor backing you? A sugar daddy?"

I steered the conversation back to him. "You were running a first-class enterprise out of Fritch Designs."

"That. That took a hell of an investment. Wiped me out. And the moment I locked in the payout, my sister springboards to the cement below and so only now I'm looking over my shoulder."

"She wasn't really your sister," I said.

"Jealous? You could be my sister."

"Maybe we could run the same operation."

"Elsewhere. Far off from this side order of hell." He took my hands. I let him. He said, "I'm being spooked, some midnight shadows, or I guess, midday, in this case. I know when someone's on my back. My means of living gives me a full spin of vision. A bluecoat has been tugging on my shirttails since I skipped the station house. I didn't go losing him on account of a couple of junior hoodlums also hanging about. Those nippers are the ones you got to fret over. Just up from the street gangs, they don't play by the big-boy rules. You give them cross-eyes and they'll gift you a new navel. I've got to shake this town. You've got the bundle. How many C's you got in your snap purse? Don't matter. Let's blow."

"I've already got a partner."

"Figures. I couldn't shoot seven with fixed dice. All luck, all bad. Who you working with?"

"Rothstein."

I couldn't have gotten a bigger jolt out of him if I'd tipped his chair.

"Rothstein?" he said. "Holey Moley. I should have… I should've seen. Any pill as sweet as you had got to be poison." He grabbed his hair and pulled, leaving a ruffled peak. "Listen, tell Rothstein all I want is out. Just only, I'm broke. For fifty bucks, I'll go my deathbed, my lips sealed like a weldered hatch."

"Fifty? That's selling yourself on the cheap side."

"Yeah? Well, for a hunderd he could get me killed. So, I figure he'll maybe show some pity if I spare him some scratch. Fifty bucks is enough for a train ticket to nowhere and that's where I'll be, digging a hole to hide in."

"So, what's this secret you're taking to your grave?"

"You don't know?"

"That's what Rothstein sent me to find out."

"Rothstein don't know?" His voice rose. "Then who's them punks following me? Who the fuck is trying to kill me?"

Our fellow diners gawked our way with feral glares.

"You know what?" he said. "Count me gone. I'm legging it. I'm solid gone." His chair toppled back as he got to his feet. Then he dashed out the door.

I ran after him. Alan abandoned his booth and trotted behind me. When he caught up, he tugged at my shoulder, trying to slow me down. I shrugged off his grip. The policeman who had been spying on us, dropped the handset at the call box and joined in the chase. The two kid thugs ran to their automobile and fell into the procession. An entire parade followed the lead of Mr. Gomorrah.

Ivan jumped around and between motor cars, threading the middle of Platt Street. When he came up to an intersection, the heavy traffic on Pearl brought him to a halt, stopping long enough for me to catch up.

I grabbed his wrist and he whirled, seizing me by my upper arms and shoving me into the traffic. I landed on my rear. One car swerved around me and, as a second one barreled my way, Alan grabbed my hand and yanked me up with such force that not only did I rise to my feet, I toppled into his arms.

Ivan bolted, trotting up behind a hay truck and hopping on the back. He wagged a finger our way and at the cop who continued to pursue him on foot.

"Are you all right?" Alan asked me.

"Never better," I said. I broke from his clasp and brushed the grit from the bustle of my skirt.

We looked up Pearl Street to where the Keystone Cop scurried and skidded ever onwards, in futile pursuit.

I linked my arm inside Alan's. "That was a kick," I said. "What's next? Another gunfight?"

"Running down Fritch? You're a remarkable woman," he said.

"Yes, I am." I added a purr. As I leaned against him, we paused for an uncomfortable moment searching each other's faces. He seemed in pain, his soul long ago stabbed and the blade broken off.

Finally, he said, "I was thinking there may be evidence on Carolyne Fritch's body. I've got a source at the city morgue."

"The morgue?" I asked. "And still on our first date? You do know how to thrill a lady."

My stomach rumbled. A vendor stood behind an oven on wheels. Fumes roiled out of its tin smokestack. A drawer in the middle hung open, displaying sizzling sausages on spits. They drooled grease. I just plain drooled.

Alan focused on hailing a cab. I was about to suggest lunch when a motor car pulled up behind us. Two hoodlums got out. The morgue and the meal would have to wait.

CHAPTER 13
A HEARSE AND A CURSE

Alan

A MOMENT after Lorraine and I stepped up to the curb to hail a cab, a flaming matchstick struck my shoe.

Once upon a time, cigars and pipes provided a dignity and ritual to tobacco: smoking generally took place indoors and at leisure. Cigarettes brought smoking to the streets, although, at first, you'd find this "more vulgar" form only among the working stiffs. Now it seemed every Joe, high and low, tucked a short fuse between their lips, including the pair of human bombs who greeted us.

They stood in front an old Crossley motor carriage, a vehicle every bit as boxy, black, and cheerless as a hearse. It might as well have been a 19th century funeral wagon. Needed a buggy whip.

Its motor sputtered and chugged. Its tailpipe grumbled, cleared its throat, and belched out a sooty exhaust.

The two who blocked our way were juvies from the sort of gang whose members seldom see twenty. Too growth-stunted to rely on muscle, one kept a hand stuffed under his jacket, a gunslinger keeping company with his peacemaker. The other extracted a peanut from his pocket, then crumbled its shell in his fist. The remains of the husk rained down. He massaged the skin from the kernels and dropped the meat in his pocket, then proceeded to work on another. He had it down to a machine-like procedure, mesmerizing, fascinating to watch for man or squirrel.

"Mr. Price?" the nutcracker asked.

"Priest."

"We've been sent to fetch you."

"Rothstein cut us loose."

"That so? Well, we ain't Rothstein," the gunman said. He opened the back door.

"Thank you," Lorraine responded, gathering her skirt above her knee as she stepped in. I realized that her attitude of "they are only killers if you treat them like killers," was deliberate, using her beauty as a ploy and a shield. I had no ploys; I had no shield.

Not so deferential to me, the gunman jammed the muzzle of his pistol against the small of my back and patted me down.

Up ahead, I saw the policeman returning, the one who ran after Fritch. I tried shouting with my eyes, flapping my fingertips, anything I could do to say there was a gun at my back.

I did catch his attention, but only for a second before Peanuts shoved me in the vehicle.

———

I don't hold faith in the power of curses, that is, beyond the type I employ to flush out my mouth as part of my daily verbal hygiene. As for jinxes and that breed of hoodoo, they're a bunch of hooey. Which doesn't mean I'm not beyond adding a spooky contrivance or two to my news stories to provide a dash of drama, a tonic to gin up the interest of my readers.

A year back I wrote a Sunday feature titled *The Curse of Stanford White*. The preeminent architect of his generation, White populated New York and beyond with his creations, each a temple erected to the gods of enterprise. But gods are fickle, and today's acclaim is tomorrow's bullet in the brain. In 1906, while dining on the terrace of his masterwork, the second incarnation of Madison Square Garden, White was gunned down by the husband whose wife he had raped. The murder held that year's title of "Crime of the Century." Over the twenty years since, many of White's greatest achievements had been razed and built over, the city seemingly purging itself of reminders that he ever existed. One of the buildings demolished was his version of Madison Square Garden. Another of his works, set for the wrecking crew, was our destination.

In 1879, William Kissam Vanderbilt, scion of the robber baron of the railways, commissioned the construction of "Le Petit Chateau"—"petit" in the sense of Versailles. Gargantuan, gaudy, it sported the sort of towering spires where damsels stick out their necks and wave their hankies at passing cavaliers. WKV's son, Will Kiss'm the Second, commissioned Stanford White to design a next-door palace, "Petit Junior."

Not quite as elegant, not quite as ostentatious, 666 Fifth Avenue resembled its senior neighbor but as a runtish offspring.

Upon WKV the elder's death, both mansions were placed on the auction block. The purchasers wanted land and not castles. Now vacated and gutted, the structures waited for the wrecking ball. And waited. In New York, even destruction is corrupt. The right permits needed to be paid for, the right palms needed to be greased. Like the construction business, demolition had fallen under the control of racketeers.

———

Why is it that, given time, all old mansions begin to look like insane asylums? Perhaps, along with the concrete, a madness gets slopped into the foundations, the megalomania of their tycoon owners.

Number 666 Fifth Avenue stood upright and tall, but its walls didn't seem quite vertical, as though the structure had sprouted from the ground and grew wider as it snatched at the sky. Over the years its unscrubbed limestone had turned sooty, brooding. A skirt of marble fencing bordered its front. Cast-iron cresting provided a thorny crown to its pitched roof.

While the husk of the building looked about as charming as Bedlam, the interior possessed a thrilling vertigo: doubledoors beneath a stone archway opened to a grand foyer. Its already tall ceiling was dizzying now that the walls were vacant. Ghost outlines indicated where paintings once hung, paintings on canvas the size of circus tents. I imagined the now-absent art to be the same as in any rich man's mansion: family portraitures of stern men and matronly women, their lofty foreheads vast enough to hold a second scowling face; idyllic murals of the forests where they went to hunt. An occasional Babylonian panel and Renaissance masterpiece thrown in to declare that the Vanderbilts, in their omnipotence, possessed not only this era but had subsumed all centuries past.

The foyer emptied into the Great Hall. Here, a winding stairway spilled down, its lower fringe flaring like the skirt of a proscenium. Its balusters supported filigreed grilles which bore the ornate letter S: Stanford White. A chandelier rested on the floor, its constellation of bulbs lit, its worn cloth-covered cord snaking over to an electric socket.

A half-dozen hoods occupied this room. Several gathered around a table, counting, stacking, and squaring ratty bills. The door to the ballroom stood slightly ajar. Inside, I could see a warehouse of crates. Booze. The gunman had said they weren't with Rothstein. Rum-running without The Bankroll's blessing? Gutsy and insane.

The legs had been ripped from a Louis the Umpteenth stool and its plump velvet seat rested on the broad bottom step. The head of the operation sat on this improvised throne and picked at his fingernails with a stiletto. I recognized him, although the newsprint photo in my mind was several years out-of-date. Jake Whelan. The Demolition King. Killer Jake. The lunatics ran the asylum.

Although in his mid-thirties, his face retained an angelic baby-fat. His straight hair swept across his wide forehead. His neck was thick and tall, more like a pedestal for an emperor's bust. He kept a cigarette pinched in the corner of his mouth, its tip angled upwards. His expression appeared earnest, serene. Nothing seemed evil about him until he slit your throat.

He blew a kiss at Lorraine and then asked me, "Are you acquainted with my reputation?"

"I've heard you'd just as soon kill a man as spit on him."

"Heh. You can always spit on him afterwards." His accent was British, but as he was once quoted as saying, "I'm as Irish as I need to be." He drew back his upper lip, a grimace which revealed his incisors.

He said, "I hear you did show-biz back in your day. What did people call you? Stumpy? The Cripple Kid?" His patter amused him, the words coming out slick and ending with a snicker.

"The Amazing Alan," I said. "When I was in my teens, I had a sleight-of-hand act good enough for the carney crowds. Before the war."

"Heh, the war. Killing for chumps. Doughboys without the dough. What a buncha suckers."

If this was a bar and he was the fair-fighting sort, I might have challenged him. However, he was the type to have a pair of thugs hold you down while he gouged out your eyes and then, when done, he'd tell you to feel around on the floor to pick up your nose on the way out.

He plucked his cigarette from his smile and flicked an ash on the oakwood floor.

"These Vanderbuilders," Jake said, "they rigged up these castles thinking they're so mighty, like their piss and shit is communion. Well, now destruction rules and I'm the Demolition King." He took to his feet and ambled over to Peanuts, the nutcracker. The mug passed off a handful of skinned peanuts to his boss.

Whelan sucked on one. "Before any new tower goes up, a fresh hole goes down. Convenient for planting a body or two. I've plugged stiffs in the bedrocks of, I suppose dozens of projects by now, probably counting into the twenties or the forties, I've never been one for figures. Rotting bodies makes for a sort of fertilizer. Helps grow the buildings."

I didn't like the way this conversation was going. Too revealing. It sounded like the kiss-off to a one-way passage.

"Why did you invite us here?" Lorraine said.

"Mmmmm," he purred, his engine running, his eyes half-shut, his mind seemingly in neutral. "Invite," he said, the word seemed to amuse him. "Amazing Alan, say I called together a poker game, could you spin some magic to rig the deal?"

"I've only got one hand now." I could still stack a deck, I just didn't want him calling on me. On the other hand, maybe he was probing for reasons to let us live.

"Mmmmm."

"Mr. Rothstein," Lorraine said, "Arnold. He's promised us his protection."

Jake exploded, spraying as he spoke. "Rothstein has his nose, his fucking kike nose, in my business. Yuh, I know you went to him and that's cause enough to stew me. Yuh, and I know you worked in that dead dame's office. And that's the account of why you're living. I gotta hear from you about who else worked there."

"We never worked with her," Lorraine said. "The police called us in as witnesses, that's all."

A bit more than witnesses, but I liked how Lorraine was handling this. Maybe, in spite of all his menace, if we sounded boring and harmless, Whelan would toss us back out on the street.

"That's all?" The Demolition King echoed, spitting his cigarette nub on the floor. A burn mark for the burnished wood. No matter, like all of this grandeur surrounding us, it was destined for the junkyard. Why not set it on fire?

"This meeting is done. I got no use for know-nothings. Nick, Peanuts? Take 'em for a trip to Ghost Row. And you two? Have yourselves a swell ride."

CHAPTER 14
THE SAVIOR OF GHOST ROW

Alan

LORRAINE and I sat in the back seat of the Crossley. Nick, the gunman, kept us at the business end of his pistol while Peanuts drove. Lorraine was stiff, quiet, and drained; her face knotted in a frown. She was no longer enjoying the adventure. Danger makes for a brisk tonic until the risk is death.

"I don't suppose you two would consider a bribe?" I asked the driver.

"We'll definitely consider it," Peanuts said. "Fork it over."

"I was hoping to drop by the bank."

"Heh. Just leave it to us in your will."

We stopped at the intersection of 52nd and 5th. I looked about for a policeman to hail. No such luck. I did see a police wagon three cars back, but I had no way to signal them.

"Eyes front," Nick said. Why did he care? Unless, I suppose, he wanted me to focus on the threat of his gun.

————

Ghost Row, near the southeast corner of Central Park, consisted of a series of luxury buildings, all of which had been either set for demolition or else were partly demolished. These include the Riding Club, The Netherlands and the Savoy Hotel.

The Savoy was once the most sumptuous hotel in the world. Like the Vanderbilt castles, it mimicked the palaces of Europe. One of its suites was fashioned as an exact replica of Marie Antoinette's room at Trianon. Paneling was constructed with three layers of insets: satin wood filled with mother of pearl carvings, brass filigrees, and white holly. Archways were supported by Corinthian columns made of mixed Numidian and Kilkenny marbles. Spotlights illumined the ever-glistening floor. The ballroom ceiling was painted with a heavenly mural as though it were the goddamn Sistine Chapel.

The Great War had left America disillusioned: kings and Kaisers were revealed to be petty, cruel, and reckless. America turned its back on Europe and continental glamor. We rejected lavish: we wanted big. Big was brutal, it made no apologies. Big was American and our country no longer genuflected to the Old World. Opulent temples were torn down to make way for buildings that were cheerless, functional slabs.

————

Across the street the vacant Netherlands Hotel stood tall and haunted. On our right, a fence surrounded a pit with the Savoy ruins. Slats of a splintery wooden fence pressed side by side, preventing even a peek. Next door to this, the walls of the Riding Club still stood, a tall, empty box with its floors collapsed into heaps of rubble. Cutting between the Savoy and the remains of the Riding Club: an alleyway for waste trucks. We entered that alley, the car bounding through puddles, swerving along muddy ruts until we came to a stop.

Nick nodded the gun telling us, no, don't move. Peanuts cut the engine. Even after being shut off, the motor rumbled, its pistons banging and its tailpipe chugging up to a final gasp of death. Peanuts hopped out.

I trotted my fingers along Lorraine's thigh, catching her eyes with mine, signaling to her that we needed to run.

When? she said with silent lips.

"None of that lipping," the gunman said, his finger twitching.

I had to chance it. I leaned in to whisper in her ear. "I suspect that they'll play us for chumps. Ask us to walk ahead before gunning us in our backs. Split from me and race off as fast as you can, zigzagging. Now slap me." A little drama for our captors.

She walloped my face: a little harder than necessary. The gunman responded with a leer.

"And when were you planning to do that?" she asked me.

"First chance we get."

We didn't get one.

———

The day's rain had turned the alleyway's fresh topping of dirt into muck and puddles. Hoof and shoe prints mixed with the ruts of iron wheels and wide tire treads, but, at this moment—perhaps because of the rain—the work site was empty, the wrecking crew had called it a day. To further seal out witnesses, Peanuts closed and latched a slab of paneling at the entrance to the alley. The gate was made from a broad pane of wood, ragged, apparently salvaged from the hotel. It bore a scarred mural depicting a frenzied, groping crowd of supplicants: lepers straining to touch the healing, haloed finger of Jesus. Artsy, well-done, even poignant. It must have been ripped out of the Savoy. America: we throw away only the best.

A sidewalk made of loose boards flanked the slat-fence. Beyond that, a broken floor hung over the pit of the Savoy ruins. I realized Lorraine and I would be literally walking the plank.

We entered the demolition site through a gap in the fence. I suppose that if I had to pick a place to be buried, I'd find no place more regal than the Savoy, that is, if only some bit of grandeur survived. All that remained of the stateliest of hotels was a vast hollow. Covering a city block, its pit extended down to the basement level, an open grave with fractured sculptures of fallen caryatids and angels cast among the piles of broken bricks. The remnants of beams that once rose to challenge God in the heavens were reduced to being mere splinters at His feet.

Peanuts and the gunman guided us along an earthen ledge to a dead end with a drop-off. Below, shafts had been drilled down through the foundation to sink new pilings—and to fill with fresh corpses. The nearest one had a concrete pillar rising from a well of water. After our insertion, they'd seal us in cement.

"Make this easy for us," Peanuts said, drawing out a trench knife: brass knuckles with a blade attached. He slipped his fingers through the holes of its grip. "Show us your backs and we'll finish this all quick and quiet."

"Why would we want to make this easy for you?" Lorraine asked, still facing him.

She had a point.

I felt paralyzed, clinging to an irrational belief that this was mere theatrics: a show to frighten us, to send us a message.

The four of us stood strung out along the earthen shelf: Lorraine the nearest to the brink; Peanuts confronting her face-to-face, his knife held in a raised fist. I stood on the other side of Peanuts, paired with the gunman three feet away, tickling his pistol's trigger.

My army training told me that in case of multiple threats, prioritize my response. The firearm represented the primary danger: death as immediate as a finger twitch. The gun needed to be neutralized or redirected.

Before I took action, Lorraine pulled up her skirt to her knees and dropped to all fours, declaring, "I feel sick." Her back was level with and in front of Peanuts.

The schoolyard pushover? *Why not?* With Lorraine having diverted the gunman's attention, I chopped his gun hand down so that the pistol discharged into the dirt. As I expected, Peanuts turned his back on Lorraine and swung his knife at me. I didn't need a well-aimed blow. I just needed to evade the blade while delivering a hefty shove. I dipped down while launching a hard kick against his thigh. He tottered backwards a half-step, then tumbled over Lorraine, disappearing into the excavation, on down into the piling hole, ending with a yelp and a splash.

The gunman backed up, six feet away, wary of my reach. Now he stood beyond the threat of a surprise attack and there'd be no more surprises. He held us point-blank and had spent only one shot from his magazine.

"How clever was that?" he asked, and then answered, "Not so clever. Only now I got to go and shed some lead. Peanuts? Are you okay?"

"I could use a pull." A single mud-covered hand flailed, reaching out from the side of the pillar.

"Not from me," the gunman said. He waved his pistol in the direction of where Peanuts fell. "Lady, you sent him down there. Before I shoot you, I want you to grab the hand of my friend."

Lorraine, still on all fours, said, "No."

"Do it!" I said, forcing an anger to my command. I had a plan, but I needed a few seconds of stalling. I couldn't turn to check on her, hoping that she trusted me. She growled.

"You usually do your business here at night," I said to the gunman.

"Why you say that?"

"You figured the rain would clear the workers and you were right," I said. "You figured the wooden panels would block out any view from the street and sidewalks. Only you didn't count on the tall building behind you, the one with balconies."

The gunman wasn't an idiot, he didn't look back. He continued to pin me with a stare.

Although he didn't, I did glance over my shoulder. With the help of Lorraine, Peanuts clambered back on the earthen shelf to join us. Covered head-to-foot with a watery brown clay, he could easily pass for a human-sized turd. He wiped mud from his eyes.

"Tell your partner, Peanuts," I said. "There is a tall building not thirty yards from here."

I suspect from the way he blinked that he had grit in his eyes. Nevertheless, the building was hard to miss. His mouth gaped and his head tilted. He nodded.

"Someone is standing on the third-floor patio," Lorraine said.

That much was true. She didn't mention the white cane in his hand.

Finally, the gunman took a peek.

I charged him, my left hand locking to his right wrist and twisting. He discharged a shot. Rather than fighting him, I crouched down, thrusting my shoulder to his chest while shoving him to the side. For a moment, his footing scraped at the brink of the pit. He clawed at me as he fell, not firing until he thudded in the mud below.

I turned towards Peanuts and Lorraine. With the knife-blade fixed to his brass knuckles, the killer took several awkward swings at Lorraine: it was clear that he was still mostly blind. Lorraine stepped back, staying out of reach. He staggered her way.

I seized Lorraine's mud-smeared hand. "Let's leg it."

We ghosted for the alleyway where we found a well-earned gift waiting for us: that old and ugly Crossley.

I climbed into the driver's seat and Lorraine took the passenger's side. They'd left the key in the ignition. Didn't they know anything about crime in this city? I turned on the motor.

It made a gorgeous and hideous chug.

CHAPTER 15
CINDERELLA ON ICE

Lorraine

WITH MY FEET planted on the windshield, I unclipped my muddy stockings, rolled them down and tossed them out the window, a silken gift for the wrecking crew. As we approached the gate with the painting of Jesus, it opened. Not exactly a miracle, a pair of cops stood there as we barreled toward them. They must have been summoned by the sound of gunfire. The moment after we bounded out of the alley and on to the street, a squad car entered.

Alan worked the clutch in such a way as to bounce us against the dashboard. "When you jumped into the driver's seat," I said coolly, "I had imagined that you knew how to handle a motor car."

Handle. An unfortunate word choice. Paying closer attention, I saw that he steered using his right forearm which he threaded through the wheel while his left arm reached across his gut to wrangle the shift.

Back when we stood across from that demented

"Demolition King," I hadn't told Alan that I had visited the Vanderbilt mansion before. Will 'Kiss 'em' Vanderbilt, Junior, was an avid race car driver, and a separated-but-not-divorced playboy who let his female prospects take the wheel. He allowed me a few spins around the Vanderbilt Cup racetrack.

I told Alan, "Let me. I've blazed off in a roadster or two in my time."

He braked so fast that he could have thrown us through the windshield. Getting out of the car, he rounded it to the passenger's side, holding the door open for me. Too late. By then I had scooted into the driver's seat. He got in and slammed the door shut.

I tried to read his face. He seemed hopped up from our brush with death, more so than I was. Did he feel humiliated by not being able to manage the shift? Or was he that rare man who could let go and allow a woman to take charge? His shoulders slumped; he offered a weak smile. I read relief in his eyes. His left hand squeezed my right as I shifted into gear.

"Alan?" I asked. I felt afraid to broach the subject. I sensed that his injury was too intimate, too personal to be discussed. It was shrapnel lodged in his mind, a pain which squeezed the air from his throat and yet, perversely, kept his eyes forever dry. Nevertheless, I plunged ahead. "Have you ever thought of using a wooden hand?"

"I own one," he said. "I call it my mask. This is who I am." He twisted his empty wrist.

He looked out the passenger's window, perhaps to avoid facing me. "Where are we going?" he asked.

"To the morgue, of course."

A line of vendors served the employees and visitors of the vast Bellevue Hospital Complex, and we stopped beside them to get something in our bellies: a pair of fresh apples for each of us and for me, a shaved ice cone. At another cart, I finally got the sausage I'd been craving. I washed it down with seltzer water—I bought a cup for each of us—adding a nickel for one of the man's drying rags to clean my still filthy hands.

Alan took a sip and sputtered. "I didn't know anyone sold seltzer without liquor."

I swept a strand of hair from my sweaty cheek. "I bet I must look like a wreck," I said. I wasn't casting a hook for a compliment, I just figured that this never-ending escapade and the humidity had smudged my make-up and ruined my coif.

"You look magnificent."

I suppose he spoke the truth. I have that talent: beauty even after being assaulted by the world and its elements. I'll make a glamorous corpse someday.

On the south side of the hospital, the Bellevue morgue stood where 26th Street dead-ends against the East River. The building was a squat, chunky brick structure as long as an aerodrome. Inside, what must have been fifty hip-high dissection tables spread out in rows and columns across the length of a vast room. Each occupied table had a slat underneath which held a block of ice. A sheet covered each corpse. Even with this valiant attempt at refrigeration, the place had a rank, abusive smell: sulfur mixed with the ammonia of spoiled meat, formaldehyde, and several unclassifiable fumes. My eyes and nose ran, and my feet *wanted* to run.

I looked over this barrack of cadavers, all lying on their backs, all dressed as Halloween ghosts, and tried to determine which was Carolyne Fritch. *Ah,* one covered corpse had a red slipper on a shelf beneath its table.

True to his word, Alan had a "friend," a newspaper contact whom he quickly cornered.

"Bob," Alan said in greeting as he shed the last few dollars from his billfold. The way Alan plied money, I was glad that I was the one who held on to Rothstein's largesse or we'd be broke by now.

While they vented the small talk from their systems, I marched over to Carolyne.

Leaning down, I picked up the shoe, the partner to the one I had seen in her 24th floor office. T-strap. Open-toed. Vici kid leather. Expensive. A sumptuous red. Tiny. I measured its length with a stretch of my fingers. Size three, maybe three-and-a-half.

Never trust a woman with small feet. I, personally, possess the sort of stompers you'd expect from someone who dwelled atop a beanstalk.

And so did Carolyne Fritch. Her sheet ended with a sharp rise. I could imagine feet swelling after death, but stretching? That was clearly not her shoe.

I pulled back the end of the sheet for a peek. No stock-ings. A lunar pedicure gave the tips of her toenails the shape of a gibbous moon. They were painted forest green. The skin of her soles and the tops of her feet had a white sheen. She used foot powder. Foot powder, no stockings, and garish nail polish set inside T-strap open-toed, expensive slippers? Never.

The stench of this area was overwhelming, so I had to lean in to take a close-up sniff to learn whether the powder was simple talcum or scented. Talcum and peppermint. Little by way of sweaty odors: she hadn't walked much. I filed all of this away in my olfactory memory book.

If her shoes had been lady boots, those would have sealed in the smells. So, instead, she had probably worn a pair of simple loafers and ankle-high socks, something to hide the naked foot and its talc.

I figured that, with the feet telling me so much, the rest of the body probably had more to say, so I threw back the sheet to have a look. The biggest mistake of my life. The horror of seeing her purple, pulped body, her splintered bones ripping through her flesh… I gagged and turned away.

Alan saw my distress. He had been to war. He'd probably met many times with his contact at the morgue. He knew these horrors. For me, the image seared itself in my mind, so that I could see it equally well with my eyes closed. When I again opened my eyes, the corpse was covered.

Alan said, "My friend here tells me that the throat wound had both a cord burn, and a roundish bruise in front. That says the killer tied a knot in his garrote. Cuts off the windpipe, stifles a scream. That's the sort of thing they teach you as a soldier. This wasn't just anybody who grabbed a curtain cord. The man we're looking for had training."

"Or else the man was a woman," I said. "This shoe does not belong to this corpse."

"Why do you say that?" Bob asked.

Men. I held the shoe beside the dead woman's foot and made a sweeping, sarcastic gesture with my other hand.

Alan nodded. "Near the window," he said, "there were scuff marks, a fight. The partner of this shoe got left behind so there's a good chance the shoes belong to the killer."

"Obviously," I said. "And the shoe is expensive and fashionable. Our suspect is well-off and has good taste."

"The person I chased down the stairs was a man."

"I know, I saw him."

"Yes, of course, you did. I'm saying there must have been two of them."

"Adds up," Bob said, proudly confirming the sum of one plus one.

Bob was about fifty and his face possessed the puttied wrinkles and half-hooded eyes of a hound dog. At least that is how the folds creased when he tried to concentrate. He finally caught on. "That means you could go around getting folks to try on this slipper and catch the killer. That makes it a valuable piece of evidence." The cash register in his eyes punched several keys before ringing up. "Thirty bucks."

"You've already picked my wallet clean," Alan said. He looked to me and my clutch purse. "We've got a hundred-dollar bill, if you can make change."

"Or I could keep the hundred," Bob said.

Men. "You are an idiot," I told Alan.

"So, you've already informed me."

"Well, it's a recurring theme. You are willing to pay one hundred dollars for a shoe, when we have the size, the color, the make, and the brand. We can find a copy to fit Cinderella in any luxury department store."

Bob seemed crestfallen. "You can have it for twenty," he called after us on our way out.

CHAPTER 16
SIGN OF THE CROSSLEY

Lorraine

CROSSLEY MOTORS MAKES EXCEPTIONAL AUTOMOBILES. The one I drove was an exception. Even in my experienced hands, the vehicle bucked and chugged as I piloted it back to mid-town. I suspect that it had never had its sparks changed or its pistons timed since the day it was coughed out of an assembly line, a dozen dark-years past in the dim pre-Great-War world. Alan beamed, vindicated, this car had humbled both him and me. This was bronco-busting, not motoring.

"How did one shoe that didn't belong to Fritch get tossed out with the body while the other stayed on the floor?" Alan asked.

"A quite obvious question," I replied, "with no obvious answer."

"If it wasn't her shoe, why toss even one of them?" Alan continued. "And, since that makes the corpse shoeless, where are Carolyne's shoes?"

I pulled over. We were on 50th near Madison, in-between my two favorite temples: St. Patrick's Cathedral and Saks department store. "Alan?" He responded by leaning in. I suppose my voice sounded conspiratorial. "Do you have a piece of paper and a pencil?"

"As a reporter, always." He nabbed the items from inside his jacket pocket.

I dictated and he wrote down in large block letters:

HEY, CARDINAL HAYES, POPE-BOY. I HOPE YOU AND YOUR ROMISH WAFER-EATERS ROT IN HELL.

666 Fifth Avenue

The Vanderbilt address. I leaned the page against the inside of the windshield and then I parked, blocking the cardinal's driveway. Whoever followed up would head straight to Jake Whelan, The Demolition King, just three blocks from here. To hell with the police: let those hoodlums deal with the full wrath of the Catholic church.

I signaled goodbye to the motor car, making the sign of the cross. We got out, laughing as we trotted across the street to Saks.

A doorman stood back and extended his arm toward the parted entrance. Alan, in turn, swept his arm for me.

Upon entering, Alan craned his neck and turned his chin in an arc as he surveyed the vast floor of merchandise. The layout had a deceptive elegance and allure. Few items for sale were visible, but each of these demanded to be seen: single flairs of the latest style draping from swank mannequins. Plump rich ladies who garnished sofas were gushed over by shop assistants who looked every bit as beautiful as the patrons wanted themselves to be, as beautiful as they imagined themselves to be. These assistants were flattering looking glasses, still kind long after the patron's own mirrors began speaking a harsh truth.

Alan said, "How do we find the shoe?"

Where I saw a cathedral, Alan could see only a big empty box of a store, lounge-abouts, and elevator dials which climbed to the number ten. I couldn't help but think: Macy's, the Gimbel Brothers, Lord & Taylor's; Alan must have never visited any of these. I needed to take charge.

I answered, "When we ask, they will find the shoe for us. But we're here for more than that. We need clothes. We can't go home."

"You've got a point. Not for a few days at least. If not the police, then I expect some hoodlums are right now arranging a homecoming party."

"Rothstein gave us five hundred. We need fresh clothes and supplies and a hotel room to camp out. Let me handle this. This—" I swirled an upraised hand as though I held the store on my fingertips "—this is my domain."

His smile was humble, sheepish—and a wee bit cute. "Just show me to the dance floor," he said, "and I'll follow your lead."

I approached the floor manager. Stiff and genial, he wore his tailored suit with his shoulders tall and a hand-kerchief puffed out of the vest pocket like a white flower blossom. He cocked his head and listened.

"Mr. Margolis," I said. It's always polite to check name tags.

"Vincent, please."

I unclipped my purse. "We had our luggage stolen in a scuffle and we're in need of a variety of clothes: elegant, basic and undergarments. Men's and women's." I took out a hundred-dollar bill and let him see there were several more. "This should get us started."

He gave me the once over. He could read the residual mud on my shoes and under my nails, assessing me in a way in which someone like Alan was blinded. He discreetly eyed the bill. I supposed that he'd give it a better inspection when he had the chance, being not certain that it was real. "I am sorry for your loss. Where do you wish to start?"

"Is Sylvia on duty? Seventh floor?"

"Yes, madam." I was impressed: he knew his people.

"Fetch her. And find Feldman in men's wear." Feldman didn't like first names.

"Anything else?"

"Yes, Vincent. We'll be trying on a variety of items, and it would be best to locate us somewhere between men's and women's departments. We could use a private area to lounge."

"On the fourth floor. Ask for Marcia. And I will personally bring you coffee."

"With cream," I said. "Sugar on a tray. I'll stir in the lumps."

"Black," Alan said, "with a shot of whiskey."

Vincent didn't even blink at that request.

Feldman, who must have been pushing seventy, had that British manservant mix of authority and deference. He corralled Alan and treated him as a clothes dummy, first goosing him in the small of his back so that his posture popped up, then stretching his arms out to full wingspan. Feldman shot a tape measure up, down and under, never bothering to take notes, only tossing out an occasional, "splendid," in his Queen's English accent.

I asked Sylvia to sit on the sofa beside me. Although thin as a straw, she had a plump, round face. Her wide eyes gleamed with such awe every patron must have felt that they were royalty.

"Miss Marquette," she said. How refreshing to have one's name remembered.

I crushed a sugar cube between my fingertips, sprinkling crystals over the surface of my coffee. I plunked a cube inside; I enjoy having one slowly dissolving, sweetening my coffee more and ever more as I downed the last sips. "Sylvia, I'll be on the go. What do you have by way of ladies' slacks?"

"Nothing in the latest styles."

Which meant nothing.

"Unless you'd like breeches," she continued. "Are you headed out riding?"

"Oh, yes, a spot of hunting."

"Foxes? We've had some folk here from the North Salem club."

I leaned in. "We're hunting a murderer." We laughed together. "Find me a riding outfit, perfect for the great outdoors, but which will start a panic when I take the floor on the Plaza Ballroom.

"Choose me an evening dress, I recall you have impeccable taste. Something both classy and daring. Find me a corset that trumpets my derriere. And a pair of Maiden Form brassieres, they are a heaven-send." We both sighed in agreement. "What use is a woman's right to vote if she doesn't have the right to breathe?"

I went on to describe the shoe in minute detail. A light burned inside her. She knew exactly what I meant. We were partners in crime. I finished by specifying size three.

She glanced at my feet. "Size three?" she asked, her voice tentative.

"They're a gift."

She nodded in relief. I was not one of those crazies who blamed the shoes for not fitting their elephantine feet.

Finally, I said, "And Sylvia, for a tip, I want you to choose that dress you've most lusted after but knew you could never afford."

By the time she parted on her mission, tears budded in her eyes.

———

Meanwhile, Alan was trying to argue Feldman down to practical clothes and, horror of horrors, to denim.

I intervened. "Feldman. Use your good sense."

"I'm not some laze-about nobleman," Alan protested.

"Darling." That word just slipped out. "Anything less than trusting him is an insult. This is what he does."

"One stylish suit and one casual for about-town," I told Feldman.

"A riding outfit?" He must have overheard my conversation with Sylvia.

"No."

He nodded and spoke to me when he said, "You will not be disappointed." No, I would not be disappointed. Alan, however, might be.

———

With the shop assistants on their way, Alan sat down with me and knocked off his cup of coffee in large gulps. His head jolted back, and he shook his jowls. "Not enough whiskey."

He said, "You know, at the Savoy, when I looked at the vast hole in the ground? I saw trenches."

I stroked his right forearm. He didn't brush my hand away. "My hand…" he said…and went silent. When next he spoke, he changed the subject. "Did you notice that while Rothstein wanted whatever information we could find about Carolyne Fritch Designs, Whelan only wanted names? He already knew what's going on."

———

Twenty minutes later, after Feldman had returned with his selections, after Alan had a stay in the fitting room, he reappeared. He wore the clothes—uptown elegance—but not the attitude, leaning at an antagonistic angle, a skyrocket in a launch tube. This is how I saw it: he didn't want to rip away the clothing. It was his own hide, sewn on too tight, that he wanted to peel off.

"Is this what you like?" he asked me. "Some tippy-nosed snob who should be out and about with a diamond-crusted walking stick?"

I patted his silk shirt, smoothing it against his chest, lingering in the touch, trying to help him relax.

"May I speak freely?" Feldman asked.

"Go ahead and shoot," Alan said, his arms raised in surrender.

"I have some insight from my years here in New York and at Harvey Nichols in London. You, Mr. Priest, are conceding to this costume show solely to please your lady friend. That is wrong. You must wear these clothes for yourself."

"Thank you," Alan said, crisply.

"I have not finished," the sales assistant protested. "Mr. Priest, you are jealous of the man in your suit. You believe that Miss Marquette prefers him, and that you could never be that man. You are wrong. Allow me five minutes of leave, and I will reveal the man whom you are." He nodded and parted.

Alan plopped down on the sofa and slumped, his jacket shoulders rising and crumpling. He looked at me with weary dog-eyes.

I sat beside him and said, "I've been with wealthy men. Whatever single-mindedness made them rich also made them intensely boring. Fashion was something they purchased, a disguise. Clothes were like a sheet they put over their summer house furniture to keep them from gathering dust. It didn't work: they were nothing but dust."

He gave me a sideways stare: maybe because I was taking the sideways route to get to my point.

"Do you know of Vernon and Irene Castle?" I asked. He nodded. "Back in the 'tens, they were the most elegant pair in Manhattan. And where did they come from? His father owned a pub. Her father was a physician. No millions, no peerage. But when they stepped onto the ballroom floor, when they danced, whatever they danced became the new sensation. They epitomized grace, not through breeding or ornament but because refinement blossomed from their souls. They represent my ideal. The clothes don't make you classy. You make the clothes classy."

For a moment Alan sat silent, sullen. He said, "Vernon Castle died during the Great War."

That was true, he did. Training others to fly.

———

Feldman returned with a pair of white silken long-sleeved gloves, saying, "You are not the first of our customers to have sacrificed a body part for the welfare of your nation and in support of my beloved homeland."

The right glove was puffed out, full. Feldman demonstrated: the prosthetic inside could be folded, it had a frame which could be bent at the fingers and knuckles, and when bent, it retained its form. A fist, a wave, an A-OK. A pinch between thumb and index for holding a cup.

"Will I be able to write?" Alan asked.

"With practice you can make loops and lines by pivoting at the elbow. Please stand."

Alan stood and spread his arms as though surrendering. Feldman removed Alan's dress jacket and rolled up his shirt sleeves. He tugged the left-hand glove over Alan's trembling hand. Then he slipped the right-hand glove with its sleeve over Alan's forearm. He cinched it in place with a buckle. The assistant proceeded to slide Alan's shirt sleeves over the glove sleeves. He pinned the cuffs in place. Finally, Feldman hefted the jacket back over Alan's shoulders.

With this done, Alan played with the prosthetic, trying out various positions. It bent in the same form as a flesh hand would and even when he tugged on a joint, it wouldn't flex in an unnatural direction. Satisfied, he went to the mirror. He changed the pose of his right hand to several forms and mimicked these with his left.

Even while looking at him from his back, I could see him grow to fit his suit. Sylvia appeared beside me, and we both shivered as we gazed on.

Alan cocked his head to the side and then whisked away, disappearing behind a display. When he returned, he was wearing a top hat. He stepped onto a podium in front and center of us, in between a pair of voguish lady mannequins and locked his arms with theirs. He smiled so widely, he seemed, in that instant, the handsomest, most elegant man in Manhattan.

He took a flying step down and told Feldman, "The top hat is too much."

"I would have said so myself, sir."

"Do you have any gloves to fit this hand other than white silk? I feel like I'm in a minstrel show."

"Silk serves best for tactile chores, but for a combination of delicacy and practicality, I would recommend evening gloves, lamb nappa, chrome-tanned or, for you, a midnight blue. We will need to tailor them."

"Do that. And… Feldman? You are very skilled at your job."

"Thank you, sir. I have had decades of experience in determining what best fits a gentleman." He narrowed his eyes to slits. "You've heard of Prince Albert in a can? I'm the one who put him there." Alan and I laughed, while Feldman maintained an expression every bit as deadpan as Buster Keaton's.

Feldman gathered the jacket from Alan's shoulders. "We can have both this and your other purchases tailored and ready for a five o'clock delivery."

"I'll keep the white gloves as a second pair. I'd like to step out in these pants and shirt, they fit well-enough as is. As for the clothes I came in and those tailored, send them to the Gotham. We'll be staying there tonight."

Alan then shocked me by stepping my way and kissing me. It felt like my first true kiss. Every other pretender to that moment in my life had been puckered lies. We began a slow, swaying dance.

Sylvia cupped her hands over her chest as though her heart might burst.

CHAPTER 17
A GOTHAM HOLIDAY

Alan

In 1908, the newly opened luxury hotel, the Gotham, went bankrupt and had to be sold. This occurred because, prior to Prohibition, obtaining a liquor license was necessary to serve wine and spirits. The sale of liquor was necessary to attract well-heeled guests. However, with the hotel being built across the street from the Fifth Avenue Presbyterian Church, state law prohibited the owners from obtaining such a license. The hotel regrouped and hobbled along until, years later, the Volstead Act resolved their dilemma and quenched their patrons' thirsts. With Prohibition in place, no one could get a liquor license and, paradoxically, every hotel served liquor.

Lorraine and I promenaded the several blocks to its front doors, arm-in-arm. She wore her riding outfit: boots high up on her calves, pant legs and cuffs stuffed inside, a bustle over her bottom, and her button-up shirt exploding in ruffles from beneath her vest. She garnered stares, even from a passing horse, but maybe the riding crop looped to her thigh unnerved the beast.

I wore my new knife-creased pants and a white silk shirt. I had two hands co-equals inside the silk-white gloves. If Whelan's hoods saw us, they wouldn't have recognized us. Well, not me, anyway. Who could mistake Lorraine for anyone else?

The Gotham was a little less jazzy, a little more chintzy, and a little less costly than the nearby St. Regis, but it was princely enough to allow us to act as swells about the town, or at least until our cash supply ran dry.

We'd spent just short of three hundred on clothes and tips, including one hundred on my new hand, more than I paid for a month of staying alive. Of course, for a complete comparison I'd have to toss in the fifty-or-so I shelled out for booze while trying to kill myself—an undertaking which had thus far failed. I should write the speakeasy owners and demand a refund.

We registered as Mr. and Mrs. Joseph Collinswood. The name came from my mother's fourth husband, the one she kept; the surname she used for her show biz career. Lorraine confided to the clerk, "We're newlyweds," and we were grinning so stupidly that it could have been true. I told the concierge our luggage would be arriving soon and to look out for some packages from Saks.

———

Twelfth floor.

The bed was vast enough to reenact the Battle of Waterloo. The bath, claw-footed and ready to gallop, could have held its own alongside Teddy charging up San Juan Hill.

"Tell me about your family," Lorraine said. She draped herself across the bedspread, her elbows sunk as posts into a pair of satin-covered pillows as she propped her chin in the cups of her hands.

"Mom and Dad had only me," I said. "My dad deposited another eight, count 'em, eight half-brothers and -sisters all over the states and one in Hawaii. My parents were stage actors. My mother still is an actress, if you consider performing in the flickers to be acting."

"Gail Collinswood." Lorraine hmm-ed. "I've seen her in films. She doesn't seem old enough to be your mother."

"She's younger than I am," I said. And then, to unknit Lorraine's brow, I added, "So she tells me. Hollywood magic."

I took a seat on the edge of the mattress. "I was my parents' first kid, back right after they met while touring the theater circuit together. My father skipped out when I was still young enough to play a prop."

"A prop?"

"A baby in a blanket. Only one talent required: don't cry. My mother taught me to read, and by the time I was five I was feeding her rehearsal lines. Mostly for classics, prestige productions. I can still taste the Shakespeare in my mouth. I suppose I got my interest in the newspaper biz while helping her to rehearse a Jesse Lynch Williams play."

"But you became a magician?"

"That was my attempt to dabble with the stage. Didn't last long. The war put an end to The Amazing Alan." I gazed at the glove with my false hand. I had always treated prosthetics as a lie. What had changed now? I wanted to believe I was whole. I wanted to believe I was half of the glamorous team of Lorraine Marquette & Co. "Your turn."

Lorraine rolled onto her back and studied the ceiling. I looked up. It was a boring ceiling, only useful to empty the mind. I scooted alongside her. She took my right wrist and tucked it and my gloved prosthetic under her riding shirt, over her belly. I felt the skin of my forearm flush and my pulse pound painfully against my wound. How could I explain to her? At that moment, my ghost hand entered her body. Any other time and I'd say my right hand didn't have skin or flesh. At that moment it did. Her skin, her flesh.

The way she trembled, the way she sighed: perhaps she felt it, too.

"I have two younger sisters," she said. "In their 'teens. They live with our aunt. My father is a physician. Was. My mother helped him with his business. He came up with a patent medicine which he was convinced would cure the addiction to booze. This was back in the nineties when anyone could slap their face on a bottle. Dr. Marquette's Sure Cure for Dipsomania. People started calling it Dr. Dipso's. That's what I called it."

"Did it work?"

"It was four-fifths alcohol. If you drank three bottles of Dr. Dipso's 160-proof cure, you could completely swear off drinking three bottles of 160-proof hooch. Sure enough, soon enough, the government came knocking on our door, nice at first, told him he couldn't sell alcohol as a cure for drunks.

"My dad knew about the contents, but he had long since convinced himself that, by adding in a few herbs, it transformed the liquor into a health tonic. Transubstantiation. Are you Catholic?"

"No."

"My mother took his side, ran the business end. They spent all their profits on lawyers, fighting the government, and doing a smart job of it. They kept on fighting and staying in business for more than twenty years. When the country went dry, sales shot up. My dad convinced himself it was because people were trying to get sober."

She turned on her side. My hand fell away.

"Well, now the revenuers stepped in, and the confrontation got serious," she said. "They threatened my father with jail time, saying he was just another liquor profiteer. But my father stood on principle and cited all those souls he was saving, the repeat business proved him right, he said. He fought his way all the way to the state pen. My mother kept the business going for a couple of more months before they collared her, too."

Now I understood why the ceiling, in all its blankness, appeared fascinating. Sometimes a great emptiness feels better than a filled moment.

I suppose the act of sharing these stories and our vulnerabilities was the last crack before the dam burst. We both had tears topping our eyes.

As she rested there, draped alongside me in that riding outfit, in those slacks and boots and ruffles, Lorraine possessed a combination of masculine and feminine strengths, a commanding, seductive energy that made me equally a conqueror and an object of conquest. She could pin me to the bed and mount me. Her beauty was like a magical door in an Arabian tale, it would open when I called to her depths and her depths would echo and answer and echo.

I unbuttoned her shirt, beginning from below, each snap sundering with a satisfying pop. She slipped my shirt buttons free from their holes, beginning with my collar and continuing down. I gasped, my chest expanding as her hungry hands swarmed over my undershirt. I clawed it up and over my head, wrenching and twisting to free myself from its straitjacket.

Voila! Houdini couldn't have done better.

She rose over me, her shirt parted. Her brassiere lifted her breasts, offering the view of a sumptuous feast. First, she swept a hand over my chest hairs. They rose to attention. With a conductor's gesture she could command my body, both as a whole and each orchestra section. She bent her neck to suckle a nipple. I could hardly wait to return the favor.

I wrestled with her riding pants secured by a top button, a largish disk threaded through a smallish hole, difficult for one hand to liberate.

"I l-like you," she said. I supposed that her stuttering came from avoiding the complications and vulnerability that came with the word 'love.' "But I don't want to get pregnant."

"We'll work around it," I promised. And we did.

———

After we finished, both satisfied, I lay alongside her. I nibbled her earlobe and whispered a suggestion. Time to explore the pleasures of the galloping bathtub.

———

As for the murder case, we decided to wait for the evening before continuing our investigations. We slept until 7 p.m. at which time I was woken up by someone at the door.

I bolted up, gasping. The knocking dovetailed with my dream: I had imagined Whelan's men, Peanuts and the gunman standing in a line, noisemakers in hand, ready to drill a few gushers in my chest.

I looked around for what could make a weapon: a brass lamp, an ashtray pedestal. I was wondering how I could both hold a weapon and turn the doorknob, when I heard a reedy voice say, "Packages, sir."

Saks. With sacks. Still, anyone could say that. "Leave them there." I took a dollar from my billfold and wiggled it under the door. It was snatched up in an instant.

"Thank you, sir. Thank you."

His footfalls receded.

I hesitated to slip the door catch, turn the knob. I was being paranoid. Still…

Lorraine sat up in bed, a sheet drawn to her throat. I stood in my trunks. I listened closely. The faraway elevator dinged. I opened the door. The leaning packages tumbled in.

Why was I being sapped by this sense of doom? I remembered how it was months after leaving the trenches before the trauma hit me, a dread that haunted me for years. Recently, I blunted its edges with booze, until it seemed gone for good. Until now. Lorraine, in her ardor, by making me feel alive, unstitched old wounds, ones that had never healed.

Lorraine got up, nuzzled me on the cheek, and then attacked the bags, going after a bundle of feminine items. She gave me a private show standing in the nude as she powdered her underarms and brushed her teeth. When she was done, she asked me to rub creme over her sore feet.

———

New York has a 'tween hour. With the sun still hovering over the horizon, but having fallen behind the westward buildings, daylight fades into a hazy memory. With their shadows having taken flight, humans become shades which trundle along the dim streets, heads and shoulders skimming the brick walls, bodies slipping between each other, and, when crossing the streets, these specters dissolve into the tar.

This ends when the city lights flash on, an electric dawn announcing an all-night party. The air trembles with the blues and high-time music. Neon blazes. Spirits rise out of the asphalt and become flesh. Colors return to the skin, painting the faces of the partygoers.

Our suite was situated in the northeast corner of the Gotham, overlooking 55th and Fifth. One window faced the Presbyterian church, dour and unlit.

Once upon a time, cathedrals were the most imposing and lordliest of structures in Manhattan. Now, all but the crowning spire cowered beneath us. Out the other window, the brawnier, more monstrous, St. Regis beamed as patrons lit their rooms.

"These curtains," I said. They were red velvet, the kind of fabric that would look good draped over a king's shoulders. But I didn't mean these curtains. I meant, "Lorraine, you had thick, luxuriant curtains in your office. That's unusual, most offices settle for shades or blinds, something modest and functional."

"We tried to make our clients forget they were inside an office building."

"Fritch's office also had thick curtains. Why?"

She added blush to her cheeks and a kissable line of lipstick to her lips.

I rasped at the stubble on my chin with my fingers. I'm not a twice-a-day shaver, though maybe I should be.

"The telescope," Lorraine offered. "They wanted to see out, but they didn't want to be seen while spying."

I imagined the end of the telescope, peeking out from a swaddling of heavy drapes. What were they doing? Collecting blackmail?

I recalled the view from the 24th floor of the Adams Express. With my head stuck out the window, I was looking east toward the Columbia Trust, near the rooftop level of the shorter building. In the morning, the sun would laze just over the top of the other building and the lens of the telescope would flash in reflection, revealing the snoops.

What was Carolyne Fritch's game? On whom was she spying? We needed to return to the 24th floor to determine which offices were in view. And we needed a telescope.

"We should contact Daisy Yinger," Lorraine said.

"Who?"

"When I was at the police station, I sat across from a Patrice Somerset. A sweetly sad sort of lady. She said that Carolyne was friends with a Daisy Yinger. Maybe Carolyne talked. Maybe she told Daisy what was going on."

I jiggled the cradle on the room phone and got the Gotham switchboard. "Hello, could you connect me with the *New York Evening World?* BEekman 4000." When the call connected, the operator clicked off. I spoke to the switchboard at the Pulitzer Building and asked for the journalists' floor.

A kid answered, a choir boy's voice. "Evening." That word acted as a greeting, the time of day, and the newspaper edition.

"This is Alan Priest. Who is this?"

Perhaps my phrasing confused him. "This? Me? Um… Jeffrey."

Ah, Jeffrey. A runner, an errand boy, and a capable one. He went on to say, "They told me you were in jail, Mr. Priest."

"Listen, Jeffrey. If I was in the Tombs, would you be my one phone call?"

"Um…no?"

"I have a favor to ask. I need you to find the address and the telephone for a Daisy Yinger. Y-I-N-G-E-R. Include D. Yinger, with D as the first or middle initial. Check the city guide and the telephone directories. Most likely Manhattan, then Brooklyn, and if not those, keep looking. Got that?"

"Yes, I do."

Of course, it could be she was married and then only her husband's name would appear. Or, for that matter, she could be living with her aunt Eulalee.

"Ring me back at the Gotham Hotel, CIrcle 2200, and leave what you find as a message under the name of Collinswood."

"Okay. Um…Mr. Priest, I suppose someone heard me speak your name and that someone is Mr. Gould and he's here and wants to talk to you. He's got a story coming out with your photo and on the first page and everything for the morning edition downstairs and which says you are in jail, um…custody, for a whole bunch of murders. Um…he says two."

Crazed World Journalist Nabbed For Murder Spree. The insult wasn't so much that my own paper would invent a story saying I killed two people, it's that they didn't give me the byline. Damned if I'd let Gould the Ghoul get the scoop on my execution. "Tell him it's a lie. Tell him to nix the story. And don't tell him where I'm calling from."

"You can tell him. Or not tell him. He's right here."

I hung up.

"Trouble?" Lorraine asked.

"My stupidity. We've got about fifteen minutes to scram or we'll be hunted down by a hound from the *World.* He'll probably bring along the cops for the exclusive on our arrests."

We dressed quickly, Lorraine taking the riding outfit again.

"It's practical," she said, "and if you don't believe me, you can wear a dress and high-heels."

I had the tailored jacket to go over my white shirt, but best of all, I had the midnight blue gloves to wear.

I took the prosthetic out of its white glove to exchange its covering. Once unsheathed, it was a marvel to see. Modeled after the skeletal hand, its bones were Bakelite and its joints were brass balls. It would crumple to any natural position and stay there. The prosthesis was somewhat smaller than a normal hand. Its flesh and its softness came from padding inside the glove. I threaded the prosthesis into its new home and strapped it to my forearm.

I used my left hand to close my right fist. It was perfect. I felt the midnight blue.

———

We made it to the lobby in a quick ten minutes with all our bags in tow. We were ready to pass outside when the desk clerk hailed me: "Mr. Collinswood, you have a message."

He handed me an envelope. The contents read:

Daisy Yinger. 17 Lispenard, Rm. 502, Manhattan. From City Directory, no phone.

D. L. Yinger, 85 Middagh, Brooklyn. ST George 384.

Gabriel D. Yinger…

Spencer Y. Yinger, M.D.….

I guess I could have been more specific when I asked for the initial D. The note ended with this bit of encouragement: I told Ghoul nothing.

Two possibilities. First, Jeffrey lied to Gould, holding

back the info on my whereabouts and his assignment to find the Yingers, which he went on to do the moment Gould wasn't looking. Or: Gould shook the whole story out of Jeffrey and then told him to lie to me. Hell, Gould may have sent the message.

"We've a line on Yinger," I told Lorraine. "And better news, my source at the newsroom says we don't have to run."

"So, what do we do?"

"We hide out in the darkest nook of the restaurant. If a reporter doesn't race in the door in the next ten minutes, his heels on fire, I figure we're home free."

And so, we enjoyed a romantic, candlelit dinner, made all the more delicious by the fact that Gould never showed. Jeffrey was a loyal kid.

CHAPTER 18
TEARS FROM THE GLASS EYE

Alan

I had a reporter's hunch: D. L. Yinger of Brooklyn was, in fact, Daisy Lee. I slotted a nickel in the payphone in the hallway just off the hotel lobby and asked the operator to connect me to ST George 384.

An elephantine "HELLO" blasted my eardrum.

"And hello to you. I'd like to speak with Daisy Yinger."

"Davy! Davy!" He called to someone far from the phone.

"Daisy! Daisy!" I corrected.

"Hello! This is Davy!" Loud. A whole family who shouted like they used ear trumpets.

"Daisy!" I yelled.

A squeak like that of a church mouse: "You got the wrong number, mister."

I've had better hunches.

———

Not having to flee the hotel, we deposited our bags with the concierge. It was theater hour and a cab line waited for us out front.

Lorraine and I crowded into the back of a cab, and I gave the driver the address of Daisy Yinger of Manhattan, Lispenard Street, no phone listed. The ride would take us back to downtown, just south of Canal, in the direction of the Adams Express Building. She lived near where she worked. Hunches be damned: the most obvious choice is usually the correct one.

Lorraine rested her head against my shoulder, her silken hair swaddling my side, tingling as though it passed through my jacket and shirt and connected to my skin, sinking roots. Her flesh, even her bone within, felt pliant, molded against mine. I'd swear we were breathing in unison.

I leaned my head against the stiff window, looking over to and seeing the reflection of my smile. I saw through my smile.

This is how the time passed. The tires thumped over the lumps and pits of the road. Smeared slabs of the city lights stretched and shrieked across the window. Traffic signals like ship-to-shore semaphores blinked between stop and go. Lorraine's fingers tapped, trotting over my chest.

All of these counted down our allotted moments together. When our money and quest had ended, I couldn't imagine Lorraine joining me in my fourth-floor cave over-smelling the docks. Hell, even I didn't want to go back.

"Stop!" I shouted. The driver slammed the brake pedal.

"What is it?" Lorraine asked, shaken out of her reverie. She retrieved the paper sack which had flown from her grasp to the floor of the taxi. In it, the red shoe.

We were still three blocks from Yinger's place, but a sign outside a corner business read: "Gordon Nursey's Astronomical and Scientific Supplies."

"The telescope," I said. I passed the cabbie a sawbuck and waited as he slowly measured out the full change.

I suppose he thought that with the swell clothes we wore, I'd tell him to keep a dollar or two for a tip. As my threads grew more expensive, I became cheaper. Just an hour ago, I would have been more generous. Now every coin was a grain of sand waiting to drop through the neck of an hourglass counting down until my fantasy was over. I gave him an extra dime.

———

Although the entry light was still on in the establishment, it was clear the owner was closing shop as the lamps in the back flicked off. I rattled a bell on the counter.

"Oh, do pardon me!" he said, appearing from the back room. We had startled him.

Perhaps seventy but spry, he wore wire spectacles with lenses the size of silver dollars. Bow-necked, the dome of his bald head tilted our way. It was spattered with a constellation of liver spots. His left eye jittered about as he studied us. His right eye was off-kilter and didn't move. It was glass.

He pivoted his head to the side to view us with his one

good eye and to not distract us with the false one. The jittering stopped. His pupil dilated to engulf us.

"You are lucky to catch me," he said. "I was just preparing to haul my reflector scope over to Columbus Park. We've a waning gibbous moon and the rain stripped the humidity from the air. An excellent night to view the heavens. I treat passersby to glimpses. Sort of an educational mission. You should see the wonderment grow on their faces. We're all child-like beneath God's eye."

The innocent rapture he described also filled him. I was so caught up in the intensity of his rhapsody that I didn't notice his outstretched hand. Even with the prosthesis, my right hand still made for an awkward shake and Lorraine stepped in front to intercept his offer. They shook and she beamed a smile.

"Gordon Nursey," he said.

"Lorraine Marquette."

"Alan Priest."

"We are fortunate to have found you in time," Lorraine said. "We need a telescope."

"Such eagerness. For personal use or as a gift?"

"For us."

"Excellent. Scholars or enthusiasts?"

"Enthusiasts," I said. "But strictly beginners."

"Then let me say that I am honored to initiate you into the congregation of those who bask in the marvels of the skies. I understand the lure that brought you here: like the three wise men, when the stars summon us, we must obey. The study of the heavens is the most vital, the most noble undertaking of mankind. Ptolemy, Galileo, Dr. Einstein, all recognized this. Do you have an idea of the magnification that you seek?"

I looked to Lorraine. She looked to me. I didn't want to step on this man's passion, but we just needed to buy a simple spy scope and to get out of there.

"It needs to be about this thick," Lorraine said. She held her fingers apart to the width of the tripod brace.

"That thick? That's a requirement?" He squeezed his lips together as tightly as his squint. A tear leaked from the duct beside his glass eye.

"We already have the tripod and mounting," I explained.

"Oh," Gordon said, "why, of course." He rounded the counter. "Then you will need a refractor scope, direct view. We have a lovely model from Watson & Sons, brass casing. Three-point-five-inch aperture, precision ground lens. Forty-x native magnification. Excellent for the novice."

He lifted the model reverentially from the molded inset of its velvet-lined case. Golden and gleaming, it measured four feet in length.

"How far can it see?" I asked.

Gordon chuckled and the joy returned to his face. "What the early astronomers called 'nebula,' mere smudges, have, under careful observation, proven to be full galaxies—each containing thousands, or perhaps tens of thousands, of stars. The Andromeda Nebula alone is twenty-five million trillion miles away. And we here on our humble planet can witness its spectacle, its festival of lights! And, what's more, think of all the living beings out there in this magnificent universe. Some of them may well be using their own telescopes and peering our way, right now as we speak!"

"Including this afternoon?" Lorraine said, pursing her lips and delivering a mischievous glance my way. "The perverts."

Gordon glowered. In these matters, he had no sense of humor.

His dome reddened. I imagined I could foretell our future by connecting the liver spots on his scalp. "A steal at two hundred-fifty."

I whistled. "Perhaps you have something less pricey?" I asked. "Let's say about thirty bucks."

He nodded, a bit grimly. "Yes, I do. I have one for near exactly that amount. The quality, of course, will be compromised. But once you are underway, I am certain you will return for an upgrade."

"We only need to see a short distance," I said.

"Steamship-sighting?" he said with distaste. "You should have told me. You wish to have a terrestrial telescope?"

"Let's say we want to spy on our neighbors?" Lorraine asked.

Gordon's face became a wooden mask. Without comment, he took out a white enamel tube, about three-and-one-half feet. It had a twenty-five-dollar price tag.

Lorraine hefted the telescope in both hands. "Would I be able to read over someone's shoulder?"

"Fifty yards will appear as two." His flesh eye glazed over.

"We'll take it," I said, to end his misery.

"I have a special price for Peeping Toms," Gordon said, all enthusiasm drained. "Forty dollars."

"The tag says..."

"Forty dollars."

I counted out four sawbucks, thinking that, when we sneak a peek at our neighbors, it's voyeurism. When Martians spy on us, that's astronomy. It seemed so unfair.

CHAPTER 19
LISPENARD

Lorraine

Gordon wrapped the telescope in butcher's paper, not even bothering to offer us the rather lovely display box. All bundled up, it looked rather like a mummified rifle, and when Alan strode down the street with it, the fat end in his palm, the slender end of the cylinder resting against his shoulder, he took on the air of a hunter marching into the woods. We got a few stares from the street crowd, him being armed, and me wearing riding pants and a crop.

Release the hounds!

We had ditched our taxi ride a mere two blocks from Lispenard to buy the telescope, so the final stretch to the boarding house was brief.

We arrived at a grimy five-story building tucked away just south of Canal, just around the corner from Broadway. A hand-painted sign posted in the first-floor corner window declared:

Furnished Rooms for Proper Ladies.
Reasonable Rates.
No Tobacco, Gin, or Men.
Fire-Proofed!
Inquire Within: Mrs. Coldmere, Rm. 101

Upon catching sight of us, a matronly lady got up from her sidewalk chair and posted herself in the entryway, her feet apart, shoulder-width. With stringy hair and a lumpy frown, she looked like the sort of person who used the same industrial detergent for every job: to strip yellowed wax from the floor, to add to the pot where she boiled her undergarments, and to peel the luster from her face and hair. Her thick arms were crossed, twined together, twin boas strangling each other. She smelled of ammonia and lye.

"Mrs. Coldmere?" I inquired.

"Call me Myrtle," she said. Nothing about her spoke of chumminess or first names.

"Myrtle. I'm Lorraine. This is my friend, Alan."

She gave both of us the once over and then settled her eyes somewhere between us, beyond us, scowling. She offered an unconvincing, "Pleased to meet you." And then, "You came about Daisy, didn't you?"

"How did you know?" Alan said.

"On account of there's been a whole parade of strangers buzzing by, zipping around like flies. All of 'em making noise, saying they want to see her, just to talk, poking about and snooping. That's why I'm out here, guarding the steps, to spook off you and 'em, one and all.

"Daisy's not in. I've been telling them that then, and

now I'm telling you. Daisy's not been home the entire day. And don't go bothering my girls."

"What sort of visitors have been asking about her?" I asked.

"Some 've been police, some ladies, and some weaselly punks who think they can persuade me with their showy blades. Thugs don't impress me. I've got a whacking board to teach their scrawny bottoms a lesson. I kept it from when I ran a boarding house in Hell's Kitchen. In Hell's Kitchen! Here, I got decent ladies, all of them holding respectable jobs except for the green ones in the secretary school. Proper gals.

"So, I'm telling you same as I told them others, you're not coming in." She spanked the board against her palm.

"I've lived in one of these sorts of rooms," I whispered to Alan. "She's bluffing."

"I heard that," she said. Her ears had thick sprouts of hairs which probably served as antennas. "Daisy's not even home. Look for yourself. She has the fifth-floor room, second down from the left-hand corner. Step right back and you'll see the light is out."

Alan and I backed to the gutter and craned our necks. "The light is on," I said.

Myrtle Coldmere joined us and looked up. "Well, I'll be…"

I saw Alan tense as though he wanted to bolt and run for the fifth floor. I felt the same sort of restrained panic: If Daisy could sneak by Myrtle, so could the punks with their knives. Her life could be in danger.

"We're going up," Alan said.

Now that all of us stood on the curb, no one and no paddle blocked the way in.

"Don't you try," she said, "or I'll be calling the cops."

"Give them a ring and tell them Alan Priest says hello."

She stepped aside as we passed. "Stay out of her room, mister," she called after us. "I don't abide with that kind of mingling. If my board don't scare you, I can wrangle me up a skillet to sap you with a decent braining."

Urgency is urgency. Daisy Yinger may have been in peril, but a five-floor walk-up is still ten flights of stairs. I'm ashamed to admit that Alan left me behind in a trot. When I arrived at the fifth-floor landing, he stood, waiting.

He explained, "The hallway is clear. I don't think there's an emergency. I thought, if she knows someone is after her, we'll appear less frightening by approaching her as a pair."

Since I don't consider myself particularly alarming, I supposed he meant his presence would seem less of a threat. Probably true in general, there's lots of male mayhem in this world. Still, the shoe in the paper sack told me that a female killer was on the loose. Daisy Yinger might know that and would be more afraid of me. Or, maybe, she was the murderer.

As we began heading down the fifth-floor hallway, a woman stepped out from Room 502. She nervously strug-gled to shut the door behind her. Once, twice: it wouldn't stay secured, and each time she tried to close it, it rebounded, cracking open.

"Daisy Yinger?" Alan asked.

She couldn't have looked more startled if Alan had called out, "Stick 'em up." Jumpy, jittery, this woman knew quite well that a menace stalked her, and she had been expecting its arrival.

"Yes," she answered. "And who are you?"

"Name's Collinswood," Alan said.

"And I'm his wife, Nora," I added, using my mother's name. "We'd like a moment of your time."

"I haven't any. Any moments." She laughed nervously. She tried shutting her door again, and upon failing, turned toward us, hands clutching the closed mouth of an expensive peccary-skin purse. "I'm sorry. My door acts like that sometimes," she said. We stood between her and the stairway, which is where her gaze went.

She had a pinched face and, when she tried to smile, the thin red line of her lipsticked lips framed yellowed teeth. A nicotine stain between her index and middle fingers. A smoker. Her eyes lay deep-set in their lidless sockets. I'd seen this in Scandinavians: it gave an intense, Viking-like stare to their every glance. Her hair was a false blonde, the roots dark. Although cut in a bob, she had passed beyond the age to be a flapper. Pushing forty, I estimated. She wore a tube dress that flattened more than flattered.

"May I pass?" she asked, on the frantic edge of politeness.

Leave without closing her door? I noticed at the bottom of the doorjamb, a brass cylinder. That was what prevented her door from shutting. For a moment I thought it was a spent bullet casing. No, too large. It was a metal canister of lipstick. Its top was off, and the pink shade inside didn't match her smile. Her door sometimes refused to shut? Liar. Something prevented it from sealing.

I also noticed while peering downwards, she had small feet. Her toenails were painted a ruby red. Pedicured to match her expensive shoes.

She stared at my hands as I squeezed on the fold of my paper bag containing the shoe, glancing up to meet my eyes in fear. What did she think I carried? A gun? She strangled her purse. Stuffed to the point of distension, its side bore the boxy imprint of an automatic. She was armed.

Never trust a woman cruel enough to torture a peccary purse. Its plumpness tugged against its fastener, that sort of zipping device popular on modern boots. She pulled back the metal slider ever-so-slowly.

I decided to play along as though the shoe in my bag was indeed a gun, and grasped it by its tall heel, aiming the toe her way. She stopped opening her purse. We had a détente.

Alan noticed none of this.

"We need you to answer a few questions, before you go," Alan said. "Just a quick sit-down. I see that your floor has a kitchenette."

"Yes. Yes, it does," she said in surrender. She turned her back to lead the way and with her purse hidden I heard the fastener clicking again as she discreetly pulled it open.

I signaled to Alan: a slitting gesture across my throat. He appeared puzzled, questioning my judgment, but not so dense as to dismiss it. He tensed and gripped the tele-scope as though it were a baseball bat.

Daisy took a seat at a small, round dining table where someone had left a pile of study notes, secretarial scribblings.

The kitchenette was spartan. Neither faucet nor plumbing, I suspected that the residents washed their plates and pans in the bathroom. A single cupboard. A small icebox, its chunk of ice melting and dripping into a catch pan, plink by plink. A hotplate rested on top of a burn-scarred counter. An open window overlooked a fire escape and beyond that to a view of the ragged rear of a building that fronted Canal Street.

I hung back in the hallway, keeping my shoe well-aimed. Alan took a seat across from Daisy. A resident peeped through a crack in her door and then shut it. I heard her throw the bolt.

Should I warn Alan about her gun? Perhaps. Or… maybe Daisy was guilty and with her jitteriness, a warning would precipitate a shooting. Or maybe she was innocent and playing it safe, protecting herself, not knowing who we were. Or, finally, by pretending as though I had a pistol, I was provoking her. One thing for certain: my shoe would not accidentally misfire.

Daisy dropped her purse into her lap and below the tabletop. Her hand slid into the purse. I wagged the sack with the shoe. Daisy got the message and put her hands on the table, folded and prayerful.

Alan beamed a smile. He had that male sort of obliv-ion: women will not outwit me; women are never a threat.

"Thank you for your time," he began. "You've heard what happened to Carolyne Fritch?"

"Yes."

I didn't see the sadness of loss or the rage of a killer, only shivers and twitches.

"And I'm told you two were friends," Alan said.

"Really?"

"Yes. Patrice Somerset said so. She works on your floor."

"That dreadful busybody. Sticks her nose into anyone and everyone's business."

"Did Carolyne ever talk about her work?"

"No."

Another of those one-word, get-me-out-of-here responses.

"For how long did you know Carolyne?"

"Since she moved in."

"And how long ago was that?"

"A month."

"Her calendar said January."

"Then it was January. May I go now?"

A splinter of a thought lodged in my mind. The door that wouldn't close. That canister with pink lipstick. A memory, a connection. I sniffed and recognized a distant perfume. I slowly drew away, moving backward toward Room 502. Daisy cast her eyes my way.

"You've visited Carolyne inside her office?" Alan asked.

"Maybe to have a peek."

"And you never asked her about the telescope?"

Daisy stared at the bundled package. Her eyes lit. "A telescope?"

As I approached the door to her room, Daisy became

jumpier and jumpier. She was no longer looking at Alan, only at me.

"This might sound crazy," Alan said. "But we'd like you to try on a shoe."

"A shoe?" she asked. She stared at the sack in my hand. I reached the door to her room and with a light push swung it open.

And there I stood for a moment, not looking in. I had to keep my eyes on her making sure she didn't go for her purse.

Down the hall, from the stairwell, came a rising thunder of footfalls.

A resident came out of her room and into the hallway, looking toward the stomping on the stairs.

Then everything happened at once.

The resident peered inside Daisy's room before I did. She screamed. I looked in. There on the floor of Room 502, her purse spilled, her throat cut, was the dead body of Patrice Somerset, the witness at the police station, the one who had pointed out Mr. Gomorrah.

Daisy's fingers sunk into her purse, jittering too much to quickly latch on to her pistol.

"She has a gun!" I yelled. I hurled the sack with the shoe at her, missing her, but distracting her just long enough to allow Alan to lift the table, flipping it toward Daisy, a blizzard of papers taking flight. The tabletop struck her hand just as she fired, the bullet skimmed its surface and continued its flight, lodging in the icebox.

The police, guns drawn and led by Santarelli, stormed through the stairwell doorway at the end of the hall.

"Don't move!" the detective cried. Alan raised his

arms. Daisy slid behind him and ducked out the window onto the fire escape. Alan looked her way and then back at the barrage of cops, weapons in hand. He stood still, stiff, unable to prevent her flight.

The resident, continuing to scream, swayed as though on the brink of collapse. I suppose I should have offered her a comforting shoulder or else at least caught her when she fainted. Instead, realizing I had very little time, I ducked in Daisy's room.

Patrice Somerset lay there, tall hair, pink lips. She had told me she planned to drop in on Daisy. Now, with her neck muscles sliced through, Patrice's head lolled backwards to an unnatural degree. Her windpipe was open and deep as a well. The wall and sofa had sprays of blood. The puddle on the floor had already begun drying at its edges.

The discovery shocked me less than it should have. Maybe I was getting used to this. In the past few hours, I had seen a woman drop past my window and seen her crushed body when I pulled back the morgue sheet. I'd been chased through a crowded theater. I had almost been shot by a gunman who cracked peanuts and a gunman who cracked wise. Another corpse seemed normal, the next logical event in this mad endeavor.

A policeman halted in front of the open door. He looked over the dead body and my living body, his gun hand trembling.

I ignored him. Before they hauled me away, I had two things to do. First, I checked the closet and immediately found what I expected. Next up, Daisy had a dresser topped with powders and blushes. I opened one drawer and then another. In the bottom drawer, there among rayon stockings, I came across the other item I was searching for. At that moment I knew where to find Daisy Yinger.

From down the hall I heard Alan. "Take it easy! Don't shoot! The person you want has gone out the window. Look out the window."

CHAPTER 20
MY TURN TO PLAY DETECTIVE

Lorraine

A POLICE SERGEANT STOOD, back against the kitchenette wall, the steel cables of his forearms woven together crossing his pigeon chest. His nightstick dangled from a loop around his wrist. His face was doughy and damp with sweat. His mouth hung half-open. Puny black pupils peeped out from eye sockets nearly swallowed by the flesh of droopy brows. He looked past us to the hour when he'd get home. Waxen, the only proof of life appeared with the measured rise and ebb of his ribcage. I supposed he was stationed as a guard to ensure neither Alan nor I tried to escape.

Several officers stood strung out along the hall, quietly questioning the fifth-floor residents. One hung outside Daisy Yinger's door, looking in on and sketching the scene.

Alan and I sat with Lieutenant Gilberti Santarelli, the three of us around the tiny kitchen table. The detective's teeth and eyes gleamed; he pinched the nub of a pencil and arched his brows, leaning forward in anticipation. The table had been set right, and the glancing bullet meant for Alan had scarred the table's surface, leaving a flight path etched as a line and now pointing to the detective's diaphragm. Secretarial homework lay scattered all over the floor, covered with a shorthand which could pass for Arabic.

The smell of baby powder had worn off the detective. All that remained was the clinging scent of parched sweat that accumulated over a never-ending workday. The window behind him framed him with the brick backside of an unlit building: a dusky red and as dark as the circles under his eyes. I suppose his job didn't offer him the opportunity for the sort of invigorating tumble that Alan and I shared this afternoon. Poor man! And here we were, keeping him busy until all hours after he had spoken so highly of his family life.

Nerve-worn, but always the genteel knight, he gave us each a courteous nod before saying, "Miss Marquette, hello."

"Good evening," I replied.

"And Mr. Priest. I see that you've grown a new hand."

"It's a talent of mine."

"And your clothes are most elegant. Watching over us is Detective Sergeant Huyzen. He will serve as my second set of ears." Not a twitch of life from the sergeant, not even a wiggle of his vigilant ears.

"Down to business," Santarelli said. "First, let me apologize that my men permitted the lady who shot at you to escape. From even the most cursory glance, I observed that our victim has been dead for what must be hours. You two—and the woman who fled—did not kill her. Or, at least, not recently. And, so it is, that I am addressing you not so much as suspects, and not even as witnesses but rather— because of your persistent ability to appear in the most critical places, and your habit of getting there before I do—I am compelled to treat you as capable investigators. Mr. Priest, I suppose the success is due to your newshound instincts."

"Thank you," Alan said. "I pride myself in being able to snuffle out a story."

And me? I bridled. This was boy-chat, and I was the fair maiden adorning their manly tête-à-tête. The Centaur-like sergeant turned his sleepy gaze my way, recognizing the slight.

"As to how worthy you are of my compliment, that will depend on whether your investigations have been competent. I, myself, have been busy at work on this case and have made several significant discoveries. But, before I spin the tales of my achievements, I defer to your accounts of what must have been a most remarkable adventure that brought you here, this evening, to yet another murder scene. With apologies to the fairer sex,"—he nodded my way—"I yield to Mr. Priest's journalistic skills to tell the story." He poised an expectant pencil over his notepad.

"Do you want a full accounting of our day, or how we arrived here?" Alan said.

"Both, please." He flattened his moustache with the heels of his palm and sniffled, explaining, "Summer allergies."

Alan remained quiet for a moment, presumably gathering and ordering his mental notes. Then he said, "After leaving the Fourth Precinct Station we met with Rothstein at Lindy's."

"And my men followed you there. Why did Rothstein summon you?"

"He wanted information about the Fritch murder."

"How intense was his curiosity?"

"He acted as though it was no more than a casual concern. At the same time, I had the impression he was keenly interested."

"He would kill to know what happened," I said.

Santarelli added a couple of exclamation marks to his notes. "I suspect that part of the secret to Rothstein's success comes from downplaying the ardor of his pursuits. And what did you tell him?"

"At that moment, we had nothing much to say," Alan stated. "Nothing more than what we knew when speaking to you at the station."

"And I have every confidence that you've uncovered a thing or two since. Why did he want this information?"

"He didn't say."

Santarelli signaled Alan to wait a moment to allow him to finish a line of notes. Then he flipped a page. "Go on."

"After we left Lindy's, we were chased through the Capitol Theatre by a gunman. I doubt that he worked for Rothstein, since Rothstein had just asked us to delve into the murder."

The detective raised a halting hand. "Allow me to interject at this point and offer an apology. My men languished behind you, not maintaining a close-enough surveillance. One, however, did provide a most revealing description of your stalker. We've identified him as a contract killer by the name of Frank Hyatt. He's called "The Lip" because he possesses a most distinctive scar. A rival, who resented his smirk, carved the meat off of Hyatt's upper lip. Hyatt responded by growing a curtain of bristles which cascade down from the residual strip of flesh to hide the gap which would otherwise expose his upper teeth. This serves as an effective veneer: from a distance. And, should you get close enough to see through it, and should you react in horror or gasp, you are near enough and likely enough to get a blade sunk between your ribs."

"So, we were lucky to shake him," Alan said.

"Yes, indeed. Without a doubt. But I daresay my men, when they entered the theater in force, had a hand in cutting off his pursuit, thereby advancing the good fortune of your deliverance. Sadly, Hyatt managed to get away."

"Who does Hyatt work for?" I asked.

"He's independent, no allegiances. Sometimes Rothstein, other times not."

"So, Hyatt's still free, and there's a good chance he's still hunting us?"

"Yes to your first statement and, as to your conclusion…quite likely."

I shivered. I thought of the man with the forearm in front of his face. Perhaps the gesture was performed more than just to confound me as a witness. Perhaps he was hiding his disfigurement.

"Hyatt," Sergeant Huyzen muttered. The name conjured a flicker of terror in the beads of his eyes.

Alan used his left hand to crunch his right glove into a

fist. He said, "Hyatt kept your men busy while we hopped a cab to meet up with Mr. Fritch."

"Who was being tailed by another of my officers. And what came of your meeting with Fritch?"

"Ivan Fritch is a flim-flam man."

The detective nodded. "I concluded as much from his card."

"Clever observation," Alan said, complimenting himself as much as Santarelli. "Along with his sister, the two ran a spy operation out of Carolyne Fritch Designs. I don't know the target of their set-up, but it involved months of patience. And a telescope."

Our eyes were drawn to the bundled-up telescope at Alan's side.

Alan continued. "I believe that, this morning, while Ivan was out, Carolyne was caught spying. Perhaps when peeking in a window, she saw this 'Hyatt the Lip' guy kill someone. The killer spotted her, headed over and strangled her, and then tossed her out the window. I appeared a moment later, while he was about to leave. He ducked behind the door, and then after I went to the window, he tried to kill me."

"Intriguing," Santarelli said, pinching at a sniffle. "But may I point out one problem with your analysis?"

"Go ahead."

"It doesn't make any sense."

Alan bit his lip. I stifled a laugh. "How so?" he asked.

"Why strangle her and then throw her out the window? If your intent is murder and escape, and you are a professional, why not leave the corpse in the office to be discovered a goodly time later? Why draw extra attention before you've made your getaway? Why try to kill you at all? Furthermore, the timing doesn't make sense. It takes minutes to strangle someone. The murder took place while you were riding in an elevator. Non-stop, that would have been less than a minute.

"And no one surprised Fritch. The occupants had time to bundle up whatever incriminating evidence lay around, even taking the telescope. And finally, Hyatt wouldn't panic at being seen as a killer. He knows the police could charge him with at least three killings, if we could catch him."

Alan didn't have a response. I did, but it was not my turn—yet.

Alan said, "Okay, we'll set that aside for the moment. What happened next, we were picked up by two punks. One, who went by the name of Nick, liked to flash around his gun. The other, they called Peanuts. They took us to the old Vanderbilt mansion, the smaller one on 53rd and Fifth. There we were grilled by Jake Whelan, who had also taken a personal interest in the case. The situation was dicey: these were the sort of punks who would gut you just for a good laugh."

"The police have known for months that the old Vanderbilt place is a liquor warehouse," the lieutenant said. "Fine stuff, nothing home-brewed. Whelan runs it down from Canada. They continue to exist much the same as all of the bootlegging does. If the police should bother to call a raid, the campaign would have been ratted out before we fired up our wagons. An enterprise both futile and lethal. Personally, I've made my peace with not taking on Whelan or Rothstein or the whole of Tammany

Hall. I choose battles I can win." He flipped back a page, checking a note. "What did Whelan ask about, specifically?" he said.

"The names of those who worked at Carolyne Fritch Designs. And when we couldn't give those to him, we got a one-way ticket to Ghost Row. We managed to escape, no help from the police you put on our tail."

"According to their reports, my men had lost track of you," Santarelli commented. His head tipped back. He sniffled.

"So," the detective said, "Rothstein wanted to learn what was going on, while Whelan only wanted to find out who else knew. Therefore, I surmise that Whelan is fully aware of the story behind these crimes."

Hours ago, Alan and I had come to the same conclusion. It was only now that I mulled over the full significance: Whelan was behind this. But what was he behind?

Santarelli said, "Ghost Row. There was a report of gunfire at the ruins of the Savoy…was that you?"

Alan nodded.

"The gunman, Nick," I said.

"And where did your adventures lead you next?"

"We went to the morgue to visit Carolyne Fritch," Alan said.

With this cue, I set the shoe-sack on the tabletop. Even through the paper, the blunt heel gave out a sharp rap. I peeled back the brown wrapper to unveil the exquisitely sculptured bit of footwear within.

"Ah, yes, I recognize that," the detective said. "The victim's shoe? While at the morgue, you purloined a piece of evidence?"

"I noted the shoe size and make and then purchased an identical one at Saks on Fifth Avenue," Alan said.

Again, I had been edited out of the story.

"A copy of the shoe?" Santarelli stopped writing. "At least I won't have to arrest you for stealing evidence. Still, an odd and capricious gesture."

"Not when you consider the reason," Alan said. He paused for drama. "The shoe that was found with the corpse, did not fit the corpse. Several sizes different."

My discovery.

"Several sizes?" Santarelli traced a finger along the arch.

"And," Alan added, "considering the signs of a scuffle near the window, the shoe probably belongs to the murderer."

"Could be," the detective said.

"More than 'could be.'"

"But why would this killer leave one of her own shoes behind on the floor and toss the other one out the window? And then spirit away the shoes of Carolyne Fritch?"

Alan laughed or else scoffed—he gave a throaty tut-tut while exhaling. "All your hesitations about my theories boil down to 'why?' In the reporting biz, for a murder case, *why* is just a ribbon to wrap around the story. *Why* is a palliative for the readers, added so that they believe everything makes sense and that we, outside the mind of the killer, can decipher his thinking. The *what,* the *where,* the *when,* the *who,* and the *how,* that's the meat of the story."

I knew why.

"All right, then," the detective said. "Who?"

"Daisy Yinger," Alan announced. "The woman we met here in the hallway. The woman who tried to kill me just before fleeing down the fire escape. Attempted murder demonstrates that she is capable of the crime. Attempted murder of me suggests that she recognized we were on to her. She must have been more than mere acquaintances with the Fritches, more than just someone who worked on the same floor: she was part of their scam. And, finally, in this hallway, a brief glance at her feet showed that she wore small shoes."

Santarelli looked at me for confirmation, perhaps because I was clutching the shoe. "Oh, yes," I said, "the woman did have small feet."

"Excellent observations," Santarelli said. "Perhaps the woman who tried to shoot you was Daisy Yinger, or perhaps she was another, as yet unknown, party in this crime intent on invading Yinger's room." Looking over his notes, I was beginning to decipher his writing. The scribble "Daisy Yinger" was accompanied by question marks large enough to hook sharks.

Santarelli continued. "I assume, Mr. Priest, that you also picked up your change of apparel while at Saks. Miss Marquette, your outfit is lovely and provocative. Mr. Priest, you could pass for an Italian prince."

Alan muttered thanks.

"After our time at Saks," he said, "Lorraine and I checked into the Gotham Hotel where we attended to some private matters."

Santarelli showed us his palm. "No. No need to detail how you spent the personal portion of your afternoon. As a gentleman, I will not pry. However, I do observe from the moon-eyed glances which you now exchange that you have become a great deal fonder of one another since the time we last met. Although I do also note Lorraine has been annoyed at you several times during this conversation, Mr. Priest."

Alan considered me with a rumpled brow. I popped my eyes and shrugged.

The detective flipped a page and once again poised his pencil. "Let's just say you've had a very busy day. One more matter: how did you come to arrive here?"

"I spoke to Patrice Somerset at the station house," I said. "She told me that Daisy Yinger was a close friend of Carolyne Fritch. Alan used his contacts at the *World* to find Yinger's address."

"Quite a straightforward chain of events," Santarelli said. "As for me, during my interview, Somerset told me much the same about Miss Yinger, directing me to go see her. My officers and I attempted this when Yinger was not home. Beyond that, the landlady, a fierce and watchful matron, would not allow entry without a warrant. And now upon returning, we find Miss Somerset, here, dead. Mr. Priest, I shall enjoy hearing your theory on how this latest murder came to pass. Or is 'how' considered lowly among the collection of a reporter's list of questions?"

"I included 'how' on my list," Alan said. He clamped his jaw shut. I supposed he was tiring of Santarelli's barbs.

I answered. "I'm afraid that I inspired Patrice to go spying," I said. "In the waiting room, she told me that she liked my questioning and how I was acting like a sleuth. She said she could do some snooping."

Alan patted my hand, saying, "Her death is not your fault."

Of course, it wasn't my fault. Alan can be pretty damned condescending. I suspected this: Alan acted differently when there was another man around. He had to prove who wore the trousers. Well, I was wearing some pretty nice riding pants.

"Let me convey how I see it," he said. "First, Patrice would have tried entering through the front door. Madame Coldmere, the house matron, is a tough dame and would have turned away a busybody like Miss Somerset. As for the exact hour Patrice came by here, you can ask Coldmere."

"I intend to," the detective said.

"Undaunted, Patrice snuck 'round the back where she found the door ajar. Jail-warden Myrtle wasn't the sort who'd allow that, so you can bet that the door had been jimmied by the killer who had entered shortly before her. You can take a look at the lock, and you'll find that I'm right. The killer, who had come along first, had made his way to the fifth floor, and busted into Yinger's apartment. Patrice surprised him there, but before she could call out, he cut her throat. Later, Yinger came home, found the body, knew she was the target and took it on the lam. We surprised her as she was preparing to leave."

"Interesting," the detective said. "Quite interesting." His tone declared that it was uninteresting. "Mr. Priest, you told me you were not impressed by matters of *why*, but I often find *why* to be the key to the puzzle. You presented a jumble of events without rhyme or reason. Why was the apartment torn up as though someone was looking for something? And in refutation of your theory, Miss Yinger's door did not appear to be forced open. As for the downstairs door, I can have Sgt. Huyzen inspect it when he goes to query Coldmere. My comrade here may seem inanimate, but I can guarantee he has listened to and has set to memory every word of this conversation."

The bear leaning against the wall popped open an eye, as if aroused from a fine sleep. That one bug-eye jerked around between Alan and me, landing on Santarelli. "Pardon me, Lieutenant, but may I ask a question of which you have overlooked?" He had a bullfrog of a voice.

"Yes, you may."

"Mr. Priest, where'd you come across the lucre to secure such dandy threads?"

"Ah, yes," Santarelli said. "I didn't ask that question, my dear sergeant, because I had surmised the answer. Mr. Rothstein is the only patron who has both the funds and the interest in purchasing our friends' souls. How much did he pay?"

"Five hundred," Alan replied.

Santarelli flipped to an earlier page in his notebook, the one where he noted Rothstein's level of interest, and added more exclamation marks. "Excellent. With that settled, it is my turn to play detective."

Sergeant Huyzen slipped out of the room, presumably to speak with Coldmere and to check whether the back door had been jimmy-cracked.

Santarelli flipped over his notebook. These notes were spelled out in block letters and proceeded backwards from the final page. "I am sharing with you the revelations resulting from my inquiries with the hope that when you have been fully informed, together we may very well realize the key to this mystery."

Santarelli cleared his throat and began. "The Fritch design office has been in business for four months. You may have noted that there is no telephone installed. The drawing pad appears to have been used but once. No appointment books or business notes were found. I suspect that no designing took place. The Fritches were behind on their rent and short on excuses. They were to be evicted the first of June; that is, tomorrow. Perhaps this pressure prodded them to take unsafe risks."

Hrr-hrrm. This time he both cleared his throat and sniffled. "The only two people who regularly visited the office were Carolyne Fritch and her brother, Ivan. Or, rather, not Ivan and not her brother.

"Ivan Fritch fits the description of a small-time grifter named Roger Planck, out of Detroit. He's been playing scams on our island and in Brooklyn this past year, mostly selling phony fire insurance. HQ had issued a BOLO—be on the lookout. During a previous arrest ten years back, his Bertillon measurements were taken, but no printing. The oversight has been resolved, we collected fingerprints during his morning visit. We've forwarded a copy on to Washington to the Bureau of Investigation, Division of Identification, to learn if he is wanted elsewhere. However, the comparisons must take place against many in their files, and the response could take weeks."

"There are no Fritches in the phone book," Alan said.

"And not in the city directory, either," Santarelli added. "In case I haven't been clear enough, they are using aliases. Excuse me. He *is* using an alias, she *was*. For matters dealing with Carolyne Fritch's case, she is properly addressed in the past tense. We took her fingerprints at the morgue. These I've sent off to Centre Street where an expert in the Henry system will compare them to those in our city files. Patrice Somerset, also in the past tense, had informed me that Daisy Yinger, two offices down, visited Fritch Designs on several occasions, and that she, Miss Somerset, saw Carolyne pass money to Yinger. How much…is hard to estimate. Miss Somerset tended to exaggerate matters during her original statements, making definitive declarations and then quickly scurrying back to uncertainty.

"In the absence of interviewing Daisy Yinger, we looked into her background. She's from Oklahoma and she's been in New York for the last two months, a moth to the big city lights. I spoke to the sheriff's office in her hometown and to her pastor. Nothing in her background to suggest her prior involvement in criminal activities. The other notes I have before me came from following Mr. Fritch and the two of you, and add nothing to what has already been discussed, other than to say that Mr. Fritch has escaped our tail." He closed his notebook, and it took Alan and I a moment to realize he was finished.

"As for making sense of the case, as I said before, I very much disagree with you, Mr. Priest. If I can determine the why, then all the fragmented details will assume their natural order and tell a narrative. And, for all my efforts, I don't understand this case. These are the questions I wrote down which needed answering. 'Why a telescope?' We have speculation, but no specific knowledge as to what they were viewing. 'Why was Carolyne Fritch killed twice?' 'Why was she killed at all?' As a more recent addition: 'Why was Patrice Somerset murdered?' And finally, I have a new uncertainty, assuming that you are correct. 'Why did Daisy Yinger kill Carolyne?'"

"I answered some of those," Alan said.

"Not to my satisfaction."

And that was it. That was all that Santarelli's police expertise and Alan's journalistic skills had figured out. I had waited patiently with my version of events to learn whether either of them would have sussed out the most basic parts of this mystery. Since they hadn't, I declared, "It's my turn to play detective. And I've solved the mystery."

CHAPTER 21
I HAVE THE ANSWERS

Lorraine

THEY LOOKED TO ME. Alan had a trembling, worried love in his eyes which I suspected was condescension or, at the very least, doubt. Santarelli glared my way. He probably supposed I'd be every bit as off-mark as Alan.

"I've learned a thing or two from reading mystery novels," I said, an opening which inspired expressions of incredulity. "What appears to be a puzzle is just an illusion that fools you into thinking something mystifying has happened. The proper solution, in any good mystery, is simple and makes perfect sense. I have my own set of questions that I've been bouncing around in my head, and I have their answers. First: is Daisy Yinger a murderer? No." I paused for effect. That's what the book detectives do when summing up solutions.

"No?" Santarelli gritted his teeth, his dismissive smile stretching to the tips of his mustache. "How excellent that you've found the answer: 'No.' An insistent no." He could have allowed me to elaborate before launching into his sarcasm. "'No' means nothing. Tell me, how is it that you came to such a conclusion?"

"Because of the answer to question two: Where do we find Daisy Yinger? In the morgue."

"Are you saying there's been another murder?" The detective was still humoring me, but he'd become intrigued. "And how would you know?"

Alan kept quiet, his lips slightly parted. At least he recognized that I was on to something.

"The corpse in the morgue who had been identified as Carolyne Fritch used a foot deodorant that I'd never come across. Just minutes ago, I encountered that same deodorant in Daisy Yinger's room. Peppermint and talc. You'll find tins of each inside Yinger's dresser's bottom drawer. She mixed them herself and the results are in a third tin. You'll also find size-nine shoes in her closet, a little on the dreary side, what you would expect for an office worker. The woman pushed out of the window was Daisy Yinger."

"Foot powder and shoe sizes," the detective said. "Keen observations, Miss Marquette, leading to a most remarkable conclusion. Most importantly, your proposition can be checked and verified—or dismissed. I'll ask Coldmere to visit the morgue to see if the body is that of her tenant. Now, you declared that the solution was uncomplicated. Let's say, for a moment, that Yinger was the first victim, how does that simplify the story?"

"Because of the answer to the next question: Why was Daisy Yinger killed? Carolyne and Ivan Fritch were spying on someone out of their office, someone very dangerous. I suspect that someone first saw a glint of the telescope lens. Then that person used binoculars and saw Carolyne—and only Carolyne—who immediately recognized that she was doomed. Probably, it was the man you called The Lip. Distinctive and well-enough known.

"Carolyne and Ivan packed up their things to escape. Then, to cover up her trail, Carolyne and Ivan decided to fake Carolyne's death. First, they lured Daisy into the office, and then they strangled her. Ivan had mentioned to me he had a service revolver: he was ex-military. He would have learned how to use a garrote during his army training. After Ivan had strangled her, Carolyne undressed Daisy and switched clothes, so that those who had seen Carolyne's polka-dotted dress that morning would, from a distance, mistake the fallen body as Carolyne's. They tossed the body out the window because, if they had left the body behind, anyone on the 24th floor could identify Daisy. To bolster the story, while in front of the building Ivan ID'd the body as that of his 'sister,' and I imagine he made sure the body was quickly covered so no passersby would recognize that the corpse was, in fact, Daisy."

"If they weren't Daisy's shoes, then why throw one shoe out the window and leave one shoe behind?" the detective asked.

"Ivan must have done that. Carolyne, who exchanged clothes with Daisy, was probably still finishing dressing when he casually tossed one shoe out with the body thinking that he needed to complete the outfit. The other one stayed to show that the body came from the office. It would be just like a man…" I glanced at Alan, "…to not notice the size of Daisy's feet. If it was up to Carolyne, she would have kept the shoes. They're elegant, they're expensive, and, of course, they fit her."

"So, it was Ivan whom I chased down the stairs?" Alan asked.

"No. I saw…well, I sort of saw the killer. I couldn't pick him out of a line-up, but I'm sure it wasn't Ivan. Ivan and Carolyne planned this with time to escape, but I suspect they cut it close. They spied on the killer until they knew he was coming their way. They had to have him pass the sidewalk before the body fell. They wanted him caught, red-handed, shortly after Daisy's murder. When the killer arrived to dispatch Carolyne, he looked out the window to find what seemed to be Carolyne on the sidewalk below. When trying to leave the room, he hid behind the door as Alan entered. Believing Alan to be someone from the office, maybe someone who knew the same secret that Carolyne did, he tried to push him out the window."

I waited for their reactions, the fingers of my one hand strangling those of the other.

Santarelli nodded slowly. Then he beamed his home-in-time-for-dinner smile.

"I find your account quite compelling," he said. "It tells the story and divines the reasons. Why was the victim killed twice? So that no one would identify her as Daisy Yinger. So that Carolyne Fritch, who was marked for death, would be declared dead."

Alan's brow furrowed. He seemed angry that I was right. Seriously, sometimes men can be such jerks.

Santarelli made surprisingly few notes on his pad and then finished by underlining the name "Fritch" twice.

"Miss Marquette," he said, "you mentioned that you

could not pick the man you encountered in the hallway out of a line-up, but could recognize him from a photo?" He extracted a mug shot from his inside vest pocket, a glossy three-by-five of Frank Hyatt before he grew his mustache. A ragged scar ran along the remnant of his upper lip and his teeth shone through as though he'd been caught snarling. I placed my pinky over the lower half of his face. His stare plunged into me like a dagger. I didn't know whether I was looking at the person I had encountered or the sum of all my fears. I shook my head and rubbed my hands for warmth as though they had been suddenly dipped in ice water.

"Too bad." Santarelli pocketed the photograph. He flipped his notepad to a fresh page. "Do you perhaps have some insights regarding the murder of Miss Somerset?"

As matter of fact, I did. "First of all, I have a built-in advantage in regards to understanding how the crime occurred. A man can't hope to sneak into a building stacked floor-to-floor with women without drawing attention."

"Are you suggesting the intruder was a woman?" Santarelli asked. After having rattled him with the solution to the Fritch mystery, he seemed to have regained his self-assured skepticism.

I said, "Any female who has ever lived in one of these petticoat prisons guarded by a warden such as Mrs. Coldmere knows how to sneak in and out for an evening on the town or for a late-night tryst. Usually, the escape and return hatch is an unlocked window away from the street and marked by some item such as a brightly colored handkerchief. Sometimes it involves knocking on the window of the designated gatekeeper. They wouldn't allow just anyone to come in, but they would let in a young woman, and with five floors of females, it must be hard to recognize a stranger. Or else, it's possible the would-be visitor simply said that she'd come to visit Daisy Yinger. When Huyzen gets back, he'll tell you the back door has not been jimmy-cracked."

"Jimmied. Just jimmied," Alan corrected me. *Is that all you have to offer?*

"Thank you, Alan," I hoped he noted my touch of sarcasm. "No one broke in." I continued, "After Patrice Somerset was turned away by Coldmere, being an enter-prising woman and aware of females-only protocols, she slipped around the back and connected with the secret entrance. She made her way to Daisy Yinger's door and found it ajar. She heard sounds inside. She peeked in to find Carolyne Fritch. Patrice had to be murdered because she had discovered that Carolyne was alive."

"Are you proposing that Carolyne Fritch was both the murderer and the shooter who just now escaped?" Santarelli said. "I must remind you that Patrice has been dead for hours. I checked. Her forehead had time to cool. Her face muscles were drawn tight in a grin as though pulled by puppet strings, the first stage of *rigor mortis*. Why would Carolyne Fritch remain there until you arrived?"

"First of all, the way the room was ransacked says she was searching for something. Detective, you said that Carolyne was seen passing money to Daisy. I'm guessing that Carolyne regularly skimmed money from the opera-tion—look at the shoes she wore. She hid money from

Ivan, using Daisy as a confidante, money which she came here to collect.

I pointed to the papers scattered across the floor. "Secondly, these school papers tell me that someone had camped out at the kitchen table to study. Whoever it was had a full view of the hallway and would have seen Carolyne leaving what would soon be recognized as a murder scene. Carolyne stayed in the room, trapped, waiting for the student to take a break from her studies which she did just before we arrived."

"Intriguing," the detective said, "we can ask the ladies on the floor."

Alan fidgeted with his new hand, bending, and straightening the digits. He seemed far away.

"One other matter: how did Carolyne get into the apartment?" Santarelli asked.

"There were no purses, neither in the design office, nor on the street below. Carolyne took Daisy's purse before dumping her body out the window. Carolyne had the key."

Sergeant Huyzen returned and bent over, whispering in the lieutenant's ear. Santarelli returned a whisper.

The sergeant stood up, mushed a frown, and said, "No."

Santarelli said, "I have been informed that one Miss Somerset asked Mrs. Coldmere permission to visit Daisy Yinger approximately two hours ago. Not too long a time for Carolyne Fritch to be trapped in the room. Furthermore, he found no signs that the back door had been pried open, and its lock was in no way faulty."

"Sometimes the marks are subtle," Alan said.

Santarelli dismissed him with a flick of his hand. Stretching his arms over the tabletop, he inhaled and exhaled a sinus-rattling yawn. "Lorraine, I find your theories most credible. Do you have more to share?"

"No," I said.

"No," Alan echoed, as if the question had also been directed to him. "If there's no further need for us here, are we free to go?" He took to his feet with a revived urgency.

"I will allow you to leave if you answer two questions," Santarelli said.

Of all the detectives in the world, we had to hook up with a bridge troll from a fairy tale.

"Question one," the detective said. "What do you intend to do with the telescope in that package?"

"We plan to go to Fritch Designs to see what Carolyne saw," Alan said.

"I suspected as much. So, you are confessing that you plan to trespass on to a crime scene." Before Alan could reply, Santarelli added, "I meant that as a statement, not as my second question. Question two: May I join you?"

Alan glanced my way and I nodded. "Consider yourself invited," he said.

"That would solve the problem of having to break in," I added.

"And arresting you again would be such an annoyance."

"We'd like to do this now if you can see your way free," Alan said.

"Now?" Santarelli tutted his tongue. "I've been a detective for fifteen years. The most important lesson I've learned over that time is: go home. It has been a long day and my children have gone to bed without their father's kisses. I do not desire that my wife should suffer that same cruel fate.

"It is late. The buildings we may hope to spy upon are shuttered for the night. If we were to set up the telescope now, we could join hands and gaze at the twinkly stars. Instead, let us convene in the morning and together we shall venture to the Adams Building. At that favorable hour, fortune may illuminate the trail of a killer. In the meantime, let me declare this a most productive day and turn the case over to Sergeant Huyzen. I am certain he will compose a most informative report for me to pore over. As for the two of you, we will meet tomorrow early in the morning. Until then, you may consider yourselves at liberty." He flicked his hand as though brushing us away.

"Goodnight, Detective," I said. Alan merely muttered something unintelligible.

Alan and I headed down the hallway past a half-dozen officers standing in the entrances of dormitories, some interviewing, some flirting. We continued on past Daisy's room, the door still wide open, Patrice's body unmoved. Her white-stockinged legs, one with its knee bent, drawn up, one extended downwards, together appearing as though frozen in place while pedaling a bicycle. The puddle of blood seemed as dark as a bottomless crater.

I walked with Alan on the side of his prosthetic hand, his arm drawn tight to his body, no room to pry my way in, to lock with his arm.

Damn you, Alan. You can't be like that. You don't have the right to treat me like an equal and then shrink back the moment I outperform you. The lovemaking, the elegant clothes: he wanted to be the rescuing prince. He wanted to dazzle the damsel. Well, this damned damsel has a few moves of her own.

We passed down the stairs in a tumbling quickstep: the percussion of a drum roll ending with a slap as we smacked a landing.

Alan checked his watch. "We have time to fit in one more chore before sleeping tonight."

"What's that?" I asked.

"Sex." He leered.

Hmm. A chore?

At the bottom of the stairs, when we passed the back door, I noticed that it was secured with a heavy bolt. Nothing subtle could have jimmied it.

CHAPTER 22
SEX IN THREE ACTS

Alan

I'VE KNOWN compulsive chatterboxes whose occasional moments of silence come as a blessed relief, a restorative balm to the eardrums. In contrast, there, as she sat next to me on the back seat of the taxi, I wished Lorraine would say something. Anything.

I had my glib answers ready.

"How can you be so detached?" she might ask me.

Then I'd detach my hand and show her. Or she could ask me about *Sex*.

Sex. I'd left that one word dangling. Sex. The chasm that divides and the bridge that unites man and woman. I tossed out the word as a private joke. Private jokes are for the smug and insecure, a way of declaring a personal victory in a game that no one else is playing. I can be a pompous ass sometimes.

Why did I resent Lorraine? Right now, this moment? I was accustomed to dealing with one emotion a day: self-pity. Here was a woman who flooded me with emotions. Here was a woman who challenged me.

Our destination was not sex. *Sex* was our destination. Another inside joke. *Sex* was the name of a Broadway play.

The *World* hated *Sex*. When Mae West opened her play with that one-word title, the critic at my paper, along with those at our competitors, all became born-again Puritans proclaiming that the theater had gone too far this time. *Sex* not only attacked our country's morals, it mounted the bareback of the American nation, and humped us, deflowering our God-given purity. Sex, the "S" capitalized, italicized or diminutive, was not to be discussed, and this show incarnated all the loose morals of the roaring, carnal twenties.

Newspapers panned West as an actress, and as a play-wright, and shamed her as a libertine. Preachers denounced her from their pulpits; aldermen censured her from the back steps of their favorite brothels. Half of the critical newspaper reviews were penned in speakeasies. Everyone concluded that Mae West had a bust on her hands to go along with her handsome bust.

Of course, *Sex* was a hit. And then some. The condemnation of the shocking, shocking show brought in crowds of those who never went to the theater and soon enough a torn ticket became the merit badge of open-mindedness among the upper-crusty. Truth be told, the play was tamer than most burlesque.

The Metropolitan Tower's clock split its hands as wide as a shrug, 10:10. I was shepherding Lorraine to Daly's Theatre, but not to see the play. At this late hour, I hoped to crash the back door when the show let out. I wasn't planning to see Mae West. I hoped to see her chauffeur.

We arrived to find that the play had ended, and the sidewalk chatter had thinned. The marquis lights flicked off. I tipped the cabbie and Lorraine and I headed to the side alley.

What brought me to the backstage door was the complex machinery that comprised New York gangsterism. Owney Madden, killer and protégé to Rothstein, also acted as the hoodlum-patron who called the shots on Broadway. He helped finance *Sex*. He was Mae West's sometimes lover. George Raft, along with being Madden's chauffeur and a member of his gang, was also a Broadway song and dance man, and—also Mae West's lover. Now, two hoods vying for a single woman would usually leap at each other's throats. But Mae West…was Mae West. She wasn't the kind who loved with possession and, somehow, even possessive, obsessive gangsters understood this.

Despite his rising fame as a Broadway star, Raft kept his job as a chauffeur. That may sound like the bottom rung. In reality, his position planted him in the middle of everything, maintaining his contacts with the power players. Because of this, he was my number one source for info about the underworld.

I knew George from when I reported the aftermath of a shootout that had left Owney Madden drilled with eleven bullets (which only served to make Owney angry, not dead). I came across Raft tucked in a closet and bleeding. No coward: he was on hand to volley lead. By the time that the shooters had fled and the police and yours truly burst in, he'd stowed himself, hiding away. He explained to me that he didn't want the police to learn that he'd been shot. Still early in his stage career, he feared that the bad publicity and a hospital stay might make him lose a running part in a Broadway show. So, I told him to play-act a reporter and clipped my press pass to his jacket. The cops knew me, I didn't need a badge. Together we shuffled out the front door.

Since then, he owed me one—and another one and another one, as I arranged to get his name in the drama critic reviews. Which were not even favors: Raft had talent. He had the firecracker energy of George M. Cohan and was billed as "The Fastest Dancer in the World." He invented a dance move where he shook all over, head to toe. It looked like sexual ecstasy. Or, perhaps, he imagined his turn in the electric chair.

George stood, one foot in the gutter, the other propped up on the running board of a Rolls Royce Phantom, a motor carriage fit for a crowned prince. He tore matches from a book, lighting them with a snap of his fingers and watching them fly. I knew that trick: patches of sandpaper glued to the fingertips. Knowing George, I figured he was rehearsing an effect to go along with a new dance routine.

I caught his eye, and he fired both barrels of his glare. Then he noticed Lorraine. He had the skill of instantly sizing up anyone and then tailoring and blending his performance accordingly. In an instant, he transformed from a punchy tough guy into an ingratiating gentleman.

"Alan, pal," he said, flicking a flaming match head my way, "how'd you earn being chummy with a goddess?"

She sent him a nod and her hostess's smile: concealed contempt. She didn't like people flattering her beauty. And yet she drank in their stares. I couldn't fit those two pieces together.

"George, this is Lorraine Marquette. Lorraine, this is George Raft. 'Ranft,' before his days on stage."

George bowed and then skipped a quick, soft shoe shuffle. He ended with a flourish, holding out his hand to Lorraine, palm up. She matched it, overhand, and he graced her knuckles with a kiss.

"And what's with your funeral threads?" George asked me, sneering at my tuxedo. "You killed a rich uncle?"

"Just a night on the town," I said. "You know me."

He chuckled. He knew that my nights on the town started and ended in a bottle. "Did you enjoy the show?" he asked.

"Didn't see it."

"But you snuck out back." Even when he spoke to me his eyes kept wandering over to Lorraine. "Came to see Mae?"

"Came to see you."

"Sort of figgered. You've come to squeeze me for some dope? Some names?"

"I've never asked you to rat anyone out."

"Then why do I always feel like a rat after talking to you?"

We could have been two game roosters sizing up a fight. He had his don't-squeal pride from having grown up on the streets of Hell's Kitchen. He didn't want to tell me, but he did want to. The same motivation that drew him to the stage—the desire to be seen and heard—made him want to be recognized as the guy in the know. I said, "Tell me what you can about Frank Hyatt."

George dropped his jaw and stuck his tongue in his cheek as though I had kissed him with a roundhouse punch. "The Lip? He doesn't take kindly to feature stories."

"This is not for my readers."

"He's trying to kill us," Lorraine said.

George's face froze in a mask. He looked worried, maybe even scared. He shook it off with some banter, "Alan, you've stepped up. Before you were just a newsmutt with a stinky nose, now you're important enough to be killed by the best." He punctuated this with a nervous chuckle. His voice dropped an octave. "I've got my own reasons for hating The Lip, so I'll give you what I can, straight up. You're no great loss, Alan, but I suppose it would be a tragedy if he knifed a peach like Lorraine. Come with me."

George led us to the stage door. He rapped once, paused, then twice more. Not the most sophisticated of codes.

A gorilla shoved open the door. A bundle of muscles squeezed into a dinner suit, he gave Raft the once over and jerked his head to the side, telling him he could pass. Then he gave Lorraine and me the long stare.

"They're jake," George said.

"We're jake," I echoed, squeezing past the muscleman, and following George backstage.

Mae West sat on the edge of her chair as though the seat hadn't earned the right to touch her bottom—and we hadn't earned the privilege of a stand-up greeting. Three panels of light-bulb-ringed mirrors worshipped her, and she returned their love.

She had changed from her stage clothes into furs, a mama bear in ermines. Restless, she percolated and sizzled, not with sex, although there was plenty enough of that, but with confidence. She was shamelessly bold: P.T. Barnum with a swivel. She gave me the once over, from feet to face, her gaze piercing me for a moment while on its way to heaven. Mae had the skill of seeing the boy inside the man. She unnerved me, past and present.

George made an "O" with his index finger and thumb; I suppose to signal that we were, indeed, O-kay folk. Mae rose. Or maybe "rose" is not the right term: she stood five feet and not an inch more.

She squared her shoulders and patted her bottom as she looked at Lorraine and said, "Mmm, George, I adore this new mirror."

Lorraine mimicked Mae's pose, saying, "And the mirror is charmed to meet you." She offered her hand and a smile. "Lorraine."

"You know my name," Mae said. She clasped Lorraine's hand and then hugged her like they were long lost sisters.

George said, "This is Alan Priest. He's been clashing with The Lip."

Mae shuddered with the mention of that name, her

aplomb disappearing. She squinched her eyes and they glistened.

"He came to visit me two weeks past," she said. "We have muscle guarding the door. They're supposed to keep people like him out. But he's the sort of hatchet that can split a crowd. Doorways part for him and people draw back. I suspect, if he wanted to, he could walk straight through hell and come out un-singed."

She unplugged the stopper of a crystal decanter and poured a honey-colored liquor into a goblet. George dutifully filled three more glasses, keeping one and passing out the other two.

I sipped some. It was a memory of how good liquor could be before hooch got watered down or else was boiled up by duffers in their home stills. It tasted too good to swallow.

Mae said, "He brought me a single rose. Blood red. He said that he saw it among the bundle of a peddler and knew it was for me. I could tell he read the fear in my eyes. I thought then and there that he was going to kill me.

"That scar. The teeth beneath that missing strip of flesh. With his mustache, it looked like a widow's veil laid over a skull. He tried to smile around it."

George squeezed her hand and she sat; this time the chair received the full honor of her rear end.

"Since then," George said, "I've showed up early, well before the show closes. I keep a gat in my vest pocket. A flat .22, and I'll empty it if he comes here again. What do you want to know about him?"

"Where can we find him?" I asked.

"No one knows where he haunts. No known family. No friends."

"Then how does he get hired?"

"The classified ads. Owney probably knows the key words."

"He works for Owney?"

"Not recently. Hyatt is too hot and too much of a maybe. Maybe he kills his man, maybe he kills his man and three more on the sidewalk. Owney and Rothstein don't like maybes." George sawed the sandpaper strips on his fingers one against the other. It sounded like a steel stylus skipping on a phonograph disk.

"Alan," he said, "did you do something to rile up Jake Whelan? Because, last I heard, that's who's been paying The Lip."

It all made sense. Whelan had gotten word, probably from a cop, that Lorraine and I were connected to the Fritch setup. Whelan learned Rothstein was calling us in, so he sent Hyatt to bump us off. He failed. Peanuts and the gunman were tagging Ivan, and when they lost him, they recognized us as the consolation prize. They brought us to Whelan who quizzed us before launching us on a one-way ride.

"Yeah," I told George. "Whelan's the guy."

"Alan Arthur Priest," George pronounced my name as though he were reading from an order for my execution. "You do know the sure way to find trouble. If you do meet up with Hyatt, don't be honorable. Shoot him in the back."

CHAPTER 23
NOCTURNE

Alan

I LAY ON THE MATTRESS, atop the sheets, sleep not coming.

That morning, when the pen fell, I just kept on walking. I never entered the Adams Express Building; I never investigated the 24th floor. Instead, I arrived at Cooper's, a speakeasy behind a pharmacy on Pine Street, a gin joint that welcomes veterans. I asked the bartender to line them up and he filled six shot glasses, each with whiskey neat, neat in a row. I took hold of the first tumbler and crushed it in my hand, the glass slicing through my flesh. I bled sawdust.

It's three a.m. and I'm on the hard edge of sober. Lorraine is sleeping, face down. Her sheet covers and clings to her body, a worshipful embrace that outlines her naked form. A sculpture awaiting the unveiling: Venus Reclines.

I'm sitting on the edge of the bed. From across the street, the glow from the St. Regis sign cleaves the curtains, a wedge of neon shooting a dart of light along the floor. My right hand lies on the windowsill, bathed in this redness. The stump of my wrist feels empty, severed anew.

Or else I'm in the speakeasy, pie-faced, swaying on a stool and sharing another lie about how I lost my hand in the war.

And I'm in a pylon hole in the wasteland remains of the Savoy, bleeding out from a chest wound; Lorraine lies crumpled beside me, mercifully shot in the head.

I'm at my desk at the *World*, the typewriter strikers leaping like popping kernels, my writing talent fighting my boozed brain, my talent winning this time, but for how much longer?

And I'm here in the Gotham Hotel and it's three a.m.

———

She stirs beneath the diaphanous sheet, a specter, her skin a skim of cream, my ghost fingers slipping through her and into her dreams.

"Lorraine?"

Her nose crinkles. I believe she heard me but doesn't want to wake.

I whisper to her, saying, "I manned a tank in the summer before the end of the Great War but still before anyone knew that the war would ever end. You've probably heard of the miracles of tank warfare: indestructible, they broke the stalemates of the trenches; they stormed across the No Man's Land, running over puzzles of scar-like ditches, craters, trampling razor wire. Truth is they were no more solid than a tin can, likely as not to throw a tread or get stuck halfway over a fallen tree. And then you'd be at the target end of a firing range, as mobile as a flipped turtle.

"Our tank bellied down in a pit of mud a hundred yards from our trenches and a grenade's toss from theirs. The treads spun, digging our grave deeper and deeper. Then began the incessant hammering of bullets. The metal plates were…with a steady barrage of machine gun fire, the shell could be breached. They didn't launch the heavy mortar: they preferred to kill everyone inside and capture the tanks. They imagined that the same tanks which allowed us to plow across the battle lines would become Germany's means of overrunning France.

"When they finished shredding our front plate, we found whatever we could to block bullets. A ripped-out shift box. A dead comrade. Those still living couldn't escape—we'd be ripped to bits—so we stuck our guns through the firing holes, emptying them, trying to hold back a foot assault. Once the Germans realized our ammo was spent, a soldier sprinted our way. He slipped a grenade through the breach. I picked it up, wrenched open the side hatch and stuck my hand through the hole, tossing it away, just as it blasted. My hand was lopped clean off. The metal plate spared the rest of me. Shocked, bleeding, I passed out.

"I next remember waking around midnight. I flicked on a match and looked around. Just outside lay the fallen bodies of the rest of my crew, shot dead at close range, intimate. The Krauts couldn't 've gotten that kind of close unless my men had raised their hands in surrender. I suppose whoever killed the others must have thought I'd already bled to death from my wrist wound. I used the dark to crawl back to my trench."

Lorraine still feigns sleep, but I can see the corner of her lips rise: she's glad to have shared in this intimacy.

And I feel glad to have gotten past the botheration of telling her how I lost my hand.

Her fake sleep matches my fake story. My tale was a longer variant of those I told in bars. This one had me as a hero, rescuing others from a tossed grenade, even if only for a moment. I suppose the details wouldn't have fooled anyone who had ridden the tanks. I never had.

The truth.

I was in the back of a truck handcuffed to a prisoner, a German officer, transporting him to HQ on his way to interrogation and later, internment. The manacle was thick and hulking, bands around our wrists, they might as well have been made for dungeons. A Gotha G buzzed overhead, a German biplane, bucking the winds. It spread open its bomb bay and dropped a half-dozen cabbage-sized bombs.

Manacled together, both the prisoner and I leaped from the flat bed just before the explosion. The driver and the other guard were killed. Now it was only the two of us, the German and me. For a moment, we lay a yard from one another with our arms splayed, our wrists bruised, lying on our backs as though watching clouds. I remained stunned as he picked up a fallen rifle.

As I struggled to regain my senses, he rolled over to me and began frisking my pockets, saying, "Where is the key?" I slipped my service revolver from its holster and pressed its muzzle against his belly. He countered by setting the tip of the bayonet against my throat.

He said in perfect, very formal English, "My name is Remus. I have a wife and daughter. I do not wish to kill you and I do not wish to be killed. If you shoot me, the weight of my body will surely plunge this blade into your throat. If you toss aside your gun and provide me with the key to unlock these manacles, I will walk away and thereby we shall both continue on our life's journeys."

I told him the truth, "I don't have a key."

"What a shame."

I said, "We don't have to draw blood. We both might die. Shoot the chain. I won't stop you."

"I had a comrade try that once. The chain becomes shrapnel, a miniature grenade."

His blade weighed against my throat. I took my finger from my trigger. "Cut off my hand," I said. "You'll be doing me a favor. I'll never have to return to the battle-front. I'll tell the story that the bomb blast knocked me out and that you hacked through my wrist to free yourself."

He closed his eyes and lifted his chin. I could see his eye-bulbs dance behind his lids. He said, "Maybe I want to be the lucky bastard with one hand who will never fight again," and he laughed.

I dropped my gun to the side and at that moment he could have cut my throat. Instead, he lay my wrist over a rock, and grabbed a stone. He smacked the stone against the blade, time and again. I screamed. Why had I imagined it would be a clean cut? Still, it did the job. And I had always thought bayonets were useless.

Before I passed out, I saw him far away, strolling down

the road as though he owned it, whistling as though no bullet, no bomb, no force of man or God could harm him.

I weep at the memory. I weep because I've never told anyone and can't tell Lorraine. I once thought myself a proud soldier. And then I gave up my hand to get out of the war.

———

She lies there beneath the gossamer sheet. Angelic. Like the story I whispered to her, I know our love is a lie. We've been thrown here together. I'm a drunk who lives in a small room near the docks. She is a beauty who romances the wealthy. The Gotham Hotel is a fairy tale castle, and when this mystery plays out, once our money is spent, our fiction will end.

How could I tell her? I went to the war believing in God and country. I became a killer to end killings in a war to end wars. I watched as other true believers marched to their deaths.

I was a skillful assassin and that was the problem. I could line up enemies in my rifle scope, their heads filling the lenses, as intimate as though we sat on opposite ends of a sofa. I pulled the trigger countless times. I saw heads cave-in or explode, the plates of skull bones shattering like porcelain. Again and again. I still see that.

Even after I understood the demonic joke of war, I kept killing. Even after I recognized that this fight had nothing to do with honor or rightfulness, I kept killing. I kept killing even after I recognized my enemies were the same as me: tired and scared and wanting to go home. To kiss their families. To have families.

In the end, I would have done anything to escape, to desert. To leave the battlefront with whatever shreds of sanity and humanity still clung to me. For too long I had kept on killing.

I could never tell Lorraine: I had become the horror of war.

CHAPTER 24
FLOOR 24

Lorraine

I DOZED off and on that night. At some hour, Alan had gotten up and moved to a chair beside the door where he slept, one hand clutching the chair's arm while his new hand rested on the windowsill. I supposed that he saw himself as the knight guarding his maiden fair. Or else he couldn't bear staying alongside a woman after sex. I've wasted too many a night with that type…

A tabletop clock read a quarter-past-five and the idea of dawn suffused the air. I opened the window. Our floor matched up with the St. in the St. Regis sign. We were high enough above the street so that the smells didn't climb to meet us. Instead, our room had the vaguely empty odors of bleach and flea powder.

Down below, a procession of horse carts. This was the hour in which those merchants who couldn't afford an automobile chose to transport their commerce, mostly free of motor traffic. But not completely free. The occasional car horn declared that, even this early, the modern day barely tolerated the past. I'd read in the paper that ten years ago there were 190 horse/motor car accidents each year in New York City. Now that number had shrunk to one-quarter. There just weren't that many horses anymore.

The phone chimed, an aristocratic jingle, not the sort of fire-alarm bells designed to summon folks from the far side of their homes.

Alan barely stirred.

I lifted the receiver to my ear and gave a timid, "Hello."

A man's voice. "Miss Marquette, this is the front desk."

First problem: we hadn't given them our real names.

"How did…?" but he didn't let me finish.

"…Mr. Priest asked us to ring up if someone came looking for the two of you."

I considered the possibility that Detective Santarelli was an early riser. He had our names and address.

"…No one has come looking, but I thought you'd wish to know that your faces are on the front page of the *World*. You're the top story. Would you like to learn the headline?"

He recited it, his voice in all capitals:

"*WORLD* REPORTER SOUGHT IN KILLING SPREE!"

We dressed, packed, and made it downstairs in Olympic time. The concierge stopped us before we headed out the door.

"Mr. Priest, Mr. Marquette," he said. "You will undoubtedly be spotted if you go onto the street."

I looked at Alan. "What do you suggest?" he said.

"Take breakfast in my office where it is private."

"You're not worried about a pair of killers?"

"A Detective Santarelli called and assured me you are guiltless. He said you are expecting him, and he will be here soon."

We dined at the concierge's desk. The waiting staff treated us like celebrities. I suppose that's how business is handled these days, now that gangsters are royalty.

They provided us with the newspaper. The subheadings read:

Daring Jailhouse Escape!
Woman Held Hostage!

"Are they always so..." I struggled to find the precise phrasing. Inventive? Dishonest? "So full of crap?"

Alan said, "They're cut-throat. They pump up the story to whatever size they need to sell the papers. Back when I first joined the *World*, having just come back from the war, our chief editor was charged with murdering his wife. A great story and we had the inside angle. The *World* proceeded to hyperventilate and spew out lurid tales of his life, his crime and his trial. They so thoroughly destroyed him that prison must have seemed like a pleasant refuge. Now he's the editor of the *Sing Sing Times*."

I studied Alan to determine whether he was making that up. He seemed earnest. I read the lead paragraph out loud.

"The police are hunting for Alan Arthur Priest, veteran of the Great War, longtime *World* journalist, and alleged underworld assassin, [I paused, taking a breath] for the sensational murders of a downtown designer and the policeman who valiantly tried to arrest her killer. The hot-tempered Priest, one-handed, crippled during the war, is said to have been seen by a host of witnesses strangling designer and ingenue Carolyne Fritch before hurling her out of the 25th floor of the Adams Express Building, early Monday morning."

Underworld assassin? A host of witnesses? 25th floor? At least our photographs seemed glamorous. Alan had once worn a mustache. His photo had a dash of John Gilbert. I went back to reading.

"Priest is said to have made a daring escape from the Fourth Precinct Station using a female hostage as a human shield, one Lorraine Marquette, from Chicago. The elegant [I paused here for emphasis] Miss Marquette has been featured in our *All About Town* column in the company of many a socialite."

"This is entertaining," I said.

"You'll be the hard-hearted queen of the underworld in tomorrow's edition. And the writer should have included the policeman's name in the lead sentence. Who got the byline?"

"Gould."

"Of course."

Santarelli marched in and gave a formal nod. "With any luck, you won't be part of the headlines come tomorrow." A quarter to six. He *was* an early riser. "In the next day's edition, you will be spoken of in the last paragraph as part of an article that details the villainy of the genuine killer."

"Good morning, detective," I said, and we exchanged greetings all around.

"My wife runs a market and receives the papers very early," the detective explained. "I rang your hotel to inform them that, although you presented no danger, you may be *in* danger. Thousands, hundreds of thousands, of New Yorkers will soon know your faces and any one of them might identify you. A word might reach Hyatt or Mr. Whelan's men and thereby lead your hunters to their prey. I asked the hotel management to sequester you apart from prying eyes and to afford you every courtesy until I arrived."

"I suppose that these must be the coffee and croissants they serve to all visiting killers," I said.

"You are merely my hostage," Alan pointed out. "I'm the one on the murder spree."

"They might have gotten my role wrong, Mr. Mad Dog," I countered. "They do get some details wrong." I'd thought of continuing, but he already seemed plenty-enough annoyed by the jest. It had worn thin rather quickly; he didn't have my taste for the morbid.

"When we finish breakfast, I will transport you to the scene of the crime," Santarelli said, "the Adams Express Building. We must avoid taking a taxi at all costs. Hacks weave the spider's threads among the underworld's web of spies."

Alan made a *hrmm.* I said, "Thank you." I'd become so accustomed to the strain that I didn't realize that I was harboring so much dread until a shiver of tension jumped up my spine and departed.

"Coffee?" the maître 'd asked.

"Cream and sugar," Santarelli replied. He sat down in the concierge's swivel chair. "And one of those flaky buns the woman is having, if you please."

I passed him my croissant. My stomach was in knots.

Alan scooted his chair back. "Excuse me, I'm going to call one of my friends at the *World* and promise him an exclusive interview for later in the afternoon. That may be enough to hold down on their attacks."

Alan departed and so I was alone with Detective Santarelli for the first time since my interrogation. I felt uncomfortable, certain that I should talk about something meaningful, but not sure what.

He sawed his croissant into thin slices of flaky rings. He dragged one to the corner of his plate and looped it over his fork. Then he slurped it into his mouth as though it were spaghetti. Strange. His mustache bobbed up and down as he chewed.

"I've never had one of these," he said.

I noticed he smelled like baby powder again.

"You spent the evening with Mr. Priest?" he asked.

"Mmm-hmm."

"I don't mean to be prying. But would you mind a personal question?"

He just did. Another? Yes, I would mind. But not so much as to stifle my curiosity. "What?"

"Do you know why people get married?"

Another one of his out-of-nowhere questions. I folded my arms. "I can think of several reasons."

He nodded. "Fools seek happiness by chasing after the illusions of castles. The castles are not over the horizon. Marriage is building that castle where you are. I know of family bliss."

He offered up a sly smile. Gilberti Santarelli. Police detective. Matchmaker.

"What do you want out of life?" he asked me.

That was a second question. I hadn't agreed to two. I countered with, "What do *you* want?"

"I want to be free of wanting."

"A Buddhist's answer."

"And a paradox."

I wanted to be independent and attached, elegant and down-home, smart and not always stuck inside my head. A jumble of contradictions that could make Buddha's chins waggle. Before I could say all this, Alan returned and the conversation shifted to an extra order of sausages.

———

I sat on Alan's right side during our journey downtown to the Adams Express Building, my fingers woven between those of his prosthetic hand. Did he choose this side on purpose? Was he setting up a barrier between him and me? Beneath the soft leather and padding, it felt like a skeleton in a glove. The bones were made of that new material called "Bakelite plastic."

I thought about Mae West. She wasn't about sex, that seemed to be merely a mask she wore for those who didn't look closely. She was an entrepreneur, a larger-than-life spirit who refused to submit to the rules of a man's world.

I was raised as the oldest of my parents' three daughters. Through the female energy of our three little women, combined with the pig-headedness of my parents' patent-medicine crusades, I acquired a fierce and anti-authoritarian femininity.

Perhaps that's why I failed as an adventuress: my heart was never into it. Men as a goal? To skip over, maybe, while aiming somewhere higher. Mae West on her throne? George Raft and others, I suppose, as her vassal subjects? Those are genuine goals.

We hold these truths to be self-evident: that all men *and women* are created equal... Jefferson came so close, and because of that omission, I sometimes wonder whether I could ever stay with a man. Because even good men, as I counted Alan to be, believe they gave women the right to vote. We had to wait on men to grant us what was for them, self-evident.

Alan saw me as equal not because he believed men and women are equals, but because he saw me as an exceptional woman. And I hated that. And yet I loved being considered as an exceptional woman. Oh, piffle!

———

Standing in front of the Adams Express Building, my workplace in my yesterday's life, I thought of how seldom I looked up at its face, at its frightening height. Thirty-four floors, the lenses of its windows gleamed in the early morning sun like those of a thousand-eyed monster, and inside of each eye, the tears of so many private dramas. With so many stories, so many tales of hope and despair, I was surprised the street below was not riddled with the bodies of jumpers. But I'm morbid that way.

I scanned the sidewalk for signs of yesterday's death. The blood had been scrubbed clean, but strangely there was a blot of ink in the middle of the walkway. Alan stared at that stain as though it were the entrance to another world. Who can figure men?

"Come along, children," Santarelli said. He stood holding open a glass door to the lobby. He tilted his head back and held out the telescope as though it were the enchanted cane from a fairy tale, a stave which would guide us onwards to a fantastical world.

Outside an elevator, I saw Mr. Winterhaven, a regular visitor to the Anglo-American Fellowship Foundation. I sent him a smile. He ruffled his shoulders and turned his back. He had a rolled-up newspaper tucked under his arm.

I thought, Hey, don't you remember? I'm the hostage, not the killer. And then I considered that the other papers might have even wilder versions of the story.

I knew half of the elevator boys by name. I hoped we'd find a cab with one I didn't know. No such luck.

"Miss Marquette."

"Walter."

"16?"

"We're going to floor 24," Santarelli answered for me.

The cage closed and Walter stared at his shoes, a pucker on his lips. That was how he always posed, too timid to look anyone in the eye. He pulled the control lever up in a smooth motion. I looked to Santarelli and Alan who seemed to be lost in their own distant lands, private crusades playing out in their minds.

After a time, the elevator boy eased off on the ascension as we approached the twenty-fourth floor. "Number 24," he announced.

I thanked him by name and, as I stepped out, I tried to catch his eyes with mine. When I succeeded, he returned the wisp of a smile. He pulled the cage door shut and disappeared, the cab sinking beneath the floor.

The three of us made the short walk and quick twist to join with the front hallway.

A warning poster was gummed to the door and frame:

DO NOT ENTER
WITHOUT AUTHORIZATION
FROM THE NEW YORK CITY POLICE

Santarelli used the teeth of a key to saw through its seal.

For some reason I expected to see something dramatic when he opened the door. A coffin. A ghost. Something to acknowledge the violence of the previous day, something that would note the seriousness of our investigations. Instead, the long narrow room seemed like the hollow chamber of an empty rifle: its action spent, the echoes long quiet.

Alan took a riverboat hat off of a hook on the coat rack. I suppose it was his. He examined it and tossed it onto the desktop. It didn't go with his outfit. It was yesterday's Alan.

The back window was closed, its curtains rehung and tugged shut. Santarelli headed to a spot in front of the window where he unbundled the telescope. He set the butcher's paper aside on top of the back desk.

"The tripod is bolted to the floor," Santarelli said as he adjusted the mounting screws to hold the telescope in place. "That explains why they didn't take it with them."

"Ivan is the sort who would grab anything he could to pawn it," I said. "That means they left in a hurry."

The lieutenant nodded.

Alan yanked back the curtains. This was an eastward view and, at this early hour, the face of the building across the street was still in shadow.

The Columbia Trust stood about sixty feet shorter than the Adams Express Building, but being on the 24th floor of this building, we were level with its roof. Alan opened the window. An unearthly breeze swept in: sweet and cool and refreshing…and nothing like Manhattan.

"Ready," Santarelli said, making a final twist.

"I can tell you right away what they weren't looking at," Alan said. "They camped out here for months. They wouldn't have been spying on the sidewalk or the roof. They might have seen a murder, but they weren't looking for something that might happen. They wanted to monitor something they knew would happen. I think they were looking in an office. Being near the financial center, I'm guessing business spies."

"Business spies?" I echoed.

"I find it hard to imagine Ivan having the smarts to pull off commercial espionage," the lieutenant said.

"Then maybe Carolyne was the brain behind the enterprise?" I asked. Again, they were overlooking the woman.

Alan split open a wide grin and rolled his eyes upwards. I surmised that this was not due to my comment, but for something going on in his mind. "Of course," he said. "The building across the street. It used to be the Knickerbocker Trust. I would have recognized it earlier, but it's been disguised."

"Disguised?" I asked.

"Not disguised…mutilated…" Alan said and, as though that weren't descriptive enough, he added, "… cursed. It's a Stanford White building. The original building was gorgeous, with Corinthian columns, the sort of bank where Zeus would keep his money. Postcard pretty. It had a huge central chamber with gleaming marble floors and a ceiling tall enough to fit a chorus of angels.

"But then the president of the Knickerbocker Trust got caught up in a huge scandal, he bet all of the bank's funds on a copper scheme and the institution went belly-up. He managed to throw the whole country into a recession. You remember, the panic of ought-seven. New owners swept in and lowered the ceilings and added a soul-crushing twenty new stories, creating a flat block of cement. They might as well have covered it with a concrete waste basket. They made it into an office building. I'd bet a dollar to a cigar that the Fritches were caught peeking in on some financial antics."

"Where do we start looking?" I asked.

Alan said, "With this angle, I can tell you from a quick glance over that there'll be only a few windows to choose from."

Santarelli rolled the swivel chair to the back to the telescope. He said, "I'd prefer to be free to take notes. Mr. Priest, why don't you take the honors?"

I felt glad I wasn't the one at the telescope. I shivered at the thought of Carolyne Fritch spying on the thing that inspired the murderer to kill her. Daisy Yinger ended up being the victim, but still, it would feel like peeping through a dead woman's eyes.

Alan settled down in the chair. He leaned into the eyepiece and kept the telescope level as he scanned the windows directly across from us. He said, "I'm looking at the top floor, south corner. I can see the logo of some sort of geographical society. Some old man at an expensive desk. Looks like he has a ledger but, from this angle, I can't see anything he's writing... I'm trying one window over on the left side. If they were looking for numbers or financial secrets, well, unless they posted something on the wall, there's nothing to see."

"Try the floor below," Santarelli said. "If the desk is near the window, the angle might allow you to look over someone's shoulder."

"Two windows to the same large room. A whole lot of women on telephones. Next window over is pasted over, covered up with newspapers. The window to its left, a desk. It has a book the size of an atlas. The book is closed now, but if it was open, I could read every word, every number. Angling a bit more to the left, I can't see anything but a sliver of wall. Another story down and I'm looking at the floor."

As he spoke, I stared out at the Columbia Trust. I had spent so many lonely days on the 16th floor gazing at that building. Then it dawned on me. Something was different. I said, "Second floor from the top. Third window from the right. The one you said was pasted over." The view through the window had been blocked with newspapers.

"Yeah," Alan said. "The angle is right. The newspaper is the *Evening World*. Great taste. Yesterday's headlines."

"It's been covered over for just one day," Santarelli said. "After they discovered that they'd been spied on, they blocked out scrutiny from any further onlookers, a rush job using the first thing they could get their hands on."

Alan backed off from the telescope. He announced what we are all thinking. "It's them."

CHAPTER 25
THE KNICKERBOCKER TRUST

Lorraine

Santarelli strode ahead of us. He had already entered the Columbia Trust Building and began inquiring at the reception desk while I stood with Alan in front. He was lost in a reverie, one of his personal intense moments, communing with a building.

The entryway was a hall. Stout columns speared the low ceiling, cut off as they just began to gain height. I felt as though we had entered some medieval torture device, a dungeon cell where the ceiling was sinking down to crush all those beneath. Offices crowded in on both sides. They seemed no better built than market stalls. In contrast, the marble floor appeared gorgeous, even though it begged to be polished. Down the hallway, we passed into a central room with breathing space, a bank.

"They destroyed so much of the original beauty," Alan said. "So much."

Having finished his inquiries, Santarelli informed us,

"The window which we viewed corresponds to suite 2415. The occupant is Vachel Ruby Investments. I showed the receptionist Frank Hyatt's photo, and he made a positive ID. He also picked out the two thugs whom you know as Peanuts and Nick. He said that they escort Mr. Ruby, serving as his protection. Mr. Ruby had been attacked recently."

"2415?" The 24th floor again. I suppose that made sense. They were being spied on by the Fritches at approximately the same height. I looked at Alan about to say something, then noticed that he seemed far away. He blanched, his mouth dropped half-open, and his lips moved wordlessly. He used his left hand to flex and unflex his right hand's fingers.

"It fits," he said. "It all fits. It's perfect." Santarelli and I were staring at his snugly-fitting prosthetic, so he clarified, saying, "Vachel Ruby, we profiled him in the *World*. He's the wunderkind of Wall Street. His investment fund pays out 10% per month. He's made a lot of people wealthy, most especially himself. It's natural that the Fritches would set up a spy nest to discover his secret."

"And that secret is somehow deadly," Santarelli said.

"Charles Ponzi," Alan said and Santarelli nodded. Alan recognized my confusion and so he went on to explain. "When an investment is too good to be true, it's not true. Ponzi used the money coming in to pay back the previous investors. He kept ahead of the game by collecting more and more new investors eager for the fantastic payouts while skimming millions. This sort of strategy works, but it's like pumping a handcar in front of a train that's gaining speed. Someday there comes a reckoning."

"The Fritches are bunco artists," Santarelli said. "Perhaps they saw the ledgers and recognized the scam. And then like fools, they tried blackmailing Ruby."

"I doubt that," Alan said. "Ivan seemed clueless. They were probably simply caught looking in. These people are paranoid and dangerous. Ruby's sort of operation only works if no one knows the truth. Maybe Ruby or one of his flunkies caught a glimpse of the telescope."

"How is Jake Whelan involved?" I asked.

Alan hitched his shoulders, the closest thing he made to a shrug. "As a partner? I doubt he's the kind who bankrolled the operation from scratch. He must have come across Ruby's secret and cut himself in. And now, to protect that cut, Whelan is trying to stamp out anyone who knows or may know that Ruby is a fraud and that means everyone with any connection to the Fritches."

"What about Rothstein?"

"Rothstein is in the dark or else he wouldn't have hired us. I'm guessing that he knew that Whelan had some sort of operation going on and used us to run down the story."

"Using Ruby's association with Frank Hyatt and other thugs," Santarelli said, "the question of his promised payouts, adding in a flexible judge…I can return here with a search warrant in under an hour. Unlike rumrunners who scrupulously pay off everyone, financial racketeers pinch their pennies, and the judges I know are happy to get their names in the papers for bringing them down.

"Wait here for me. Station yourself near the bank guard in case Whelan's men appear. When we're done with the raid, you can ride along with me to the station to get the inside report on the genuine assassins along with the financial crime of the year."

"Exposing Vachel Ruby," Alan said as though lost in a dream. "Just his connections with the underworld will be enough to kill his racket."

The detective made a low bow, arm across his belly.

Alan watched, glassy-eyed and stone-faced as Santarelli exited the front door out on to Broadway. The moment that door closed, he said, "You stay here. I'm going up." He made his way to a bank of three elevators.

At first my heels stuck like magnets but then I popped them free and followed. He waited, staring at the floor indicators. Each of them had dials pointing to the locations of the elevator cabs, each on the middle floors. One was descending.

"Are you crazy?" I wanted to say. I did say, "Hyatt or Peanuts or any of their kind could be up there."

He presented a nervy sort of smile. "Last year, there was a gas leak in a line along the subway," he said, "and the transit chiefs stopped a trainload of commuters between stations, not wanting to run the train forward or backwards or out of harm's way because they were afraid of an electric spark. So, they dithered while everyone down below was set to be gassed. I thought back to my time in the trenches and how any day could bring a cloud of poison our way.

"So, I snuck past the cordons and into the tube. I wasn't being a hero, it was a story and I had to head into the trenches to get it.

"Lorraine, you're a hell of a snoop. You've got an eye

for the details and heaps of savvy. I'm just a crusted-over doughboy and bull-headed news-hack. Charging into the thick of danger is what I do."

I was prepared to snap at him, but first I had to know. "What happened to the people on the train?"

"They had gotten fed up with waiting and started walking back to the last station. I didn't rescue them, but I did grab a few good interviews."

I understood. Alan was a news reporter: he had to see, to bear witness. Ruby's office was the beating heart of the animal which had killed Daisy Yinger, Officer Baxter and Patrice Somerset—and which had tried to kill us. I understood him, but didn't forgive the slight.

"I'm coming with you," I said. To my surprise, he didn't argue.

Danger brought out a stupid streak in me, just like it did in Alan.

As an elevator cab came down to take us, I noted the dial above was numbered 1 to 25 with no 13. This building had exactly 24 floors. I was beginning to hate that number.

CHAPTER 26
VACHEL RUBY INVESTMENTS

Lorraine

"Say, bud," Alan said to the elevator boy, "what sort of stairways you got in this building?"

The boy eyed him strangely and then looked me over up and down, deciding he must be okay since he was with a doll like me. "One set alongside the elevators and another at the far end of the hall."

"That'll do. How much do they pay you?"

"A dollar a day and some tips."

"Well, twenty bucks tells me that today you are feeling too sick to go on working."

"Twenty bucks? Jeeze, mister, who do I gotta kill?"

"Me and my friend here might need to make a quick, safe exit and we don't want anyone following us. I need you to station yourself in the back stairwell on the 24th floor. When she and I come to see you, you run down the stairs and make a big noise with your feet. Stay near the wall so no one can look down and see you. We'll soft-pedal it up a flight. A few moments later, whoever followed us to the stairs will be chasing down after you."

He shut his eyes, the lids twitching as if in deep thought while trying to visualize this. Finally, he said, "Sure, swell. A double sawbuck and that's all I got to do?"

"That's all. The men racing down after you could be dangerous, but if you meet up, just sell them some line about being in a hurry."

"Can I see the twenty now?"

"Ten and ten more when you get the job done," but all the folding money that Alan had on hand were twenty-dollar bills, so he passed one over.

"Floor 24," the boy said, adding as we parted. "My boss is a swell egg. Let me arrange getting sick and I'll be back in the shake of a lamb's tail."

The 24th floor hallway stretched out before us, open-throated and sarcophagal. That last 'word-a-day' word means either like a stone coffin or like a flesh-eater. It was both. I shivered. Okay, my imagination was working overtime.

The lighting was dim. On our end, the cables of the sinking elevator whined on their pulleys. At the far end, a muffled chirping leaked through closed doors: women talking, seemingly all at once. A dull red carpet with hypnotic zig-zagging lines covered the middle of the wooden floor and deadened our footfalls. The air smelled of dust, and as for the floor, walls and ceiling, the whole place needed a good hoovering. The hall ended faraway, at an open window, which allowed in a skewed slab of light. To its side, a door to a stairway: our escape hatch.

"Why didn't you ask the kid to just hold the elevator cab for us?" I asked as we walked down the hall.

"Too long a hallway. Too much an opportunity to buy a bullet in the back."

As I continued down the hall, I felt the floor and the walls rocking, amplifying the gentle sway of my walk, a dizziness that increased my sense of doom. I knew it was all in my head, my pulse pounding, the world throbbing…

"Don't worry," Alan said. "I've run that trick with the stairs a dozen times. The suckers will always chase the big commotion."

A dozen times? I tried to imagine what need a reporter would have for such a ploy, but my head felt clouded. I focused on the here and now, on the details, the mesmerizing pattern on the carpet, the doors that read Vachel Ruby.

Vachel Ruby Investments filled the final three offices on our right-hand side. The first door served as the formal entrance. Its wooden frame supported a head-to-foot frosted window which bore gold-leaf lettering, the name of the firm set in a rainbow arc, a gay Oz-like presentation. Underneath, the business hours were spelled out: a leisurely 8 a.m. to 3 p.m. Inside, a typewriter clacked. I had thought that, after they had discovered the Fritches' spy-game, they might have closed shop and scrammed, but no.

"They haven't skipped out," Alan said, echoing my thoughts.

I stooped down to open the mail slot and peek inside. I

saw a pair of knobby knees below the tasseled fringe of a flapper's skirt shuffling by while a spectral shadow glided across the frosted glass. I saw no one else, just an empty waiting space with empty waiting chairs. A desk for a receptionist. I don't know what I had expected. Tommy-guns and corpses? I stood up.

The doorknob was oval and ornate; brass, antiqued with a coppery stain, and engraved with golden fleurs-de-lis. Set below it, a knocker fashioned in the form of a lion biting down on a ring, suited to a Dickens tale. I expected Marley's ghost to snap at me as I reached out to give the door a rap. Alan stayed my hand. Without a word, he turned the knob and swept open the door.

The reception room was lushly appointed with burgundy drapes and matching carpet. Six armless chairs stood in two neat rows. Elsewhere, arm-chairs upholstered with vermillion leather sat in pairs around reading tables. The air tasted of cigars, as though the fabrics and furnishings had been cured in a tobacco smokehouse.

Through the windows I could see over to the Adams Express Building. I imagined myself there, on the 24th floor, peering back at me.

Atop the table an open box of cigars and a book: *Prospectus 1926.* I riffled through pages of numbers. Even without stopping to study them, all the figures looked impressive, lots of plus signs and four-digit payouts.

The only person present was an orange-haired secretary: a tiny pixie who glanced at Pitman scribbles while banging typewriter keys. The typewriter was one of those tall, old demons that battered the page into submission.

From the way in which she slugged away, I supposed that her fingers could deck Jack Dempsey. "May I help you?" she said, not looking up until Alan answered.

"I'm Alan Collinswood and this is my wife."

"Collinswood? Like the photoplay star?" she asked.

"Yes, but no relation." Alan peeked my way, holding back a smirk. "We have several thousand dollars we'd like to invest, and we've been told that Mr. Ruby is the wizard."

"I can vouch for that." She continued to type, one-handed, glancing at the scribble. She gestured with her other hand as she spoke. Talented. "I sink every penny I can straight back into his pool and now I'm making double my salary."

"Incredible," I said.

"Sounds too good to be true," Alan added.

"Mr. Ruby has a very busy schedule," she said—no one else was in the reception room— "but I'm sure he can find time for a serious investor." I noticed she didn't have an interoffice telephone, just a set of colored buttons. She pressed a green one and, in a moment, a green bulb flashed in response. She pushed a buzzer beneath her desk and the lock clicked and the door on our left parted from its jamb. They'd wired up a remote, electronic lock. I'd never seen one. Nifty.

———

Vachel Ruby was a small, frail man with a long face, plumped out at the bottom by a healthy set of whiskers.

He sat, swallowed by an enormous oak desk. Its top was inlaid with parquet-tiling, spit-shined so that his reflection appeared sealed beneath its polish. On one corner of the desktop was a series of three lights, red, yellow, green. The wall to his left was a floor-to-ceiling bookshelf with leather-bound ledgers titled from A to X-Y-Z. To his right, the reception room. The secretary shut the door and its electronic lock snicked into place. Muttering, like that of a theater crowd, filtered in from beyond a back door.

Towering over and behind Ruby, a tall bank of windows had been recently covered with dull, dead news-papers: they might as well have slopped on as papier mâché. It was easy to imagine someone peering over his shoulder from the Adams Express Building.

"Pardon me for not rising," he said, a grin raising his whiskers. "I sprang an ankle yesterday and, in losing my balance, rammed an elbow through some windowpanes. I've scheduled a handyman to come fix them, but what with that squall we had, my partners insisted on covering them up right away."

I could see the tumescent bulge of a cast beneath the forearm of his shirt sleeve. I noticed the shudder of his breathing: bruised ribs. I glimpsed the hollow of the arch beneath the desk. One leg projected out, stiffly. Elbow, ribs, and ankle: when his partners had learned the Fritches were spying they went on to make Ruby pay for his lapse of security. This self-made man was a self-made prisoner. He hid his fear—and pain—behind a salesman's confi-dence, exposing only brief twitches of strain in the corners of his smile.

He said, "When the late afternoon sun comes

streaming through this tall window, it reminds me of my choirboy days, the stained glass sparkling. I enjoy having my office here on top of the business world. It's as though I've made a nest in the clouds, bathed in the aura of the heavens."

Just as I began wondering if he would feed us nothing more than sunshine and daisies, he continued with, "God has blessed me, endowing me with genius. Newton discovered gravity, and the Curies, radium. I am a prodigy at prosperity. My extraordinary talent humbles even me. It is my deepest desire to share this gift with all those discerning enough to join me in my wealth-making crusade. No, not a crusade: a voyage. A search for the treasure that is our due. The prize is a 10% return per month, compounded, payable at thirty-three-and-a-third, each quarter. You will double your investment each nine months."

Back in my catechism days, I'd snuck off with a Presbyterian friend to visit a tent-revival. The preacher came across as a rabble-rousing blowhard. In contrast, this soft-spoken humbug tickled me with his patter. Who among us can refuse God's endowment?

"You're asking us to risk a lot of money," I said. "How does your system work?"

"No risk involved. As to the details, the recipe is a secret. I can tell you that we identify growth stocks by applying the latest advances in algebra and trigonometry to intelligence reports gathered domestically and from around the world via the magic of wireless communication transmitted by my patented code.

"A Ruby membership starts at $2,000. So how much

should I put you down for?" His fingers galloped and jumped in place, tapping on the desktop as though a steeplechase scrolled beneath them.

As I said, I liked his soft-spoken pitch, but now that it was done it felt too brief. I like a bit more seduction, just enough to maintain the illusion of my dignity before I give in.

Alan put an end to any spell cast by Ruby's words. "I suppose you have a full-length speech, the one you run by high-priced suckers. All I heard was 'Give me your money, I have to feed my partners or else they'll break my other leg.'"

To Ruby's credit, Alan's broadside barely flustered him. His steeple-chasing fingers halted. His lips flattened and he drew in a quivering breath. His eyelids jumped. He asked, "Who the hell are you?"

A commotion began in the reception room. I heard muttering and heard what worried me more: the rustling of a newspaper. Alan and I were front-page fodder. The red light blinked on Ruby's desk. His eyes zig-zagged, not knowing where to settle.

"Excuse me," he said. He pressed against the desktop, rising to his feet. His right leg filled a gypsum cast and he used it as a peg to trundle past us and to the door. He slid a key in the lock. When he opened the door, I caught a brief glimpse of the secretary and the gangsters Peanuts and Nick, huddled around a spread-open *Morning Herald*. Our photos were on page three. The headline, all that I could read from where I stood, focused on Alan's mother.

SON OF PIX STAR
GAIL COLLINSWOOD
ACCUSED OF MURDER

The trio looked our way, wide-eyed. Peanuts and his fellow killer were either amazed by the fact that their prey had wandered into their lair, or else they were impressed by the fact that Alan was the son of a photoplay star. Ruby stared at the page and then glared at us in horror. He rushed the door to his office and slammed it closed, shutting us in. The bolt thwacked into place.

Up to this moment we had been stupidly still, lambs in the slaughtering pen. I jumped to my feet and Alan rose slowly.

"Quickly," he exclaimed—a little late to be quick —"before they lock the back door."

I could see the gap in the jamb: that door hadn't been fully shut.

Alan pushed open the door, peeked in to make sure the way was safe, and together we entered a room made stark by its whitewashed walls and flimsy furnishing. Here stood a three-by-four array of small tables. On each tabletop, a yellow notebook, along with a phone set, cradle and speaker, black and tall, like chess bishops. The devices were being operated by a dozen jabbering ladies. All the operators were young and stylish, a virtual brigade of flappers. They spoke into the mouthpieces of their receivers, twelve voices all at once.

"Your second quarter return is forty per cent. That reflects a dividend for two cycles with no withdrawals. Let me set you down for rolling over your earnings."

"Yes, there is a bonus for referring clients to us. Yes, and an extra family bonus."

"Mr. Sherman, I don't know why you haven't received your quarterly check. I can look into that for you. You know that you'll make a lot more if you let your proceeds ride."

None of the women looked our way, it was as if we didn't exist. Or, perhaps, they existed only for show. Prospective clients were introduced to a bevy of beautiful professional women, all engaged in making the Ruby investment machine run.

Telephone cords snaked across the floor, bunching at a nearby hole in the wall.

Peanuts and Nick entered from the hallway door across from us. Perhaps the back door to Ruby's office had been left open on purpose: they had herded us this way. Peanuts said, "Ladies, heads down," and they all obeyed, eyes dropping in unison as though "no witnesses" was a routine part of their jobs. Maybe it was.

Peanuts sprang a switchblade. Nick tucked his hand in his jacket, over his heart, pledging allegiance to the gun that peeked out from his vest holster. Peanuts slid between the tables, coming directly towards us, while Nick scooted along the side wall, blocking our path to the hallway door.

Alan stooped and yanked on the bundle of phone wires. The women quickly seized hold of the cradles to prevent their phones from tumbling to the floor and together these actions elevated a web of cloth-wrapped cords which, for the moment, halted the killers' progress.

"Back inside," Alan said. The best of bad options.

We ducked back into Ruby's office and closed the door.

"If that's how you choose to play it," I heard Peanuts say.

In a moment, I heard the electric bolt slide into place. We were sealed in until the moment they chose to unlock one of the doors. This must have been their plan all along: trapping us here. Peanuts and Nick were the sheep dogs. The Lip, when he arrived, would be the butcher.

Alan ripped through the newspapers covering the outside window. He stuck his head through the gap in the broken glass. He soon reappeared, frowning. "Not enough of a ledge to make an escape."

Not enough might be our best option. I guessed that the attack was going to come through the front door. As much as the killers depended on the obedience of the phone operators, they wouldn't want twelve witnesses to our murders. We needed to get back inside the telephone room.

I climbed on the desk and fell forward, catching the bottom of the transom frame. Alan mounted the desktop and bent down on all fours. I understood the gesture and used his back to boost me up.

"The two killers," I said, looking over the telephone bank, "they've abandoned the back room." I unlatched the window and flipped it open on its pivot. "I think I can skinny my way through."

I pulled myself up and into the space, halfway over the door frame. Then, with a wriggle and lunge, I tumbled head over heels into the operator's room. Even more than the killers with a knife and a gun, my actions grabbed the attention of the ladies. The chattering stopped.

I grabbed the table away from a nearby operator and shoved it next to the door. I climbed on top and chinned my way up to see through the transom space, to help Alan up and over.

Alan was not even trying to follow me. He had shoved the large desk in front of the reception room door. This seemed to make no sense: the door opened outwards. Then I recognized his plan. The desk had a broad space for legs, enough so that Alan aligned the hollow in front of the closed door and slid hidden beneath. When they opened the door, the killers would scramble, climbing over the desk and Alan would skip out from beneath.

Although risking his life, his plan would serve as a distraction while I escaped. There was no time to argue his gallantry and I wasn't helping by standing on a table and watching. I jumped down and wove past the lady operators, some of whom had blithely resumed their calls. I heard a crash and a gunshot from the direction of the reception room.

I ran into the hallway. I screamed, hoping to divert attention from Alan, thinking that one of the killers might come follow me. An even better reason to scream came as the elevator door opened at the end of the hall, revealing The Lip. He tucked his head down and came racing my way, his arms and hands slicing the air as he ran.

I ducked into the stairwell. The elevator boy sat on a step, flipping cards into a pile.

"Now!" I cried and he dutifully began trotting down

the stairs. I climbed up to the landing and the steps beyond where I waited, hidden, holding my breath.

In mere moments, what must have been The Lip flung open the stairwell door. I didn't dare peek. The newcomer paused on the 24th floor landing, breathing harshly. Below, the frenzied footfalls of the distant elevator boy. They sounded nothing like women's shoes. But then The Lip is a man: he wouldn't even think about the difference.

He took the bait and hurried down the stairs. I exhaled.

A pair of gunshots rang out in the hallway, followed in a few moments by the door opening again. The new arrival stood on the landing, silently. For a moment, I heard only the clatter and echo of shoes cascading far below.

Then, from the hallway, a mad rush clamored toward the door as muffled footfalls slowly, stealthily climbed the steps, turning the corner to confront me.

"Lorraine." Alan whispered his greeting.

"Sssss," I answered.

Alan pressed against the wall of the landing as two more sets of footfalls entered the stairwell. Peanuts cursed and he and his partner began running down, following the sounds made by Hyatt and the elevator boy.

Alan raised a finger to his lips, then pointed. Together, we climbed up, each step silent. I thought we were being overly cautious, our pursuers so far away and on the wrong track. Then I heard someone whistling a tune. Only one of our group would be calm enough to whistle: the elevator boy.

I heard one set of footfalls stop.

Not Peanuts, not Nick—they were stampeding together. It might have been the elevator boy deciding that he'd earned his twenty dollars, but I knew that it wasn't.

With the whistling, The Lip recognized he was pursuing the wrong person.

I heard him begin to climb the stairs toward us.

The feet of those heading down created a clattering, jazzy rhythm. The feet coming up beat like war drums.

CHAPTER 27

#50

ALAN

Two flights up and we arrived at the rooftop entrance. The base of the door scraped over gravel and soon jammed. Lorraine and I squeezed through the gap. Before I shut the door, I twisted the knob to test whether it had a spring bolt. If the roof-side locks on this building needed a key, we would be trapped up here and easy pickings. The knob turned freely, and I assumed the other stairway's access would readily open.

Half of the rooftop was flat and empty, spread out like a theater stage when viewed fromthe taller Adams Express Building. The gravel covered an expanse of tar, as shiny and as black as an oil spill. Tin-capped vents sprouted through the ceiling like metallic mushrooms. A distance away stood an ungainly structure the size of a chapel. It housed the water tower, the elevator riggings, and the entry to the other stairway.

I bent to catch my breath. Not that I'd run far, but the

tension had clenched my every rib muscle, leaving them trip-wire tight.

"No time for a breather," Lorraine said. "He's coming."

We trotted across the roof with Lorraine reaching the far side stairwell before I did. This door also stuck, rasping against its frame. I set a foot against the jamb and pulled with such force I thought I'd lose my flesh hand. The doorway split open.

Hyatt burst out of the other stairway and fired our way. A slug hit the door. We squeezed through and attacked the steps, hurtling downward. I told Lorraine, "I don't know if we can outrun him. We should duck into a hallway to hide before he enters the stairwell and can hear us leaving."

Lorraine was in front of me. We skipped by the first three exits. I followed her out into the twenty-first floor hallway.

I clasped a hand over her lips as she was about to speak and listened. I heard Hyatt above us bursting into the stairway. He began descending the steps. Not hurriedly, but with a deliberate pace. Perhaps he was listening for us. And then what? Hearing nothing, he would conclude that we had exited. He would rule out us passing by Ruby Investments. He would check the next floor down, and then the next, where we stood frozen. No. I heard him continue to pass down, seemingly two floors up. He was coming directly toward us.

This set of stairs descended alongside the elevator shafts. I could hear the creak of an elevator cable as its cage approached. I leaned against the outside gate to look down. A cab was one floor below and rising. I pressed the call button. The elevator glided slowly into place and stopped. An elevator boy and an elderly couple. The latter wore a heavy bundle of covering considering that it was June, and both held hats in their hands. The woman strangled a sheet from the Help Wanted pages. The man muttered his puzzlement in a Slavic language.

"Not here," the boy said to the pair as he opened the outer gate. We rushed in.

"Down," I whispered, "it's a matter of life or death."

"We're going up," the operator advised.

"Life or death," Lorraine echoed, biting the words, and seizing the boy's collar.

The elevator boy reached for the outside gate, but before he closed it, I shoved him to the side, and yanked downward on the operating lever. With a jerk, we began to descend. The stairway door burst open, and Hyatt pivoted to witness our open cage dropping below his knees. I looked up, catching a glimpse of his figure towering over us and the skeletal grin behind the veil of his mustache. He swung his gun our way.

"Duck!" I cried out. Even the immigrant couple understood, and we all dropped to the floor as Hyatt fired a bullet through the ceiling.

As we continued to descend, I could hear the banging and echoing of feet as Hyatt rushed down the stairway alongside us, an unreal sound like the rattle of a tin sheet.

"Can't this go any faster?" I asked the operator.

"The lever is cranked as low as it goes."

As the elevator continued to descend the pursuing footfalls failed to keep pace and became the echo of distant thunder.

The two immigrants argued with one another. "Nu, nu," the man said and mimed a gunshot.

My throat dropped into the pit of my stomach; my thoughts stewed in acid. I hoped the elevator would arrive on the first floor revealing Santarelli leading a score of anvil-shouldered bluecoats, each of them thumping a nightstick against his palm. I silently counted down the floors, now in single digits.

When the gate opened, we encountered no rescuers, merely the real world going about its ordinary business, a sea floor of bank commerce, far beneath the storm.

We had passed this way before. Marble floors and the cut-off Corinthian columns. A semi-circle of teller booths. What seemed a short time ago to be ordinary and safe, now felt like the bull's-eye end of a shooting range. Lorraine and I rushed across the lobby, down the hallway, and out onto Broadway. Here, we mixed in with the midday crowd, a roiling flood of people and no matter which way we faced the current seemed to be flowing against us.

"We have to get far from here," Lorraine said.

I squeezed her hand to say, "*I know.*"

We headed south, passing Exchange Alley, a dark passageway for dark-suited investors. At first, I thought of entering the Exchange Court Building, as well-guarded an interior as any building in the city, but we'd have to get inside. A rhinoceros with a truncheon slotted at his side guarded its door, ready to chase off all but the most proper of people. If only I had a bowler hat. One more building down the street and we came upon #50 Broadway.

———

The modern world began at Number 50 Broadway—a lot of blame to place on a single building. In 1888, the architect settled on an impossibly tall and thin design. All the buildings which had come before, like beetles, had been supported by their outer shells, becoming as big and as brawny as their stone or brick walls could be stacked. Castles and cathedrals reigned as the tallest buildings in the world. The Tower at 50 Broadway took its cue from evolution: creatures could grow taller and more immense using internal skeletons. So, the architect cried, "Let there be life!" and constructed his new beast using an inner framework of steel, thus giving birth to a modern breed of titans, giants with spires that raked the sky.

Cliffs rose around Wall Street. The masses and the masters separated. Those above owned the sun and towered over the rest of us, who were cast into a pit of shadows. With the people and the prestige separated, New York became even more concentrated as a center of power, until that power became a monster, more imperious and more controlling than the cathedrals and palaces of yesteryear.

Of course, the original Number 50 Broadway was torn down. New York regularly gobbles up its past and craps its future. A new building was now being erected in its place, colossal and even more sky-scraping.

Lorraine and I rushed onto the construction site. It was lunch hour and the building crews stood crowded in front of food wagons. One cart offered a mutton stew, grilled corn and charred biscuits. Its patrons were Mohawks, legendary for their fearlessness and their willingness to "sky walk" along the girders of the upper floors. Even while standing in line, their folded arms seemed as tough as steel crossbeams, and I imagined that, if we joined them, any threat would be routed like Custer's Last Stand.

No, we couldn't risk it. Hyatt stalked toward us, pressing through the crowd, passing in front of Exchange Court, his pace deliberate, relentless. His right arm was missing from its sleeve, and I could see its outline running underneath his trench coat, his elbow bent, his hand at the height of a shoulder holster.

I remembered what Raft had said about The Lip: Maybe he kills his man, maybe kills three more on the sidewalk. Not only did we need to escape from Hyatt, we had to lead him away from anyone who might end up as his casual victim.

On the outside wall, at the far end of the building, was an improvised elevator. No more than a hoist, it had a floor and ceiling and two walls. The front and back were missing and all that prevented the potential passengers from spilling out were rope cordons.

An electric winch sat nearby with a cable rising up and wrapping over a pulley wheel at the pinnacle of the construction. No other rigging went so high. I thought that, if we took this cab to its peak, we could wait there in safety.

A Mohawk stood inside the cab, his teeth tearing into a sandwich. He was a chunk of granite, barrel-chested and long on the torso, his broad head sunk squat against his shoulders. His feet were bare.

"We need help," Lorraine said, breathlessly. "There's a killer."

"A killer?" The man pursed his lips and sucked on the words as though they were a squidge of tobacco. He looked beyond us to Hyatt who had drawn his gun. "Get in."

We ducked under the cordon as Hyatt fired off a shot, the floor rising to meet our feet before we'd finished stepping fully inside.

We remained crouching as a bullet bit the bottom of the cab.

"We call this The Crate," the man said. "It'll take you as high as you need go. Name's Lucas. Lucas Sayers."

I felt a twinge of disappointment: I'd hoped for a runs-with-nature sort of name.

"Alan Priest."

"Lorraine Marquette."

We passed a series of floors each scrolling by like individual frames of on a slow-running movie reel. Each of their floors and ceilings sandwiched great unfinished expanses.

"What's the highest story you've completed?" Alan asked.

"Completed?" Lucas seemed confused. "We don't complete anything until it's done."

"What's the highest story that has a floor we can walk on," I clarified.

"That's not going to be enough," Lucas said. "The north side of this building's got its own crate, and someone has set it a-go."

Across the ways, a cable trembled like a spider's thread twinged by a fly.

"We have company," the operator said. "But don't worry. That other crate may be faster, but ours goes to the top."

We broke above the "completed" floors, those with ceilings, and continued to rise alongside a steel support beam. The pedestrian world began to diminish below us as we passed story after story of steel skeletons. The Crate rocked against its guide wire as though bobbing on a billow of wind.

I felt nauseous, dizzied. Lorraine's eyes seemed to be in near focus. Lucas remained stone-faced.

The elevator stopped on floor thirty-six, the uppermost story, no more than a rectangle of beams held in place by their vertical supports. From street level, the girders had appeared to be as thin as needles. From here, I could see they were eight inches wide. They didn't exactly require a daredevil act to balance along, but a wobble and a slip to either side meant certain death.

At this height the building narrowed to the width of a capping tower measuring about forty by eighty feet. Three sides had crossbeams set in place. A crane seated on a make-do platform two floors below held aloft the girder needed to complete the missing portion of the fourth side. The long beam of metal was suspended by a pair of broadly-spaced cables, allowing it to stick out like a diving board over the world below. Wooden planks had been placed catty-cornered where the girders intersected, allowing for extra footing when switching directions. In the near corner stood a makeshift hut.

When I was young, while my mother pursued stardom, I'd spent several years on my grandparents' ranch in Vermont. Between the farmhouse and the town there was a finger-like lake and, rather than undertaking the long trek along and around its shoreline, I crossed an old, abandoned railway bridge. The support logs had settled causing the bridge to bow. That, together with the rising lake, placed the rusting rails and rotting ties just beneath the surface.

In the summer, when balancing along the tracks, I felt as though I was walking on water. In the winter, I had to pay close attention. The rails were hidden beneath a shell of ice. On many mornings the lake maintained a skim of mist and, if my foot slipped and I fell to the side, I would disappear beneath the frozen crust.

I had the same impossible feeling now. I stood on a cloud above the crystallized lake of Manhattan. Towers peaked below us, seemingly as cold and as out-of-place as icicle spikes. A few, damned few, rose over us: the Woolworth and Singer buildings, Metropolitan Life.

The distant elevator bumped up against the plate below its pulley and stopped four floors below, thirty, forty yards away. It swayed in the breeze and for a moment I thought it might be empty. Then Hyatt stepped out and looked around, fury on his face. He clasped a vertical beam with one hand and fired a shot in our direction but missed by several yards.

"He can't shoot worth beans," Lucas said.

"He's come pretty close before," Lorraine countered.

"You'll be safe," Lucas said. "He's no Skywalker."

Safe was a relative term. I felt as though our elevator was a bucket ready to spill us out. Safe? A twist of an ankle and Animal Control would be scraping our flattened carcasses off the asphalt.

"You should hole up in the Crow's Nest," he continued. He pointed at the wooden shelter at the corner. "I'll head down and collect some police, 'cause there's no way up here without this crate."

I recognized that Lucas was right. We needed the police to trap Hyatt or at least to escort us the hell out of here. We needed men with guns. We needed the cavalry.

The Crow's Nest was ten feet away, across a length of girder.

I told Lorraine, "If you throw yourself into it, the momentum will carry you there," but she was ahead of me. She shed her shoes and with her nail split a seam in the soles of her stockings. Then she raced headlong, stopping only after she reached the Crow's Nest.

I followed her, more slowly, unsteadily, not as willing to part with my slick footwear. Once inside the nest, I turned and looked back. Lucas had begun his descent.

The Lip stood four floors below, gun aimed, studying us. For a moment, he was as still as a coiled snake. The respite ended when he dipped his head and bolted, dashing breakneck along a girder, finishing as he crashed against and hugged a steel pillar. He rounded the vertical beam and began a second sprint. I gasped: he was heading for Lucas and the Crate.

It became a race between Hyatt's insane dashes and the slow descent of the Crate. As Hyatt crossed the final stretch, the makeshift elevator passed below him, and I exhaled with relief. Then Hyatt launched himself beyond the border of the building, scratching at the air as he dropped down, crash-landing on the roof of the Crate.

During Hyatt's run, I couldn't see Lucas and his reaction, and I had no way to tell whether he knew what was coming. Now, with Hyatt smashing against his ceiling, he knew.

Hyatt squatted at the brink of the roof, facing the center. He clasped the edge and, while maintaining his grip, he dropped back and swung down like a gymnast on parallel bars, hurtling inside the Crate.

Lucas had a Jim Thorpe physique. I would give him even odds at close quarters in a battle with a madman like The Lip. The Crate rocked as it descended. It writhed and bucked. A shot rang out. Moments later, a gun flew out the back side. I took that as a good sign. Then, the crate stopped.

What now? If Lucas had won, he'd be taking the body down to the police. If The Lip had won...The Crate, seemingly so tiny, began to rise. It came our way, its size and menace increasing like a boulder hurled at us by a distant catapult. I saw Lucas's limp arm draped over the edge of the floor.

I looked around the Crow's Nest, searching for a weapon. On top of a triangular table sat a jug and a communal tin cup. At my feet, a bucket full of rivets and a pair of empty catch-cans. Wooden planks lazed against the wall. A pair of work boots rested on the floor. I had hoped for something sharp or a club with a good hand-hold. Instead, I had a collection of clumsy objects; their only use would be hurling them at him.

We had one advantage: he'd lost his gun. If he'd come our way, he'd be balancing along a beam while we'd be set in place.

"Alan," Lorraine said, "look at the other elevator."

The one that Hyatt had first taken. It had disappeared. Its pulley turned and its cable quivered. Someone must have heard the gunshots or seen the falling weapon. Our rescue would be here soon. All we had to do was buy time.

I had a plan, a crazy plan, but it would ensure our safety.

"I hope you're not afraid of heights," I said to Lorraine.

"My biggest fear is that I'll want to jump."

"What the hell?" I gawked at her and her inscrutable expression as she gazed downwards.

"Now's not the time to ask," she said.

Fine. "Follow me." A request that was just as big a leap of faith as asking her to fly. I dried my sweating palms on my pants and grabbed a plank of wood from the Crow's Nest and set out, crossing the girder to my side. With a brief glance down, in my imagination, I saw the skeletal construction expand and contract like an accordion.

I closed my eyes and gathered my nerve. My throat felt dry, and I shivered as though I stood atop a mountain peak and the thin air had sponged the very life out of me. I pawed the toe of my shoe against the boards.

I headed toward the gap where the unconnected cross-beam was held, suspended by a pair of cables, waiting to be fit in place. It swayed with a gust of wind.

I laid the plank of wood across the five-foot space between our girder and the floating beam. I told Lorraine, "All that we need to do is cross here, climb aboard the beam and then hold on to the cable. I'll take up the plank and use it to fight Hyatt if he's crazy enough to try to join us."

"You mean, if he's as crazy as we are."

Lorraine rushed across the plank and grabbed hold of the cable, clinging for her life. As much of a daredevil as she was, she squeezed her eyes shut and trembled. I looked back at the arriving Crate. Hyatt appeared, one foot planted on top of Lucas's corpse. He held a long blade and it dripped blood. He kicked Lucas's body over the side.

Then, for a moment, Hyatt stood motionless, his eyes shifting, taking in Lorraine and me and the layout of the metal skeleton.

Lorraine raised her forearm masking the lower half of her face. Hyatt mimicked this action, then ran to the Crow's Nest.

I took a look around, thinking: where are the birds? They were probably too scared to fly this high. Smart birds.

I crossed the plank, three quick, short steps, completing my transit by wrapping my right arm around the cable. After taking in a quivering breath, I knelt down to pull up the board. From this angle, one handed, I couldn't lift it and it slipped from my grasp, tumbling end-over-end as it fell.

I stayed there, kneeling, awaiting Hyatt's next move, certain that I could prevent him from crossing over to our girder. As long as he remained separate from us, we were beyond the range of his knife. Only then did I think: what if he throws it?

He licked his mustache, momentarily revealing his glistening upper teeth, then took hold of his own plank of wood and held it crosswise, using it as a balance as he walked the span of the cross beam toward us. Was he going to lay it down to use as a bridge? That would be suicide. I could easily kick the board free.

Instead, when he came to the end of the girder, he used his plank as a pole, prodding the floating beam at its end below our feet, moving it. We swayed backward and then toward him. At the peak of our return, barely an arm's length away, he again prodded the foot of our beam and we swept back this time farther and tipping higher like child pumping a swing. The girder ground against the cables looped around it.

I recognized that, when we returned, we would be within range of his blade. With no other alternative coming to mind, I chose to meet him head on. I grasped the cable with my left hand and leaned toward him, holding forth my prosthetic hand. He took the bait, swinging the knife at it, a hard, downward thrust that cut through my glove, cleaving between my fingers and passing deep into the Bakelite. The knife split the prosthetic in two, stopping shortly before my wrist.

That blade was wedged tightly and tugged against his grip as we swayed backwards. Perhaps the shock of destroying my phony hand startled him so much that he didn't think rationally and didn't let go of the knife. He held on as we swung back away from him, and his clutching hand towed him over the edge. As he toppled from his perch, in a last desperate effort, he seized my wrist with his other hand. His grasp slid and his own knife sliced into his hand. The fasteners on my prosthetic sprung, the attachment wasn't built to support the weight of a human.

My hundred-dollar hand slipped free with its brace and Hyatt fell. One floor down, he thudded against a crossbeam. I heard his bones crack. As he ricocheted to the side, he wrapped his arms around the girder. It seemed impossible to maintain a hold, but certain death is a strong motivation.

He lay there for a moment, squirming, struggling to achieve a tighter embrace.

Then came the pings, metal striking metal. Too soft to be bullets. It was the sound of rivets glancing off of the steel beam where he clung. One and then another struck Hyatt. He flinched. He loosed his clutch and grabbed again, desperate to hang on.

I looked down. Outside the elevator on the opposite side, four stories below, stood four Mohawks. They took turns pitching bolts at Hyatt's dangling figure. They must have seen Lucas's falling corpse and witnessed the perpetrator attacking us.

I realized I was wrong. We didn't need the cavalry; we needed the Indians.

One rivet smacked Hyatt in the head. After that, he tried to swat away the projectiles before they arrived. A flying chunk of metal struck his bleeding hand and it convulsed, pawing at the air. He got to his knees. Blood drooled from his mouth. He swayed and rolled his head. Waving a hand in surrender—or else as goodbye—he toppled to his side, falling like an arrow until he crashed through a completed ceiling twelve stories below.

CHAPTER 28
A SLOW STROLL IN THE SHADOW OF THE GUILLOTINE

Alan

I MASSAGED the skin of my forearm where the straps of my prosthetic hand had raked against my skin as it was wrenched free.

"I see you've lost your hand," Santarelli noted.

"Another talent of mine," I said. "Lose a hand, grow a hand, lose a hand."

We stood in a light misting rain in front of #50 Broadway and watched as the meat patrol carried off the remains of Hyatt. A score of cops held back a crowd. I recognized reporters from the *Herald* and the *Times.* From the *World,* my archnemesis, Gould the Ghoul.

"Please, allow me," Santarelli said. Ever the Italian knight, he laid a shawl over Lorraine's hair and shoulders. Where did he get it from? Did he keep one inside his jacket for women in the rain?

Lorraine said, "Before he died, The Lip let me know

that he was the one who threw Officer Baxter down the stairs." She raised her forearm in front of her face.

Oh, right. Lon Chaney. So *that* was the meaning of the gesture they exchanged.

The detective smiled with relief. I suppose he had still maintained the possibility that I killed Officer Baxter. "When word gets out that you two killed Hyatt, you will be heroes to the boys at the station."

I contemplated that. I envisioned the killer story I'd be writing.

"And what about Ruby?" I asked Santarelli.

"Did I tell you I was born in Sicily?" he said by way of not answering. I knew I had to wait it out: he'd eventually come to the point. "I came here as a child and my parents were most forcible in their demands that I learn the American accent. I tell you this because my family expressed their extreme disappointment when I told them I wanted to be *polizia*. My father said that if I was an honest cop, I would be Don Quixote tilting at windmills. If I was dishonest, I would be the helping hand of the *fratellanza*. That's how such a career would play out in the old country. But America is a land of new possibilities, and I strive to find a middle path between the extremes in order to do what is right.

"I am telling you this because I fought with the judge to solicit a search warrant, but the clap of his gavel rang mightier than the thunder of Thor's hammer. I apologize for bringing to bear so wide a world of analogies.

"He refused to issue a warrant—not due to lack of evidence, oh no. He proclaimed nothing could persuade him to soil the name of so great a financier as Vachel

Ruby. I suspect one of two possibilities. Perhaps he needed to first withdraw his own investments from Ruby's portfolio. Perhaps. But I would wager that he is being paid off."

Who owned the city's judges? The Big Bankroll.

"Rothstein?" Lorraine said. She had come to the same conclusion and Santarelli arched his eyebrows and pursed his lips in confirmation.

But that didn't make sense. Peanuts, Nick, The Lip—Jake Whelan's men guarded Ruby and kept him prisoner. Rothstein had paid us to dig up the story behind Fritch's death. He wouldn't have done that if he already knew about Ruby's game and had wanted to keep the fraud hidden.

I wiped the rainwater from my face. I needed to find somewhere dry to think. Or else a different kind of wet: a speakeasy.

The mile-long Pierce-Arrow pulled up against the curb. Icepick, aka "Bucky," climbed out of the back seat, his frame seemingly larger than that of the car. A random question popped into my head and annoyed me: why was he called Icepick? He didn't need an icepick to kill anyone. With those monster mitts he could crack my skull like it was a walnut.

"Boss says he wants a talk," Icepick announced. I looked at Santarelli. His eyes spoke of resignation. Standing up to Rothstein qualified as tilting at windmills.

"I cannot oppose Rothstein on my own and I cannot find a brigade to join me," he said. He raised a hand and folded and unfolded his fingers, a good-bye wave.

I stepped toward the car and Icepick stopped me with a thud to my chest. "Ladies first."

Lorraine ducked into the back, and I slid inside to join her. Bucky slid in alongside us, his shoulder squeezed up against me, eye-level. Up front, Nick sat at the steering with Peanuts on the passenger's side.

Rothstein's men and Whelan's: they went together like whiskey and strychnine. The car pulled out into the street, north on Broadway. Another car trip with thugs. Lorraine and I were the best chauffeured couple in Manhattan. Our chances of surviving this particular ride depended on where we were headed.

"Ghost Row?" I asked.

"Rothstein," Peanuts said.

That was good news. Maybe. "Lindy's Restaurant?"

"Nope."

Too bad. Rothstein would never kill anyone at Lindy's.

"The boss, Mr. Whelan, is going to be plenty cross when he learns how you iced The Lip," Nick said. He took his eyes off the road long enough to meet mine and send a smile my way. "Them two was pals."

Lorraine stroked my arm, her face pinched in deep thought. Then she said, casually, freely, "Bucky, you like me."

"I like you swell," Icepick said.

"And you like Mr. Priest?"

"Sure do. But not so much as you."

"So, you're not going to kill us, are you?"

"Mr. Rothstein told me not to talk about that."

I tried a different, more aggressive tack. I said, "You know, Icepick, these two want to kill us but that doesn't have to happen. I suppose with your strength, you could grab the two in the front seats and knock them cold in a second."

"No, sir. Mr. Rothstein has made friendly with the Jake gang. He explained me and explained me hard, to hurt even none of them. Not even."

"And do you always do what Rothstein tells you?"

"Always." His nod fell like a sledgehammer on a spike.

I saw Nick's eyes floating in the rearview mirror, laughing at me. I'd prefer it if they were angry rather than dismissive. *Sure,* his eyes said, *look at that schmuck trying to get Icepick to kill me and Peanuts. No hard feelings. They're dead meat.*

I still held on to a glimmer of hope. Maybe Rothstein merely wanted a report from us. He'd paid us the five C-notes. But if he'd paired up with Whelan and was arranging protection for Ruby Investments with the judges, what was it that he didn't know?

We passed Times Square and just north of that, Lindy's. We turned east.

———

We entered through the ballroom, weaving our way between stacks of liquor crates. Not much had changed by way of the physical structure of the mansion at 666 Fifth Avenue. The demolition of the past day had been limited to the grand staircase. One side of the wide steps had been ripped out, revealing a skeletal frame of cross beams and, poking out of the ground beneath them, the pointy ends of anchoring spikes. A fringe of the intact staircase allowed transit along one side to the second floor.

A lot had changed regarding the atmosphere. The two

gangs had some sort of truce going on: divided but equal in force. One side of the second-floor hallway was lined with Whelan's men. Boys—punks, really—they assumed cocky poses, their pistols on display like flipped-open codpieces. The other side was lined with Rothstein's men. Cement blocks in business suits, they looked as polished as freshly shined brass knuckles.

Jake Whelan ruled from a stool, all smiles. He licked clean some blood from beneath his fingernails and then examined them. Perhaps the reason Peanuts, Nick and Icepick guided us this way was to show us Ivan Fritch, who lay on the rug by Whelan's feet, his throat sliced ear-to-ear. His lips were locked in a post-mortem grin.

Peanuts walked over to Whelan and passed along some shelled nuts, emptying a handful into his boss's pocket. If I weren't worried about a quick blade to the throat, I would have mentioned that the ritual seemed almost erotic.

As we passed by, Jake gave a happy-to-have-known-you smile. Nick and Icepick continued to shepherd us forward.

We climbed up the servants' stairway to the third floor. This hallway was also divided side-to-side between Whelan's and Rothstein's men.

Nick knocked on a door.

"Enter." Rothstein's voice.

Nick opened the door and then made a show of patting down me and Lorraine. Satisfied, he jerked a thumb in the direction of the doorway. Nick and Icepick stayed outside. We entered and the door shut behind us.

The room was narrow, the carpet pulled up. The only furnishings were the chair and desk where Rothstein sat.

An automatic lay on the desktop on top of a pile of neatly squared documents. It served as a paperweight and a warning.

"In a house like this one," he said, "I prefer the servant's quarters: they feel more intimate, more private. I can stretch out and rap a knuckle on the solid walls. My visitors have no choice but to keep inside the boundaries of my vision." He demonstrated this by dropping his hands in the motion of a tomahawk chop. "That permits me to see my visitors' backsides when I boot them out the door.

"Now, Vanderbilt's bedroom, down the hall, is large enough to stage a carnival. He had to be showy. When William Vanderbilt headed down Fifth Avenue on a stroll, you would recognize him instantly: a foot-tall top hat, and a cane that twinkled. If you've got to strut like that, when you got to announce to the world who you are, you got no grit."

One thing about Rothstein, he never showed signs of being insecure. This attitude didn't come from an inflated sense of self-importance. He had the certainty that he owned whoever he spoke to or if not, he had decided that the person wasn't worth owning.

"I have you to thank for leading me to Whelan's enterprise," Rothstein said. "Once I'd learned about it, I knew I could destroy it with a word. That made it easy to insist on a split in the profits. I'm here, filling out some details regarding our deal. I will receive two grand a day from Ruby Enterprises of which I will spend half to ensure protection from the police and the legal system."

"How did you learn about Ruby's scheme?" I asked.

"We've come to the part where you answer my questions and I tell you nothing," Rothstein said. "My question is who else knows about Ruby's scheme other than you two and Detective Santarelli?"

Roughly the same question Whelan had asked us before dispatching us to Ghost Row.

"Carolyne Fritch," Lorraine said. "She killed Daisy Yinger to fake her own death, and then killed Patrice Somerset to get away with it."

"I'd already learned as much from the police," Rothstein said.

I speculated as to whether Santarelli had informed him. No. Rothstein probably had a dozen sources on the police force, starting with the commissioner.

"Who else?" he said.

"No one that I know," I answered.

Rothstein looked at me as though he didn't believe me. Worse, he looked at me as though it didn't matter whether I told the truth.

There were others who knew. More police, the judge. Hell, maybe Gould the Ghoul had stumbled on to the real story. If I did name someone, that person would be marked for execution.

Rothstein said, "As part of my deal with Mr. Whelan, he was quite insistent regarding one item must be part of the agreement: he demanded that you two must die."

I looked to Lorraine. She wore a brave, unflinching mask. Or maybe she *was* brave, braver than me. Now, facing death, I realized I'd been such an idiot, wrapped up in my pity, still fighting the Great War. If I had another chance, if I could do it over, I'd have taken the $500 and run off with her.

"Because I like you two," Rothstein said, "I told Whelan that my men will kill you. Quickly, not much pain. Not like his hoodlums. They enjoy hurting others. I asked Icepick to perform the service. Downstairs, a quick twist of the neck. My orders made him sad, but he always follows my orders."

"If Whelan is worried about us talking, we can Scotch our lips," Lorraine said.

"It's gone well beyond that. Whelan hates you."

"He hates everyone."

"Agreed. But you showed him up and, by leading me to Ruby, you cost him two thousand a day."

"Come on, Arnold," I said, "with your power, you could persuade him to not kill us, force him to work out a new deal."

He shook his head. Rothstein wasn't the kind to succumb to a chummy appeal to the ego or first names.

But he might agree to some sort of wager. A sure thing. "What would you say if I told you that Icepick won't kill us, and that Lorraine and I will walk out the front door?"

"Impossible," Rothstein said. "Do you think you can find Icepick's sweet side? At times he acts like an agreeable lug but when he's ordered to do something, he's all business."

"Five grand," I said. "Five grand says Icepick will walk us out the front door."

I had intrigued him. I'd appealed to his gambling

instincts. I appealed to that part of his vanity that told him he could sniff out a rigged proposition.

"Okay," Rothstein said, chuckling, "no skin off my nose. If you manage to walk to out the door, come on back and I'll slide you five g's."

Five g's and a bullet.

"I'll pocket the money now," I said. "And you can collect it off of my corpse, if we fail."

He was smiling. Oh, how he smiled.

"You think you can bribe Icepick to turn down my orders? Or are you going to try to bribe Whelan?"

"Five g's and you'll see," Lorraine said, joining in.

"Not a penny in bribes," I promised.

His eyes slitted. He seemed close to agreeing but still needed a nudge.

"How often do you get to see a horse race where the horses have to win or else die?" I asked.

"A race?" he said. His face fell flat.

Bad analogy. He knew horse races could be fixed. And he probably actually cared about whether he killed a horse.

"We'll walk out the front door," I told him. "No running. No rough stuff, no grabbing for guns, no bribes. And once we're outside, I promise that we'll keep mum about Ruby. You'll still have the chance to hunt us down to square it with Whelan."

I suppose that it helped that five thousand barely dented his walking-around money. I suppose it helped that he believed that he'd pluck the money off of our dead corpses.

"Okay," Rothstein said, taking out his bankroll. "As

Miss Marquette suggested, I want to see what you have in mind. If there's any disloyalty among my men, I need to know."

Rothstein silently counted a tidy stack of hundred-dollar bills. He laid them on his open palm, challenging me to take them. His palm was dry; mine, sweaty. As I snatched them, I would have sworn an electric arc jumped between our skins.

"One more thing," I said. "Why do they call him Icepick?"

"An unfriendly acquaintance decided to kill him by scrambling his brains with an icepick. Stuck the pointy end through his skull. Didn't do anything, or if it did, nobody can tell." Rothstein tossed his chin. "Give the door a rap."

I knocked and that must have been the signal that it was time to go.

Rothstein summoned the giant. "Icepick, can I have a word?"

Icepick lumbered over to his boss.

Rothstein curled two fingers and shook them to say, come closer. Icepick bent over and Rothstein whispered in his ear, some extra instruction. Rothstein wouldn't think of it as cheating on the bet, merely securing the advantage.

"I hope this plan of yours is a good one," Lorraine said to me.

Icepick broke off, ruffled and frowning, saying, "Sure, boss, sure. I would never. Sure." Whatever Rothstein had told him, and I had a pretty good guess, had wounded his sense of pride. Of course, he'd kill us. A contract for a hit was a sacred vow, and to break a vow was a sin.

The giant scowled and stomped toward us. Grabbing me by the scruff of my jacket, he raised me to my tippy toes. "Come along, you," he said. He looked to Lorraine, adding, "And you too, ma'am."

Icepick shoved me ahead and I caught my balance. He cracked his knuckles just by closing his fists. We paced slowly along the third-floor hallway, Lorraine and I in the lead, Icepick two steps back. He'd drawn his gun. Rothstein had promised Icepick would deliver a quick crack to our necks. I guess the pistol was to make certain we didn't try bolting.

On one side stood Rothstein's men. On the other, Whelan's. I'd seen a newsreel of a marathon runner approaching the finish line at the 1908 Olympics. The crowd cordoned off to either side, the athlete stumbled along, so exhausted he was out of his head: falling, getting up, falling. Then the crowd surged in just before he could finish and helped him up, their actions disqualifying him from winning the gold medal.

I suppose I thought of that because if I got so weak-kneed that I fell, these hoodlums would drag me to the killing floor.

"I know Rothstein ordered you to kill us," I told Icepick.

"Mr. Rothstein told me to not talk to you about that."

"I'm only saying, that's alright. No hard feelings. It's a loyal man who obeys his boss."

"Thank you. You're okay. And I got nothing against you, neither, Miss Lorraine."

"Thank you," she said, her voice acid.

Rothstein trailed us at a distance, making sure he had a grandstand view for when the bet paid out.

We came to the top of the front stairway, the section connecting the third floor to the second. Nick and Peanuts stood at the bottom of these stairs looking up, witnessing our death march with smug glee. I plucked the bankroll from my pocket with that same jazzy move I'd seen from Rothstein and, as I walked down the steps, I peeled off five one-hundreds.

Icepick eyed the money. "Mr. Rothstein told me to not take any money from you," he said.

"Of course, you shouldn't," I said. "But before you kill us, I have to give Peanuts his share."

"His share?"

"Oh, maybe you didn't know," I said. "Lorraine and I are working for Mr. Whelan, now."

"Oh." A concentrated confusion knit his brow.

Lorraine was a genius at picking up a signal and she joined right in.

"Of course, Bucky knew that," she said. "That's what Mr. Rothstein whispered to him."

"Maybe and maybe no," Icepick responded. "But not maybe yes."

At the bottom of the stairs, I stepped away from Icepick's escort and walked up to Peanuts as though we were now the greatest friends in the world. I waved the five C-notes. He eyed me and the money with killer suspicion.

"That's Jake's cut," I told him, loud enough for Icepick to hear, hell, loud enough for Rothstein to hear from where he stood leaning against the balcony railing. "Pass it on to Jake, he'll understand."

Jake, a short distance down the hall, nailed us with a killer stare.

Peanuts headed off to talk to Whelan. I hoped he took his time getting there.

It was a short passage to the grand staircase. We'd be there in a matter of seconds, but I had to play this out casually, as though it meant nothing to our lives or deaths. I stopped short of the top of the stairs, as if just having thought of something.

"You'd never cross Rothstein," I said to Icepick.

"I'd never cross Mr. Rothstein," he swore.

"And you'd never disobey one of his orders," I said to drive home the point. Icepick nodded with grim certainty. "And yet…he told you not to hurt anyone who is working for Whelan and now Lorraine and I are working for him."

"He told me to kill you."

"Yes. But if you do that, you'll be disobeying another one of his orders."

We walked on as he mulled this over to the best of his non-abilities.

Some of Whelan's men glared our way.

"He told me not to listen to you," Icepick said. His forehead puckered. The aim of his pistol drooped from my chest to my gut. All his goofy cheer had disappeared.

We came to the head of the stairway, the steps a slender ribbon alongside a gutted hole.

He shook the gun, ordering us to keep moving.

Lorraine went first, then it was my turn, and then Icepick slowly walked down the narrow path, step by step, holding on to the banister. Icepick's pistol had recovered its sureness and was poking at the back of my head. I kept quiet, allowing the paradox to slowly seize control of his brain.

Several of Whelan's men leaned against the banister above us, watching our slow death march. Peanuts stood beside them, there in the peanut gallery. Rothstein appeared. From the tall arch on his brow and wide smile, I guessed that he had figured my ploy. I also guessed that he was still betting on Icepick. We stepped off the bottom step and into the Great Hall. From here a short stone's throw to the entrance hallway, and from there a promenade out onto the street. On one side, Whelan's men. On the other, Rothstein's. The killers surrounding us looked on. Each of them had only a small bit of the story. None of them was certain what to do.

I wrapped my arm under Lorraine's. Strangely, neither of us was trembling. I didn't want to die and I didn't want her to die. But, if we had to go, I was happy we'd be doing it together.

"All things considered," she said to me, "I'm glad I met you yesterday."

All things? Death included? Now I wanted to cry. "Me, too," I said.

I heard Jake Whelan cursing at Peanuts. "Five hundred? Five hundred? What's his fucking game?"

I looked toward the second floor and then to Icepick. "I know what I did wrong," I told him. "Both Lorraine and I work for Whelan. I didn't hand over her end of the cut."

"You work for Whelan?" the giant said. Only after I

had mentioned this a second time did the echo in his head return to his lips.

"Maybe I need to settle the money with Jake before you kill us," I said, halting.

"Oh, no you don't," Icepick said. Waving his gun at us. Dried blood crusted the floor at our feet. This could well be the designated killing spot.

"Then why don't you take the money to Whelan?" Lorraine asked.

"And while you're upstairs, you can apologize to Rothstein about disobeying his orders by killing those who work for Whelan." I pointed out Rothstein leaning against the banister. "He's looking down on you, testing you, seeing what you'll do." I counted out five C-notes. "From Lorraine to Whelan."

Icepick waved the bills at his boss, eager to show him that he was going to do the right thing. He began lumbering up the steps at the moment Whelan started trotting down.

"Walk slowly to the entryway," I told Lorraine peeking back to see if we needed to duck a bullet. "And then as soon as we are out of sight, run." We pressed on as though we didn't have a care in the world.

Whelan began screaming obscenities at Icepick, who blocked the stairway: "You fucking moron! You thimble-wit! You overgrown doofus…"

I doubt that Icepick understood what all of those meant but he understood the humiliation. Just before entering the hall, I looked over my shoulder and called back to Icepick, "Rothstein said not to kill Jake's men. He didn't say anything about Jake himself."

Icepick lifted Whelan overhead and hurled him over the side of the staircase, down onto the metal spikes that once supported the pillars.

Lorraine and I picked up the pace. Gunfire rang out. By the titanic volume of the subsequent crash, I guessed Icepick was the gunmen's target.

I opened the front door. Lorraine and I stepped out onto Fifth Avenue. The sound of gunfire had caused some to stop and stare.

"They've a big garage," I announced. "Just the backfire of an old jalopy."

There, near the corner, Santarelli stood, waiting for us, one foot on the running board of a police car. He wouldn't storm the building to save us, but at least he was polite enough to give us a ride.

October 5, 1926
Mrs. Nora Marquette
Westfield State Farm Reformatory for Women
Bedford, New York

Hello, Mom.

That little item, the one I told you about in the previous letter? We went ahead and took the plunge—although Saratoga is definitely *not* the place to get hitched when you are trying to avoid the eyes of gangsters. It was that marvelous detective, Gilberti Santarelli, who convinced me to try the domesticated life. In his last letter, he wrote telling me I could maintain my independence and demonstrate my authority by making the proposal myself and that if Alan had a problem with that, I should walk away.

Alan answered, "If you are fool enough to have me, I'm fool enough to be had."—So sweet!

I've accepted the fact that I'm smarter than him, which makes it such a relief to be fools together. Although, and you might not like this, I wish we were back on the trail of a killer. Those were swell times.

As to where we are now, the postmark on the envelope is a lie. I asked an ex-school chum in Buffalo to forward this letter. Right now, Santarelli is the only person who knows where Alan and I are hiding out. The detective is keeping his ear to the ground, ready to tell us when it's safe to come out of the woods. Probably when Ruby Investments collapses, and our secret becomes meaningless. In the meantime, we are continuing our honeymoon on the lam, courtesy of Mr. Rothstein and the four grand we had left over. That'll give us a year.

I suspect that Rothstein doesn't hold a grudge. We won the bet, square and unfair. Whelan probably would be hot on our trail if Icepick hadn't skewered him. I've heard Icepick pulled through. Silly people, thinking bullets would hurt him.

Tell Beth and Karen I miss them.

I suppose there's one good reason for getting married over staying single: I can flash my enchanted ring at the wolves and shoo them off. Most of them, anyhow.

Okay, a second reason—and I'm so glad we talk about everything. I don't have to start from scratch to teach a new man about sex, about women, about me, about what works and what is no more than feather-headed piffle.

Okay, a third reason. Alan. He has the bouncy eagerness of a puppy. I have to fight with him to make him supper to balance out how every morning he serves me a delicious breakfast in bed. He says he had time to learn about cooking while in France after losing his hand. He helped in the cafeteria in the convalescing hospital where they had genuine French chefs, the ones who cooked for their lives. As long as they cooked well and were needed, they staved off being sent to the front.

Alan told me about how he lost it, his hand. The final, honest truth. Broke down crying and everything. I think getting out of war is good common sense. It's strange what men find shameful.

I take a peek at the financial pages every day. I see the stock market is still going up and up. Like those fish, the trouts, that swim upstream and leap up cascades, defying gravity. Of course, those fish are looking for some sex—I hope the guards don't read these letters.

I think about what Alan and I did—and are continuing to do—by keeping silent about Ruby and his scheme. We're helping him cheat people, and in the bigger picture, we're cheering along that merry group on the Wall Street hayride, all of them headed for a cliff.

It seems everyone is chasing a cheap buck. Prohibition has made greed the national intoxicant. Someday the entire market is going to fall, although I can't imagine anything could be worse than the crash of '07.

After the financial collapse, I can imagine what Santarelli would say about the corpses: the American dream killed the American dream. Suicide. Home in time for dinner.

xox

L.

AUTHOR'S NOTE

This novel is mostly populated by fictional characters. Other than those mentioned in passing, the historical, flesh-and-blood characters are Arnold Rothstein, Mae West, George Raft, and Gordon Nursey. Their larger-than-life personalities were much the same as presented in these pages.

Arnold Rothstein, the Big Bankroll, ruled over the New York underworld in the period before organized crime families solidified their power. In true terms, he didn't run a gang. He financed illegal actions and took a cut, fixing any legal difficulties the criminals might encounter. He was alleged to have helped rig the 1919 World Series. He appeared in the contemporary novel *The Great Gatsby* as Meyer Wolfsheim. More recently he was a key figure in the series, *Boardwalk Empire,* portrayed with suave menace by Michael Stuhlbarg. Rothstein maintained friendships with, among others, the easy-going alcoholic mayor of New York, Jimmy Walker, and Herbert Bayard Swope, the crusading editor of the *New York World*.

Rothstein was shot by a fellow gambler over unpaid poker winnings. He died November 6, 1928, the day Herbert Hoover was elected president, an event that would presage the transition from the partying twenties to the austere thirties.

Rothstein made his headquarters over Lindy's restaurant, which was immortalized by author Damon Runyan and featured in the musical and film, *Guys and Dolls*. Although Lindy's has relocated since the 1920s, it continues to remain in business.

At age 32, with her acting career languishing, Mae West had her first big hit with the comedy, *Sex*. It ran for 375 performances at Daly's West 63rd Street Theater before the police decided it was too obscene to continue, and raided a show in progress, shutting down the play. West spent ten days in jail. She went on to play a sex siren in Hollywood comedies up into her eighties and died on November 22nd, 1980.

George Raft worked as a Broadway actor and dancer, while being a chauffeur to mobster Owney Madden. He went on to Hollywood stardom, most famously as the coin-flipping lieutenant to the gangster Rico in the 1932 incarnation of *Scarface*, and as the mob boss "Spats" Colombo in Billy Wilder's *Some Like It Hot*. He died on November 24th, 1980, two days after Mae West.

When the Victoria Bridge was being built across the St. Lawrence River in 1886, men from the nearby Mohawk village of Kahnawake signed on as laborers. The renown of their bravery in working at great heights soon gained them employment in New York City. Crews were hired to construct many of the iconic buildings, including the Empire State and the World Trade Center. They became known as the Skywalkers and their tradition continues to this day.

Gordon Nursey, an advocate of astronomy, did bring his reflecting telescope to Columbus Park to treat passersby to views of the heavens.

———

Although many of the characters were fictional, the buildings presented in this novel either existed or else continue to exist. The mansion at 666 Fifth Avenue was designed and built by Stanford White for William Kissam Vanderbilt, Jr., in 1905. Vanderbilt separated from his wife to follow his own pursuits, including auto racing. He established the first motor-race trophy, the Vanderbilt Cup and briefly held the world land speed record. His wife, Virginia, continued to live at 666 Fifth Avenue until moving out shortly before the building was torn down in 1926, the year of this story. She relocated to 660 Park Avenue which she quickly renumbered, 666.

The building currently at 666 Fifth Avenue is owned by Jared Kushner, the son-in-law of Donald Trump. During Trump's term in office, the building was renumbered 660.

Stanford White designed two buildings for the Knickerbocker Trust, the one across from the Adams Exchange and one on Madison Avenue. They each had Corinthian columns more in line with a monument than a bank.

In 1907, the Knickerbocker Trust, one of the wealthiest banks in America, stood at the center of an international financial scandal. Crooked entrepreneurs Charles Morse and the Heinze brothers used funding from the Knickerbocker Trust while attempting to corner the world copper market. When their scheme fell through, the entire nation was thrown into a recession, referred to as the Great Panic of 1907. The stock market lost half of its value. Charles Barney, the bank president, committed suicide. Charles Morse went to prison, where he met a third Charles: Charles Ponzi, who would learn a thing or two from his cellmate.

The Knickerbocker Trust went bankrupt and became the Columbia Trust. Both of its buildings suffered similar fates, their beauty hidden beneath redesigns that added more floors. In particular, the exquisite architecture of the one on Fifth Avenue made it more reminiscent of a temple than a bank. Originally four stories, the new owners decided to cap its sturdy columns with ten more floors. It lives on, across from the Empire State Building, unrecognizable when compared to its former glory, having once been a masterpiece of architecture. It was like turning the Lincoln Memorial into a condominium.

Alan Priest, fictional, worked for the *New York World*, a real newspaper founded by Joseph Pulitzer. After Pulitzer's death in 1911, his sons, the Pulitzer boys, took over. The premier award in American journalism was established in their father's name. From 1890 to 1895, the headquarters for the *World* stood as the tallest building in New York and as the tallest business building in the world.

Was the building at #50 Broadway, constructed in 1888, the first "skyscraper?" This title is disputed. The

Home Insurance Building in Chicago, completed three years earlier, used a mix of iron and steel in its frame, but also used bricks to support its height: a sort of hybrid of the new and the old.

The super-thin structure of #50 Broadway required an all-steel internal frame, and its tower-like structure presaged the sky-piercing buildings of the future. The 450-foot building constructed in the place of the original #50 Broadway in 1926-27 and which is featured in this story, still stands.

The Bellevue Morgue opened in 1866. A vast warehouse for the dead, it currently houses the Office of the Chief Medical Examiner of New York City. Among those who have passed through its doors are Arnold Rothstein and John Lennon. It was used as the site for identifying victims of the 9/11 attacks.

Horace Saks and Bernard Gimbel opened their iconic luxury department store in 1924, on Fifth Avenue, across from St. Patrick's Cathedral. It continues to operate at that site and at thirty-eight more, although with retail outlets in crisis, that number could change.

The Gotham Hotel opened in 1905 in the shadow of the more famous St. Regis. In 1938, it became notorious for an eleven-hour-long drama in which a would-be jumper stood high up on a ledge while the police tried to talk him to safety. Three hundred officers were called upon to control the crowd estimated at ten thousand. At 10:36 p.m., the despairing man jumped. The event was given a happy ending and made into the film, *Fourteen Hours.*

Beginning in the late 1970s the hotel was made-over

by an eccentric Swiss owner, Rene Hatt, who installed purple bathtubs alongside the beds and mirrors on the ceilings. After bankruptcy, its new owners renamed it the Peninsula New York. The interior and the rooms have been nearly completely renovated; little of the original work remains. The Manhattan hotel that is currently named "Gotham" bears no relation.

Opening in 1919, the Capitol Theatre on Broadway was the largest, most magnificent film palace in the world, with 5,230 seats. It pioneered radio broadcasts and over the years featured great live entertainment, including Duke Ellington, Martin and Lewis, Frank Sinatra, and Sammy Davis, Jr. The theater continued to operate until 1968, when it showed its last film, Stanley Kubrick's, *2001: A Space Odyssey*.

The Adams Express Building was chosen for its key role in this book not for its architectural beauty, but because it possesses that sort of flat-faced structure with a thousand anonymous windows which defines an aspect of Manhattan. It measures 443 feet in height, and, when completed in 1914, it ranked as the seventh tallest building in New York.

———

Within this novel, one background character connects history to architecture: Stanford White. Through his firm, White designed and constructed many of the most luminous structures of the Gilded Age. On June 25, 1906, while lunching at the rooftop pavilion restaurant of Madison Square Gardens, he was shot to death by millionaire Harry Thaw. In what was described as the Trial of the Century, Thaw pleaded insanity, saying he was driven to murder by the accounts his wife had given of her rape and abuse by White when she was a child. Thaw was declared not guilty by reason of insanity and sentenced to Matteawan State Hospital for the Criminally Insane. After the institution restored his mental health and released him, in 1916, he was arrested for raping a teenage boy. He was again found not guilty due to insanity, and again sent to an insane asylum.

ACKNOWLEDGMENTS

Thanks especially to those in writing critique groups both locally and with the Mystery Writers of America, Florida Chapter who gave me invaluable feedback on this work. These include Bob Ritchie, Iris Monica Vargas, Diane A.S. Stuckart, Holly Thompson, Lee Summerall, Allison Horton, and Michael Harrawood.

Diane A.S. Stuckart is the New York Times bestselling author of the Black Cat Bookshop Mysteries (as Ali Brandon) and the Tarot Cat Mysteries. Holly Thompson as Holly Newman is the author of standalone novels and series, including e regency mystery romances.

Thanks to those involved in historic building preservation. Their dedication and efforts to preserve these treasures are so important and their monographs on great buildings are a precious resource.

Thanks to the good folks at Oliver-Heber for believing in this book and helping to present it in the best possible way.

ABOUT THE AUTHOR

Martin Hill Ortiz is a professor of pharmacology at Ponce Health Sciences University in Ponce, Puerto Rico. He received his undergraduate degrees at New Mexico State and his doctorate at George Washington University. He is the author of three novels. Many of his short stories, including those that introduced Alan Priest, have appeared in Mystery Magazine.

He has one son who lives in Panama.

Previous books by Martin Hill Ortiz

A Predatory Mind
A Predator's Game
Never Kill A Friend (as Martin Hill)
Dead Man's Trail (a novella)
The short story compendiums, The Best Short Stories

Volumes I through III: Chosen in 1914 by the most prominent authors of the day.

More about Dr. Hill Ortiz can be found at mdhillortiz.com

9 781648 396885